FOR THE LOVE OF
HER KING

ZARIYA HONAKER

authorHOUSE®

AuthorHouse™
1663 Liberty Drive
Bloomington, IN 47403
www.authorhouse.com
Phone: 1 (800) 839-8640

Published by AuthorHouse 12/15/2016

ISBN: 978-1-5246-5555-6 (sc)
ISBN: 978-1-5246-5554-9 (e)

Print information available on the last page.

Any people depicted in stock imagery provided by Thinkstock are models, and such images are being used for illustrative purposes only. Certain stock imagery © Thinkstock.

This book is printed on acid-free paper.

Because of the dynamic nature of the Internet, any web addresses or links contained in this book may have changed since publication and may no longer be valid. The views expressed in this work are solely those of the author and do not necessarily reflect the views of the publisher, and the publisher hereby disclaims any responsibility for them.

CHAPTER 1

Sweetwater, Wyoming 1887

I n 1880, Shamus Ewen moved his family to America in search of a better life... With his wife Carlin and their daughter Blaine, along with Carlin's Sister Shannon and her daughter Roslyn. After Shannon's husband, William, died from illness brought on by the famine in Ireland, Shannon became very close to her sister and brother-in law. Leaving their home land, they made the arduous trek across the sea... After nearly a year of travel the Ewen family found their new home in the small, dusty, town of Sweetwater Wyoming.

Seven years had passed; Blaine was nearing her sixteenth year. She had grown into a fine Irish beauty with flame red hair and emerald green eyes.

She was very proud of her Irish heritage even though others made fun of her she never tried to hide where she came from.

Roslyn Ewen was just shy being a year older than Blaine. She was a beauty in her own right, with her blonde hair and azure blue eyes.

Though she had recently turned sixteen, she looked mature for her years and enjoyed using this fact to her advantage with the men in town.

Roslyn was not proud of her heritage she preferred the town's folk not to know of her Irish background.

Roslyn spoke often to Blaine of leaving their small town and going to a big city where no one would know where she was from.

Blaine could not understand her cousin but she loved her anyway.

Blaine was eight years old when her family left Ireland.

Now she considered herself almost grown since she would be sixteen in just a few months.

Even though she was much older now, her Da' still considered her to be his little girl.

Blaine enjoyed reminding her Da' she was not a baby anymore.

Shamus hoped to keep his family safe, especially his daughter and his niece. However, the two young ladies always seemed to find ways to get into trouble, much to his disliking.

One hot afternoon Roslyn came knocking on the Ewen's door.

"Hello, Aunt Carlin, is Blaine around? I wanted to see if she could go swimming." Carlin pointed toward the back door. "She is in the barn milking old Gertrude. And Roslyn darlin she has to be gettin her chores done before you two go runnin' off You Hear!?"

Roslyn was out the back door headed toward the barn. "Yes Ma'am!" Roslyn flew into the barn giving Blaine a start.

"Roslyn, you just about scared me to death! What are you up to anyway?" Roslyn was grinning from ear to ear. "We, my sweet cousin, are going skinny-dipping. So get your chores done so we can go."

Blaine looked confused; she had never been skinny-dipping before and had no idea what Roslyn was talking about.

"Roslyn, what in heaven's name is skinny-dipping?"

Rolling her eyes Roslyn replied, "Oh, cousin, I really have to get you out more. Let me just say it is a type of swimming."

Blaine looked up from milking Gertrude. "And where did you learn about this kind of swimming?"

"Last week I went swimming with Scott Johnson, he might even be there today this will be fun you just wait and see. You do realize dear cousin since moving here to this dust bowl, nothing much exciting ever happens.

Since they were young, Roslyn had taken it upon herself to create as much excitement as she possibly could.

Blaine hurried to finish her chores; Roslyn even helped... a little, which was something that rarely happened.

Then off the two girls went toward the swimming hole.

With a mischievous twinkle in her eye, hoping to shock her cousin, Roslyn said, "Blaine, in order to go skinny-dipping we have to take all our clothes off." "Roslyn, I am not stupid I know we don't swim with our clothes on."

"Dear cousin, I mean **all** our clothes.... we swim naked."

3

"What! Roslyn, what if someone comes and sees us! Wait... you said you did this skinny-dipping with Scott Johnson... Roslyn Ewen! **You** swam naked with a **man!**" Roslyn lifted her nose in the air and spoke with indignation in her voice. "Yes, Miss proper, I did! Moreover, I had a wonderful time. And if you were not so good all the time you might have some fun too."

"Roslyn, I did not mean to upset you I just can't believe, well, that you took your clothes off in front of Scott Johnson."

"Silly, he turned around while I took mine off, then I got in the water then he took his off and he got in the water."

"And you turned your head away while he undressed right?"

"Well, since it is just me, you and the woods.... Mmm... No, I did not. I watched him undress."

"Oh, my heavens, Roslyn, you are wicked! What did he look like, Blaine lowered her voice as if someone might hear "I mean when he was naked?"

"Now, cousin, who is being wicked? All right, I will tell you. You already know he has a stunningly handsome face and he is very muscular, from the waist up that is. However, from the waist down, well I'll just say it he has no behind. His butt is completely flat. And his legs are so skinny they look like twigs. And his manly parts, well, let me just say, it did not look so manly to me."

Roslyn and Blaine started laughing, neither one noticed that Scott was hiding in the woods only a few feet away. Roslyn had forgotten she had asked him to meet her. He had expected Roslyn to be alone and hid when he heard her talking to Blaine.

He overheard everything Roslyn had said about him. Scott's pride was wounded and he became very angry. Until this moment Scott believed he and Roslyn not only swam naked together but they had shared an intimate moment in time together.

Scott was convinced young Roslyn loved him. Before this moment he had prepared to ask for her hand in marriage, now after hearing Roslyn poking fun of him he realized she had only used him.

He planned to wait right there, hidden in the woods to have his revenge. Blaine and Roslyn quickly stripped off their clothes, laying them on a rock, and then jumped into the cold water.

Both squealed as their bodies hit the spring fed pond.

As Blaine and Roslyn splashed about playing in the water they never noticed Scott silently removing all their clothes from the rock.

Quietly he slipped away back into the woods leaving nothing behind, not even their shoes.

After a few hours of swimming Blaine wanted to be getting home.

"Roslyn, it's gettin' late, I am getting all wrinkled, and I think we should head home now." Sighing Roslyn replying, "Oh, just when we are having fun you always want to go, Roslyn looked at her hands seeing them wrinkled, but I guess you are right we need to get our clothes and be getting home before uncle Shamus comes looking for us."

As the two girls climbed out of the pond, they noticed something strange; their clothes were not where they had left them. At first neither one of them panicked.

Roslyn said, "Maybe an animal moved them on us."

Blaine looked at Roslyn as if she were crazy. "You really think an animal would have taken everything?"

"Well, Blaine, it must have! Everything is gone, now isn't it? Now let's start looking for our clothes I am getting cold."

As the girls began hunting for their clothes in the woods near the swimming hole they heard a noise in the distance that made them stop, the girls realized it was voices coming toward them!

After a few moments of being frozen listening to the voices coming closer they realized it was Scott Johnson and another man's voice!

Blaine and Roslyn heard the man say to Scott, "Are you sure they'll still be there?" Scott replied with venom in his voice. "Yeah I am sure I stole their clothes. They ain't goin' anywhere."

The girls looked at each other with sheer fright in their eyes not knowing what these men might have in store for them. Blaine and Roslyn took hold of each other's hand and started running as fast as they could toward home.

When they hit the front door of Blaine's house, they came blasting thru the front door as if the devil himself were after them, and just as bare as a baby fawn in the woods. Blaine's folks were sitting at the dining table talking as the two flew through the house. Her folks mouths could have hit the floor.

Both girls were so frightened they had forgotten all about being naked, that is until they saw complete shock in the faces of Blaine's parents.

Carlin was able to find her voice first. "Young ladies, I suggest you both get upstairs and come down, **Decent and Presentable**, to explain why you just flew thru *my* house as bare as the day you were born!"

Quickly Blaine and Roslyn scurried upstairs like two frightened mice.

Blaine was desperately trying to come up with a story to tell her folks as to why they just raced in butt naked but nothing was coming to mind. Both girls agreed the truth would be the only way because neither one could come up with a story that would explain why they would be naked, outside, in the middle of the day.

Blaine was satisfied with their decision it was not common for Roslyn to agree to tell the truth. Roslyn had a gift of making up stories to get the two of them out of trouble. No matter how outrageous she normally persuaded everyone to believe her that is everyone except Blaine, she always knew the truth this time however Roslyn was stumped. Blaine also thought her Da' and Mama might not be as angry if they knew their clothes were stolen.

After they finished dressing, the girls held hands as they went down stairs. Blaine felt she was about to be executed; They entered the kitchen and found Shamus, Carlin and Roslyn's mother, Shannon waiting for them with looks of disapproval on their faces. Shamus cleared his throat. "Alright, you two, start explainin yourselves."

Blaine did not give Roslyn the chance to tell it her way she nervously started talking. "Da', this really isn't as bad as it looks. Roslyn and I went skinny-dipping and.... Roslyn rolled her eyes, letting out a moan she could not believe her simple-minded cousin just blurted out "we went skinny-dipping." Roslyn covered her eyes for a moment; she had to think of something fast!

Shamus interrupted. "You and Roslyn did **what**! Have you lost your mind, girl! You have **no** business skinny-dipping and what in the devil's name happened to your **clothes**!" This was not turning out the way Blaine had hoped she was not accustomed to her Da' yelling at her. Pleadingly, Blaine turned to Roslyn for help.

Roslyn sheepishly looked to her Aunt Carlin, in a soft imploring tone, she said, "Scott Johnson had told me about this kind of swimming so Blaine and me went to the swimming hole to try it. We had no idea Scott and his friends would steal our clothes." Carlin gasped in shock. "Heavens, child, do you mean to say this man talked you into swimming without your clothes? Was he there with you?"

Blaine spoke up so Roslyn would not have to lie about being with Scott.

"No, Mama, we were the only one's swimming. We heard Scott coming, he was talking to someone else, we couldn't tell who it was but we did hear Scott tell the other man he had taken our clothes while we were swimming."

Roslyn added. "That awful man thought by stealing our clothes he would keep us trapped there for who knows what. Blaine and me, we were so scared we started running and we did not stop until we got home."

Shannon finally spoke. "Well, girls, you are both safe I don't think Scott, I mean Mister Johnson, would have hurt either one of you, but he had no business takin' your clothes." Carlin looked at her sister in disbelief. "Sister, Scott Johnson is a grown man! He has no right talkin' to a child about swimming naked and seein' he stole their clothes! We have no way of knowing what horrible thing could have had in mind for our girls!"

Shamus added. "Carlin is right Shannon the man would not have come back with another if he had not schemed something bad for our girls. Men are takin' notice of our girls especially of your Roslyn Shannon. We have to protect our sweet gentle roses even more now it would seem."

Weeks went by; it seemed Roslyn's determination for mischief was escalating. Shamus started thinking it might be better to move his wife and daughter to a bigger city where Blaine would be among young **ladies** her own age. He had taken a serious dislike to the wayward direction Shannon was allowing his dear niece to go. He had tried to give the child guidance but nothing he did seemed to have a positive effect upon her. Now it seemed as if she was becoming a bad influence on his Blaine....

All Shamus ever wanted was a better life for his family, so he decided to answer an ad for a laborer, working in New York. After several weeks, Shamus received a reply inviting him to come to New York to meet Joseph Rossi. Shamus hoped to set up a new life for his family. He left as soon as he received the invitation. Shamus was gone for two months.

Once Shamus returned, he excitedly gave his family the good news of his new job; He had been offered a very promising job working as a builder for the most prominent family in New York. The Rossi's has also offered Blaine's Mama a position in the house as their main housemaid.

The decision was made that they would move to New York late summer of 1887. Blaine was not certain she wanted to move she liked her life in Sweetwater, living in a big city was never her dream it was Roslyn's. As the day drew closer for them to leave, Blaine gave serious thought about what her Da said about their move, maybe he was right, life would be better in New York. Afterward, Blaine found herself becoming more and more excited! She stayed up one night to listen to her Da' and Mama talking about their plans from what she overheard the Rossi family was into just about everything from building homes and stables to raising horses and trading them too!

As Blaine quietly continued listen to her parent's conversation her heart broke as her Da spoke. "Carlin my love we will not be able to take Shannon and Roslyn with us I am sorry, but the offer was just for us." Carlin sat quietly for a moment then softly spoke; "Shamus I realize this move is important to you and I will do what you say, but I don't have it in me to tell Shannon she must stay here alone." Putting his arm around her, "love I will talk to her and remember she will not be alone she has Roslyn. Carlin sank into his arms and cried.

Tears silently ran down Blaine's face she never considered Roslyn not coming with her! What moments ago she thought to be exciting was now terribly painful. She found it hard to believe, she would be separated from her best friend the one she counted closer than a real sister. She decided this move was no good and she for one would say so! Waiting for a good time to tell her Da how she felt she realized how excited he was about the move. Blaine chose not to express her negative feeling her Da was happy…she would have to try her best to be happy too, at least make him believe she was.

The day arrived for the Ewen's to begin their journey.

Shamus had explained to Shannon that she and Roslyn could not come with them. Shannon did not seem to mind but Roslyn was not happy about being left behind in the dusty little town while Blaine went off to the big city without her. It was her dream to leave this place, her dream not Blaine's to move to a big city!

Blaine had the most difficult time saying goodbye to Roslyn leaving her behind just did not feel right.

The girls promised to write to one another every day.

Carlin and Shannon agreed Roslyn could visit just as soon as this could be arranged with the Rossi's.

Heartbroken the two girls hugged and said their final farewells, and then the Ewen's were off.

The completely wearisome trip lasted a total of three and a half weeks from Wyoming to New York.

Blaine was so exhausted from traveling she was overjoyed when her Da' told her they were almost at their destination.

She had seen some beautiful sights along the way, an amazing herd of buffalo grazing so close she could almost touch them, the most incredible field of wild flowers, every color she could imagine, spread out like a festive blanket on the ground; it was breath taking.

Even though Blaine was excited about the beauty she was seeing as they traveled her heart was broken over Roslyn. They had been two peas in a pod most of their lives always together and usually in some kind of trouble.

Blaine's mind drifted ….

'Mama always talks about how beautiful Roslyn is it is true Roslyn is so beautiful. People always think her to be several years older me. Roslyn likes that, she uses her beauty, and the fact she looks older than her years to her favor plying for the attention from men.

I wonder what it would be like to have a handsome man desire me, just the way Roslyn has described to me. Oh, it must feel just wonderful. I do envy Roslyn for the attention she gets; well, maybe not all of it, but some of it….'

Even though they promised to write every day, Blaine knew it would never be the same.

It was as if a huge piece of her childhood was gone forever.

As Blaine continued to daydream about her and Roslyn, she fell asleep to dreams of their childish antics.

CHAPTER 2

New York, fall 1887

As the Ewen's coach arrived at the Rossi estate, Blaine woke to see the largest most pristine house she had ever laid her eyes on. Her mind raced, 'this is just perfect!' Blaine mouth dropped open in sheer amazement.

"Da'! Are we in the right place? It looks like a King lives here!" She was overwhelmed at the size and beauty of the Rossi's estate.

Shamus replied, "yes, Blaine dear, this is the right place. And no, Mister Rossi's not a King."

"Well, he sure has a place befitin', one I would say," Carlin excitedly added.

The coach came to a stop. "Alright you two don't just sit there with your tongues wagin' out.

Get your belongings together and be gettin' yourselves off this coach."

As the Ewen's began to unload their belongings, Mister Joseph Rossi came out to greet them. He was a very tall muscular man whom Blaine would have considered scary, except for the great big smile on his face.

Mister Rossi greeted Shamus as if he had known him all his life.

Mister Rossi called her Da by his first name, but Shamus greeted him as him Mister Rossi.

Mister Rossi called for his wife, Anna; she looked just like a jolly Irish woman.

She went straight up to Blaine's Mama with open arms.

"We are so happy you finally made it. I hope your trip was not too unpleasant." "No, Mrs. Rossi, the trip was long for sure, but not unpleasant. Thank you for asking," "Mrs. Ewen, I do dislike being so formal, do you mind if I call you Carlin?"

"Please, Mrs. Rossi, I would prefer to be called Carlin." "Carlin, I insist you call me Anna. Mrs. Rossi sounds so formal." Carlin remained silent for a moment, "Mrs. Rossi, since I will be employed in your home I think it proper for me to call *you* Mrs. Rossi."

Blaine watched her Mama and Mrs. Rossi go rounds, in a nice manor of course, about her Mama using Mrs. Rossi's first name.

Mrs. Rossi finally realized she was not going to win against a stubborn Irish woman.

She surrendered and let Carlin call her Mrs. Rossi. Then Mrs. Rossi turned her attention toward Blaine.

With all the crazy bantering between her Mama and Mrs. Rossi, Blaine was thinking attention was not what she was wanting at all.

Mrs. Rossi exclaimed as she reached for Blaine, "Oh, and my heavens! Look at this beautiful young woman! She is a vision!"

Mrs. Rossi carried on and on, making a fuss about Blaine's red hair, her porcelain skin and her green eyes.

She said Blaine would be the envy of New York society. Blaine had no idea what Mrs. Rossi was rambling on about.

However, she was happy that someone, besides herself and her Da', finally appreciated her red hair.

Blaine was smiling and totally absorbed in Mrs. Rossi's compliments.

She failed to notice her Mama's disapproving look as they entered the house.

The Ewen's had thought they would be staying in an out building away from the main house, but much to their surprise, Mister and Mrs. Rossi had a small wing of the house, as Mrs. Rossi explained it, not being used, so they decided to turn the wing over to the Ewen's.

"Carlin, I have readied this wing of the house for your family. Mister Rossi and I would like for you and your families to feel as part of our family, so please, take time to get settled in, and please feel free to look around. I will come back in a little while to check on you."

With that, Mrs. Rossi turned and left the three of them standing in one of the two large bedrooms.

Blaine ran to the window and opened it.

"Mama, come here! Look, we can walk out the window!" Carlin came to the window and calmly walked out with Blaine. "Isn't this beautiful, Mama?"

Carlin acted as if she was not overly impressed, "Yes, Blaine, it is."

"Mama, do you know what this is called?" motioning to the place where they stood.

Carlin turned to go back into the room, "I believe this is called a veranda." Shamus came out to see what the fuss was about. He was amazed at what he saw.

"I think I can see all the way to Ireland from up here! Come on, Blaine darlin', let us see what other surprises we can find."

Blaine and her Da' went running thru the rooms like two little children.

Shamus called for Carlin, "Carlin my love, come here please."

Carlin entered a small room with a washbasin and a seat with a cover on it. Shamus stood with Blaine. "Carlin, my love, would you possibly know what this silly lookin' thing might be?"

Carlin was quite serious. "Shamus, I believe this is a chamber pot." "A what?" Asked Shamus.

"I have never seen one, mind you, but I have heard a chamber pot is a place to take care of your private matters."

Carlin found the whole thing something not to be discussed, so she tried to explain its purpose quietly.

Both, Shamus and Blaine found it quite amusing.

They both danced around acting foolish.

"I think I have died and gone to heaven, no more goin' out in the cold to the outhouse!" Shamus made up a crazy song about the chamber pot.

He sang: "Oh back in my sweet Ireland in the frosty cold night, to the outhouse I would wonder. Now in the new land, I found the chamber pot. So… Across the hall from my warm soft bed, to relieve myself I do saunter!"

Shamus and Blaine were laughing, but Carlin was not amused.

Carlin felt her family was acting like uneducated back woods people and found it embarrassing, even though no one was around to see their foolishness.

Carlin announced. "If you two insist on acting like a couple of pixilated leprechauns, I will have no choice but to deny you two are my kin!"

"Oh, Carlin darlin', we were just havin' a bit of fun. No one is about to see our Irish comin' out. You know, my love, you could stand to have a little fun yourself. You have been lookin' a might pale since we left Wyoming. Are you missin' your sister already, darlin'?"

"No, just feelin' a little under the weather and tired of your silly blarney, Shamus Ewen." Carlin grabbed a broom swatting at him as he ran out of the room giggling They all were laughing as Shamus ran down the stairs as if the devil himself were after him.

As he reached the bottom of the stairs, Shamus found Mister Rossi looking up at him; Quickly Shamus stopped his foolishness.

"Shamus, I was just about to go looking for you. I have a few questions I would like to ask you about the new storehouse."

"That would be just grand Mister Rossi. I am afraid my ladies have no further use for me upstairs."

The two men disappeared out the back door toward the storehouse site.

Carlin and Blaine quietly unpacked their trunks. Lately Blaine and her Mama had not been very close.

Blaine had wanted to ask her Mama what was wrong, but she was afraid of the answer.

She was afraid her Mama blamed her for their family moving to New York.

Blaine knew it was difficult for her Mama to leave the only family she had. She knew this situation upset her Mama.

Truth be told what started out as exciting had turned into a very difficult situation but Blaine did not want to complain.

Moving to New York was what her Da' said was best for them, so she pretended everything was just fine…

Not long after Blaine and her Mama finished unpacked, Mrs. Rossi came to find Carlin. "Carlin, I was hoping you would feel up to giving me a hand in my new sitting room. I realize you just arrived, if you are too tired I understand."

"Oh no, Mrs. Rossi, I will come with you right now. I would be delighted to help." With that, the two older women disappeared down the hall toward the stairs discussing the plans for the sitting room.

Much to Mister Rossi's surprise, Shamus was just as excited to start work as he was. Moreover, the two men got along with each other just like two old friends. It was not long before they began working on the storehouse.

Carlin had been working on the sitting room with Mrs. Rossi for several days, now their work was reaching its completion.

Blaine brought five books with her; she had now read every one of them.

For her firsts few weeks in her new home, Blaine tried to adjust to spending most of her time alone; not knowing what to do in her new surroundings, the house being so big she thought she might get lost.

Boredom had become Blaine's new best friend and what a sad companion it turned out to be.

Eventually, Mrs. Rossi noticed Blaine's boredom and took pity on her.

"Blaine, dear, I am so sorry you have been neglected for so long. I do not want you to feel that you must stay in your room all day you can go exploring in the house. Please, go anywhere you would like."

Noticing the books on Blaine's night table, Anna added, "I can see you enjoy reading. We have a large library upstairs; Help yourself to any of the books that interest you." Completely enthused, Blaine said. "Thank you so much, Mrs. Rossi! I do love to read." Right away, she decided to begin exploring. Blaine thought to herself; 'Well with so many rooms, I might as well start at the top and work my way down and see how many rooms I can explore in one day.'

As Blaine climbed the staircase, it seemed to go on forever.

When Blaine reached the top, she discovered a long hallway lined on both sides with what seemed to be very old family photographs.

Blaine walked up one side slowly examining the faces in each photograph then she slowly examined the next wall of photographs curious about the people.

She thought to herself; 'I wonder if any of them had a beautiful place such as this to live in? On the other hand, maybe their life was harder like ours has been? I wonder where these people came from and why do some look so sad? Oh, I cannot wait to write Roslyn about this place.'

Blaine sat down on a red satin bench, examining one photograph that had caught her attention.

The next thing she knew she was being abruptly awoken. "Blaine, sweet heart, wake up!"

Blaine woke with a jump, confused, she was not sure where she was. "Blaine, honey, are you alright?"

"Yes ma'am, for a moment I was not sure where I was. I am sorry. Blaine apologized. "Honey you gave all of us a fright we have had every one searching for you. even our stable hand is all worried about you, child."

Blaine was still in a dazed. Rubbing the sleep from her eyes, she said, "I have no idea how long I was asleep.

"Well dear I have no idea either, but we have had an all-out search for you for about an hour now."

"Oh! My goodness, I am so sorry! Da' and Mama must be ready to switch my hide!" "Blaine dear, no need to fret I doubt a switching is What your parents have in mind, they're both much too worried about you for that." Taking Blaine's arm gently in hers, Mrs. Rossi assisted Blaine to her feet directing her toward the stairs.

"Now, my dear, if you are awake, let us go down to dinner. Aggie has a nice dinner all ready and waiting for us."

Blaine touched Mrs. Rossi's arm, as they descended the stairs she asked, "Mrs. Rossi, do you think, possibly, when you get some time, you could tell me the story of all the people that are in those photographs?"

"I would be delighted, Darling.... Did you spend your entire day up here looking at the Rossi family photographs?"

"Oh yes Ma'am! I find them completely fascinating; I have so many questions I want to ask you."

With a smile, Mrs. Rossi replied, "Alright my dear, what are the questions you have?" Blaine began her barrage of questions, "Why do so many of the people look so sad? Where did your family come from? How old are these photographs'? Are you and Mister Rossi in any of the photographs'?"

Blaine's questions continued as they reached the main floor.

As Mrs. Rossi and Blaine reached the bottom, she turned to Blaine and said. "Child, you truly amaze me. Your curiosity and enthusiasm for knowledge surpasses any I have ever seen... Blaine, I just had a wonderful thought, how would you feel if I asked your parents if they would allow me to tutor you. Would you like me to be your tutor, Blaine?" Blaine thought for a moment not being quite sure of the meaning of the word tutor. Moreover, not wanting to look completely stupid in front of Mrs. Rossi, she replied slowly.

"That would mean you would be my teacher, right?"

"In a way, yes, dear that is what it would mean." Blaine said excitedly. "Oh! Please ask them, Mrs. Rossi, I would love to go back to school!

As the two of them entered the dining room, Blaine's Da' and Mama came running up, both fussing at her at the same time.

"Blaine girl, where have you been?" "We have been worried sick!"

"You should never sneak off and hide like that." "Don't ever be doin' a foolish thing like that again child!" "You had this entire house searching for you."

"What were you thinkin', child, goin, off in such a big place as this?"

The onslaught would have continued without giving poor Blaine time to defend herself, but Mrs. Rossi stepped in to rescue her.

She apologized, "Please, Shamus, Carlin, this is really my fault, you see, I told Blaine to feel free to explore the whole house. I had not realized Blaine's great desire for knowledge; therefore, when she found the library she literally spent the whole day examining it.

She is amazing, for a child her age, for her to have such an interest in history is truly a wonderful thing, wouldn't you agree?"

Blaine did not say a word, but the reference that her Da' and Mama kept making to her being a child, and now Mrs. Rossi was making the same reference, all of this was really beginning to chafe her nerves.

'What is their problem anyway; she thought,' I am *not* a child. I will be sixteen in a week.

Most young women my age are preparing to marry!'

Carlin interrupted, "My Blaine has always been wise beyond her years, isn't that right Shamus, darlin?"

"Yes, Carlin, dear, she be a smart one, my girl, god bless her," Shamus said with a proud smile on his face.

"Well, before we eat I would like to make an offer that would, one; help us keep up with Blaine's where bouts."

Blaine was not happy; she did not like where this conversation between her folks and Mrs. Rossi was headed she thought, 'How dare they talk about me like I am not even here! And what happened to going back to school.

Blaine remained silent, looking at the floor, hoping this would be over soon. But soon Blaine's attention went back to the conversation at hand. "And two, help Blaine's already bright mind grow even more."

Shamus cleared his throat, "Mrs. Rossi, I am not meanin' to be rude, but Mister Rossi and I have been out pounden' fence posts all day long. I am pretty sure if you don't get to the point right quick you are gonna' have two big lumps on your nice clean floor, that is if we don't be gettin' some food in us pretty quick!"

"Oh, gentlemen, please pardon me for being so winded. Please, Seth, tell Aggie to bring dinner now."

Mister Rossi turned his attention to Seth, the Rossi's stable hand, "and get a plate for yourself young man you will be having dinner with us."

Blaine noticed that dinner was very nice; everyone seemed to get along so well. It felt as if her family had been adopted this made her very happy.

Blaine could not wait to write and tell Roslyn. She just knew Roslyn would be happy for her.

At the end of dinner, Carlin and Blaine helped clear the table, as Aggie wash and cleaned up the dinner dishes.

Carlin took notice of Shamus going into the study with Mister **and** Mrs. Rossi.

Carlin knew she was feeling jealous of Mrs. Rossi. She thought, 'All that talk about my Blaine being the envy of New York. Why is that woman filling my daughter's head with such unrealistic notions? Blaine is a smart girl but she is not the envy of society' Although Carlin believed she would never utter her thoughts aloud, she felt strongly that Blaine was doomed to live an ordinary simple life.

However, as for Roslyn she would be able to do anything, she was such a fine beauty.

Oh, how Carlin had wished Blaine were more like Roslyn. That night Blaine sat at her window writing her letter to Roslyn.

'My Dearest Roslyn, Oh, how I miss you cousin. I truly wish you were here with me. I have wonderful news; remember I told you about Mrs. Rossi, she has offered to tutor me! I am not sure Da' and Mama are going to approve but if they do wouldn't it be wonderful! I am excited even though I have no idea what Mrs. Rossi will be teaching me. Roslyn, she is so refined yet down to earth I do believe she has found a special place in my heart. I hope you can come soon so you can meet her. I love you please write soon I regret not hearing from you. Love Blaine'

Back in Carlin and Shamus' room, Carlin lay in their bed and waited for Shamus. Shamus slowly came into the room assuming Carlin was sleeping; he quietly began to remove his clothes. Carlin softly asks. "So what did Mrs. Rossi have to say?"

"Well, Darlin', she wants to teach Blaine. Tutor is the word she used." "Oh, and what was the decision on this tutoring?"

"I told her it would be fine, as long as it wasn't every day. We also decided to include etiquette of New York society."

"What! Are you telling me there is something wrong with Irish etiquette," Carlin said sarcastically.

"Shamus, why do you want this woman to try to turn our Blaine into someone she is not.

And try to make her believe she can be something she never will be."

Shamus yelled, "Woman! What in the devil are talking about! And you better calm down and make sense."

"Shamus, ever since we walked into this house Mrs. Rossi has been trying to get her hands on Blaine. Filling her head with nonsense about her being the envy of New York society. Making such a fuss over her red hair and her eyes. Yes, Blaine is very smart, but Shamus, she is plain. She does not and never will possess the beauty like Roslyn. This woman is leading Blaine down a false path."

"No! Carlin! Someone has led you down a false path! Unlike you, woman! I want Blaine to have every chance to have a better life, something you seem to want to deny your own child! You do not even deserve to call Blaine your daughter. And right now, I cannot abide to look at you. I think your jealousy and bitterness has eaten you up!"

Shamus left the room, slamming the door behind him. Unfortunately, Blaine was still sitting at her window.

She had heard every word her parents said. She was so sick at her stomach and her heart was broken, but no tears would come she just sat there stunned by her Mama's words … how could her own Mama hate her so? At that moment, her fear was realized; her Mama did resent her for them moving to New York! 'This is all my fault,' thought Blaine.

Then Blaine thought of her Da's words. Though heartbroken she found comfort in what her Da' said about her.

Blaine could not sleep; she was very upset that her parents were fighting over her. Late into the night, Blaine crept out of her room with a heavy blanket and a pillow. she found her Da' curled up on a fairly small couch, so she took the back cushions off, put the pillow under his head and covered him with the thick blanket.

Blaine kissed him on the cheek, and then she went back to bed, slowly falling asleep.

The next morning there was a light knock on Blaine's door.

The door slowly opened. Aggie came in and opened the curtains, which awoke Blaine. Rossi's had employed Aggie for ten years she had been with the Rossi's since she was ten now she was about twenty years old.

Aggie was a buxom blonde-haired woman from England who was a hardworking, outspoken young woman.

Now destined to be Blaine's new best friend, Aggie was taken with Blaine and found her Irish antics amusing.

Blaine sat up in her bed, rubbing her eyes, "Aggie do you need my help this morning?" "Not me, Miss, but your tutor, Mrs. Rossi is waiting for you down stairs, and it is my job to make sure you look like a lady. It is Mrs. Rossi's under takin' to make you act like one! Begging your pardon, Miss, I have seen the crazy way you and your father act when you think no one is about. And even if you had the worst case of the pox in the world, I would still have the better end of the job," Aggie began to giggle.

Blaine laughed a little, then replied, "Well, Aggie, I do believe there are some who would completely disagree with you."

Aggie added playfully, "beggin' your pardon again, Miss, but, then they ain't seen what I have seen, that is all I am sayin'."

They both started laughing as Aggie began to help Blaine get dressed.

Blaine sat at the dressing table, as Aggie began to fix her hair.

Aggie added oil for shine, brushing Blaine's hair until it glistened. She marveled at the color of Blaine's flame red hair, "Your hair truly rivals the sun, Miss! It is truly very lovely."

Aggie, being proud of her handy work, gave Blaine her mirror, "see for yourself." As Blaine peered into the mirror, she saw the reflection of a beautiful young woman, someone she hardly recognized, looking back at her.

Suddenly, the hurtful words of her Mama came crashing in around her ears. Blaine's countenance changed immediately; quickly, she placed the mirror face down.

Blaine stood, walking toward the door, "well that's enough of that. I shouldn't keep Mrs. Rossi waiting."

Turning back and giving Aggie a weak smile, "we better be getting me down stairs before she sends out another search party."

Aggie was perplexed over the sudden change in Blaine's mood. She wondered what happened to disturb Blaine so drastically.

Aggie worried silently, 'oh, I hope I did not offend her with my big mouth.' she scolded herself, 'Aggie, girl, you just do not know when to stop.'

Blaine descended the stairs slowly, lost in thought, 'why did her Mama dislike her so?' Aggie reached out; touching Blaine's arm, she stopped her at the bottom of the stairs. "Miss Blaine, I was only havin' fun back there in your room, I did not mean to be offensive."

Blaine looked at Aggie, confused, then replied, "Aggie, you did nothing to offend me." "Oh, that's good. I was afraid because you seemed to be upset."

"Aggie, you are so sweet, it was not you. I was just thinking. That's all." Reassured she had not been the cause of Blaine's sudden melancholy, Aggie left Blaine as she entered the sitting room.

Blaine looked around she found no books, no writing tablets, nothing to do with school or study.

What she did see was a silver tea server, a basket with string and needles, and needlepoint. This was getting more confusing by the minute.

Blaine thought, 'What kind of class is this going to be anyhow?' Several minutes had passed and Mrs. Rossi had not come into the study yet. Blaine was tired of pacing, she decided to sit and wait for Mrs. Rossi.

Not long after Blaine took a seat, Mrs. Rossi cheerfully breezed into the study. "Good morning, my dear. Oh! I see Aggie has done a wonderful job, but it is not as if she would have a hard job with such a beauty as you. Oh, stand up, turn around let me look at you. Yes, yes... after our lessons today we will go straight to town. I will have you measured for a new wardrobe befitting New York society. Oh, by the way, Blaine, when will you be turning sixteen?"

Blaine's head was swimming from how fast Mrs. Rossi was talking when she finally caught up to what Mrs. Rossi asked, She answered, "In a week ma'am."

Mrs. Rossi became very excited and said, "Heavens to Betsy, we are just going to go to town this instant! I will send Seth to the field and tell your father."

Blaine asked, "what about Mama? Shouldn't I ask her too?"

"All I know is your father said everything to do with you is to go thru him... period!" Mrs. Rossi and Blaine found Seth in the stable.

Seth readied their carriage and then set off to find Mister Ewen and Mister Rossi.

As the two women road along in the carriage, Blaine asked. "Mrs. Rossi, will we be gone all day?"

"Child, we will be out late tonight. Have you ever dined at an inn before?"

"No Ma'am, I am sorry I have not. I have never been fitted for gowns before either. Why did you want to know when I turn sixteen?"

"First, Blaine, please do not be sorry. Not everyone is born into privilege. Some earn it, and some are helped to find it. Some are fortunate enough, to be born into privilege or marry into it. Second, a young woman's sixteenth year is special. In society this is the coming out year, the year a young woman is prepared to have suitors, possibly even marriage if she chooses. You Blaine, you are a very special young woman and I would like to see you given the opportunities to reach your personal potential. Not what someone else has decided for you. Blaine, in the next few months I can give you all the tools you will need to be part of New York society. I will show you how to dress, what to wear, and what not to wear. I will teach you how speak how to eat at social affairs. I will also teach you about people, who to stay away from, who to talk to but not to get too close to and who you are safe with."

Blaine shook her head, "Mrs. Rossi, I am afraid this will be the hardest schooling I have ever attended."

"First of all, you are absolutely right this will not be easy, but with hard work you will do just fine, Blaine, and as your tutor and your friend, I insist you call me Aunt Anna." "Are you sure Mrs. …I mean, Aunt Anna?"

Putting her arm around Blaine "I am absolutely positive my dear." The ride to the city took about an hour and a half.

Blaine and her new Aunt talked about simple things, their favorite colors, and Blaine's theory that all true Irish people love the color green and red roses.

Blaine told Anna all about Roslyn and all the fun they had and some of the trouble the two of them would get themselves into when they were younger.

After awhile Blaine noticed she had done most of the talking and she had not given her Aunt Anna very much time to tell her about herself.

She promised herself that on the ride home she would work on listening and do less talking.

Blaine could not believe her eyes when they reached the city. There were so many buildings and so many people! This was such a big place. She had never seen anything so amazing!

The carriage came to a stop in front of the gown shop.

Blaine was a little disappointed; she had hoped to get to see more of the city before entering the gown shop.

Blaine found being fitted for gowns was like being caught in a windstorm.

Fabric and straight pins were flying everywhere, Blaine was to terrified to move for fear she would come out looking like a human pincushion.

It seemed like hours before Blaine and her Aunt Anna were done with what Blaine considered cruel and unusual treatment.

Blaine thought. 'I cannot imagine women enduring this torture on purpose!' When Anna and Blaine came out of the gown shop, Anna looked at Blaine and started laughing, "Child, you are as white as a sheet! You look completely unraveled, are you alright?" "No, I do not think I am. I believe I have a few wound marks in my backside too! My goodness, Aunt Anna, why do they have to wield those pins like swords!"

Trying not to laugh Anna replied, "I am sorry Blaine dear, I told them we were in a hurry." Afterward her day much improved. As Blaine and Anna continued on to have more fun together shopping.

Anna enjoyed watching Blaine's expressions of excitement as she experienced her first shopping spree. Anna knew it would not be Blaine's last if she had a say in the matter.

Blaine and Anna shopped for hats, shoes, jewelry, stockings, and scarves.

So many beautiful things Blaine had never possessed in her life. All of the things Aunt Anna chose for Blaine were elegant and beautiful.

Blaine was having so much fun she had forgotten all about the time and all about her problems.

She was enjoying every minute with Anna. Blaine found no problem calling Mrs. Rossi, Aunt Anna for she had found a special place in Blaine's heart.

The last place they stopped before the inn was a very elite perfume and makeup shop, only the very wealthy shopped there.

Anna said to Blaine. "Come with me inside dear, I want to get a few things while we are here."

Blaine hesitated; Anna took Blaine by the hand. "Part of your training my dear, is to hold your head up and never let anyone, no matter who it is, make you feel unworthy, even if you doubt yourself on the inside never let it show. Now, you hold your head up and you come into this shop right now my dear."

Blaine had never worn makeup before or perfume but she truly enjoyed both, she felt so beautiful.

Anna would not let Blaine know how much she spent on her. Anna had no doubt Blaine's mother would pressure her to tell her how much was spent, so Anna was determined not tell anyone.

Anna and Blaine finally made it to the inn for dinner.

As they entered the inn, Blaine was amazed at the crystal and the candles, every table covered in red satin, everything was so elegant. Blaine tried to act as if she had eaten at many places just like it, but it astounded her.

Blaine quietly leaned in and whispered. "Aunt Anna, I am nervous and I am not sure what to order."

"That is quite alright my dear, try not to be nervous, I will order for both of us, if you would prefer."

"Yes Aunt Anna, I think that would be fine with me."

Blaine was relieved that Anna offered to order for them both for nothing looked familiar to her, Blaine was pleased with her food.

Knowing Blaine was nervous Anna allowed Blaine to have a little wine, however, Blaine became quite giddy and silly, so Anna did not believe that wine would be on the lesson plan ever again.

By eight in the evening, they were back in their carriage headed home. "You look tired Blaine dear, would you like to rest your head in my lap?" Blaine smiled laying her head on Anna's lap. Anna pet Blaine's hair.

Before drifting off to sleep, Blaine thought of something she wanted to say. "Aunt Anna." "Yes Blaine dear?"

"No one has ever been so kind to me, and I want to thank you, not just for all the beautiful things you bought me today, but for caring so much for me and being my friend."

Anna smiled, Blaine's words warmed her heart, "You truly are a special young lady Blaine, and I think it a privilege to be among your friends."

Everyone in the Rossi home was asleep when the carriage reached the estate.

Everyone that is, except for Shamus Ewen, who was waiting up for his little girl to return home.

He came out to meet the carriage; Shamus assisted Anna down from inside, "Thank you Mrs. Rossi for given my Blaine such a special day. I know this meant the world to her."

Anna touched Shamus's arm, "You have raised a fine young woman Shamus, you should be very proud of her. She is an incredible person I am impressed. Good night Shamus."

Anna turned and headed up the front stairs. "Good night Mrs. Rossi."

Then Shamus climbed into the carriage, picking up his sleeping little girl, he carried her into the house, up the stairs to her room.

Blaine never woke as her Da' tucked her into her bed, she dreamt wonderful dreams that night, all about the fun she and her Aunt Anna had that day, and the extraordinary sights of the big city. Blaine would never forget this special day that she shared with her Aunt Anna.

CHAPTER 3

The next morning Blaine woke early to write Roslyn. 'My Dearest Roslyn, I have such exciting things to share with you. Yesterday Mrs. Rossi took me to the big city, just as you always talked about Roslyn. She and I have become the closest of friends. She now wishes me to call her Aunt Anna. Oh, Roslyn she took me shopping yesterday for things I could have only dreamt of having although I have to say being fitted for gowns is as close to war as I ever want to get! I have pin marks in my backside from those crazed dressmakers! Aunt Anna took me to a real perfume shop I have makeup, perfume, and silk stockings. And we ate at an Inn it was so elegant and I was so nervous! I tried wine for the first time, nasty stuff, but the food was wonderful. Roslyn, we have been apart now some two months, I know you must be very busy I am distressed that I still I have not received a letter from you. Please write me soon. Even though I am having a wonderful time, I miss you frightfully bad. Love Blaine' Blaine had just finished her letter when Aggie knocked at her door.

"May I come in? Miss."

"Of course Aggie, but I did not think I had lessons today." "Oh no, Miss you don't with Mrs. Rossi but you do with Seth." "With Seth? Whatever for?"

"Well….so he can teach you to ride a horse …proper, like a lady, Miss." "You mean to tell me ladies ride different too!"

"Yes, they do, and Mrs. Rossi says you should be wearing this outfit." "Aggie! What is this? And why do I have to wear this ridiculous hat!"

"Now Miss Blaine, calm down, I realize this might be a bit overwhelming, but I am here to help you, and you know Mrs. Rossi would never do anything that ain't proper. So no matter how silly it looks to you and me. Obviously all society young women are wearing this."

Aggie held up the riding gown, "And I don't think they find it silly. So, we need to be gettin this outfit on you now?"

"Alright, Aggie you're right, but I do not see how anyone, society or not, could ride a horse wearing this." Blaine picked up the riding habit and tossed it on the bed.

Aggie finished with Blaine, both girls descended the stairs Blaine first with Aggie right behind her.

Blaine looked regal, elegant with her black and white pin striped riding gown and her perfect white gloves', and habit she was a picture of society and a nervous wreck. Then Blaine remembered what her Aunt Anna told her, she held her head up and smiled.

"Now where is Seth? I need to prove to the man I know how to ride a horse." Even though inside she was franticly thinking, 'How on earth am I going to get my leg over a saddle in this ridiculous skirt and how am I going to keep this hat from flying off, and these white gloves? Unless that horse has just been scrubbed in lye soap there is no way any of this outfit is coming back looking the same not with me wearing it. Oh, this is a nightmare! And I for one want to get this over with.'

Seth was standing next to Mister Rossi. Mister Rossi said in a calm sweet voice, "wouldn't it be a better idea if you ate first Miss Blaine?"

Blaine looked at the disapproval on her Mama's face and it was too much for her to bear.

She turned and headed for the door, she lightly called back. "I will eat when I get back, are you coming Seth?"

Out the front doors the two of them went, down the path toward the stables.

As Seth and Blaine reached the stables, Blaine asked Seth, "Seth, please tell me this is a joke?"

"I don't know what you mean Miss Blaine; I was given instruction to teach you how to ride the way society ladies do."

"Alright Seth before I lose my temper how do society ladies ride?" "Well, Miss Blaine, ladies ride side saddle."

"Seth, how in heavens name do you ride side saddle?"

Seth laughed, "Well, fortunately for me Miss, I don't have to cuz I would break my bloody neck for sure. But I can teach you how."

Blaine took a deep breath not at all impressed with Seth's ability to teach her anything, "Seth your confidence overwhelms me. Oh see, I used the word overwhelms, I learned that word yesterday and I already have use for it. Probably the last time I will ever get to use it, because this ridiculous undertaking is gonna get me killed!"

"Don't be so glum Miss Blaine; I am going to be with you the whole way."

Seth brought around the horse for Blaine with the sidesaddle ready for her to mount.

One look and Blaine started laughing. "What kind of saddle is this, and how am I supposed to ride that dressed like this?"

"Miss Blaine, this is a side saddle and I am going to help you ride. Now, Miss Blaine I'll just help you up."

As Seth lifted Blaine, they both went tumbling into the hay. He landed on top of Blaine. Blaine said with a nervous giggle. "I do not believe this was part of the, um... Riding lessons, was it Seth?"

Seth quickly jumped up with his face bright red. "Miss Blaine I...um... I am truly sorry please forgive me. I..., I... did not do that on purpose! I swear I didn't."

Seth helped Blaine up out of the hay. Blaine dusted herself off.

Seth tried to help pluck hay from her hair and gown.

She smiled and said softly. "No worries Seth I never thought you would do something like that on purpose, I never took you for a two timer."

"What are you talkin' about Miss?"

Blaine gave Seth a mischievous smile, "It's just that I have seen the way you and Aggie look at each other, when you think no one is looking."

Realizing Seth seemed completely lost as to what she was talking about Blaine quickly corrected herself, "Oh my, am I wrong, are you not sweet on each other? I am so sorry Seth. Please forgive me."

Seth grinned, shaking his head. "No Miss, you're not wrong, I just didn't think anyone knew that's all. Aggie is the sweetest girl I know, I really think she has hung my moon and stars. I am hopin' to make her my wife someday."

Seth could not believe he had just said all that to a complete stranger and a woman at that.

He felt like kicking himself so quickly he had spilled out his most prized secret! Seth was completely embarrassed, and determined to change the subject!

Sensing his discomfort, Blaine tried to put Seth at ease, "Oh Seth, that is beautiful, I am happy for you both and your secret is safe with me."

"Ok Miss, we have to stop gossiping' and get you on that horse, even if it kills us." "Uh! That is what worries me."

This time Blaine carefully placing her foot in the stirrup, Seth assisted her on to the horse.

Blaine adjusted herself onto the sidesaddle she placed her knee up over the horn, as Seth instructed.

Seth Mounted his horse as he held onto the reins of Blaine's horse.

They exited the stable, nice and slow, and then headed down the road out of sight of the stables.

Seth and Blaine started riding along gently.

Blaine was getting frustrated with Seth, being lead around as a child riding for the first time was humiliating!

Finally, she decided to say something to him. "Seth, I believe that I can handle the reins on my own."

Seth reluctantly turned the rains over to Blaine. "If you are sure you can handle it Miss." "I am, thank you, I have been on a horse before"

They continued to ride along gently. The sky began to turned gray rain softly started falling. Seth eyed the sky with concern.

"Miss Blaine, I think we need to be headin back to the stable. I believe the weather is about to turn on us."

Blaine said teasingly, "Seth, I do think you are afraid of getting wet."

"No Ma'am, I just know the weather can change fast, I really think we should be getting back now."

Before Blaine could say anything else, the sky broke forth with pouring rain, suddenly, lightning struck a nearby tree both horses were terribly spooked.

Seth's horse reared up throwing him to the ground. The frightened horse bolted down the road out of sight.

He jumped up and took off running after his horse, not realizing he was leaving Blaine to fend for herself.

Blaine's horse was running wild; all she could do was hold on to the horse's reins.

She tried her best to keep her leg held tight to the horn.

The beast ran her thru trees and briers, finally throwing her off into a muddy pond.

Brushing her tangled hair out of her eyes, she wiped mud from her face. Blaine looked up at her horse, which was calmly drinking water from the pond.

"You and I are going to have a come to Jesus meeting horse and I promise it will not be me meeting him first! You ornery four legged piece of rawhide! If I could walk back home I would have a mind to cook you over a fire right now!"

A man just happened to be watering his horse just a few feet away. As he walked up behind her, he cleared his throat. "Excuse me Miss."

Startled Blaine quickly stood up. She turned around much too quickly causing her to fall back into the water, as she regained her balance and stood up again.

She asked a little more abruptly than she had wanted. "Who are you?"

The man replied politely. "My name is Ashton, and what might your name be Miss?" "Blaine." she simply replied as she tried to smooth her drenched gown and brush her disheveled hair into place.

"Well, Miss Blaine, would you like some assistance out of the water?"

Blaine quickly calmed herself. "Oh, yes that would be very helpful. Thank you, sir." Ashton waded into the water, placing his arm around Blaine's waist he tried to pick her up.

Blaine's temper flared! She slapped his hands away, and said, "Sir! I am very capable of using my own legs if you do not mind, thank you!"

She took hold of his shoulder and waded out of the water with him. Then she turned to him and said, "Thank you Mister Ashton."

Ashton was trying to keep the conversation going, "And just as an observation that is a pretty good piece of horse flesh you got there. I personally would not recommend pitching him on a fire. However, the coming to Jesus thing, I guess no man should step in between a lady, her horse, and her lord, so that one is defiantly up to you."

Blaine could not contain herself and burst into laughter, Ashton began laughing too. After a few moments they could hear the distant rumbling of thunder, Ashton looked up at the sky.

"I have no idea where you live Miss Blaine, but there is another bad storm coming, and my family lives close by, if you want to double up, I will take you to my home. I know my mother would just love you."

"Oh, no thank you sir, I can manage on my own just fine, I do not live far either and I have to teach this fine piece of horse flesh, as you put it, a lesson."

Ashton protested, "Now how are you going to do that, seein you are all wet, in a long skirt, riding sidesaddle?"

"Because," Blaine said softly, "I plan to do it my way this time." "Mister Ashton, would you please hold the reins?"

Ashton reached for the reins. He was bemused with Blaine's actions With haste, she unbuckled the saddle, pulled it off her horse's back.

She carried the awkward saddle and placed it under a tree.

Half mumbling to herself "why on earth ladies feel the need for such torture is beyond me!"

Swearing she should just burry the useless thing.

Clearing his throat to gain Blaine's attention.

"This still does not solve the problem of how you are going to ride the horse."

"Oh yes, well…. I do not know you but I hope you will not be offended, this has been a frightfully distressing day, and well… my actions at this moment may seem, a bit, um, crass so if you don't mind please turn your head."

Ashton acted as if he was going to look away but did not.

Blaine reached down took hold of the slit in her riding skirt and ripped it all the way up to her thigh.

The last thing she said to Ashton was…"Can I have the reins now please?" Still stunned with his mouth agape, Ashton handed them to her.

Blaine took hold of the reins and her horse's mane threw her leg over and with a smile took off riding her horse bareback.

Before Ashton came to his senses, she was gone.

She was riding so hard he knew he could not catch her.

However, there was always tomorrow and he planned to find out who she was.

Blaine found Seth in the stable.

Seth was so happy to see her. Without a word he pulled her off her horse and gave her a big bear hug. "Miss Blaine, I was worried sick. I swear I looked for you, after I caught up with my horse I looked for you I was just getting ready to go and fetch your Papa." Blaine was exhausted, and quiet unnerved at the thought the rawhide might have followed her.

"Well, as you can see I am back so you don't need to send out reinforcements. Please, Seth I will explain what happened to me later, just go get Aggie for me first."

"Yes, right away Miss."

Seth hurried to find Aggie; he thought Miss Blaine must be exasperated with him for not holding on to her.

Aggie raced into the stable, she came to a sudden halt, letting out a scream when she caught sight Blaine covered in mud and her clothes torn.

"Oh my lord! My dear sweet Miss! What horrible thing has happened to you?" Blaine quickly ran to Aggie putting her arms around her.

"Aggie my friend, please calm down, its nothing like you think, I had a riding accident that's all. I was thrown from my horse and I landed in a mud hole. Anyway, I do not want everyone in the house to see me in this sad state. So I need you to help me get cleaned up... out here."

Aggie breathed deeply; relieved her worse fear was unfounded.

Right away Aggie's countenance changed, "don't worry Miss; I will go fetch one of your gown and all your trimmings."

Seth added, "And I will get you hot bath water, I just built a new trough, you can use it as a tub, if it doesn't bother you, I mean."

Giving Seth a reassuring smile, "No Seth, I do not mind."

Seth looked at Blaine sheepishly, "Miss Blaine, I am truly sorry about today. I would have come after you but my horse threw me and took off for home and...."

Blaine touched Seth's arm. "It is alright, I am fine Seth, but I do need that bath."

"I mean no offense, Miss Blaine, but I have some fine oil, it comes from the Middle East somewhere, but it works great on manes and tails. I figured since your hair has had such beating with the mud and all, you might want to try it."

"That would be nice Seth; I would like to try it."

After Seth had readied her bath and given her the oil, he left her to her private matters. Now Blaine was all alone, except for the horses, she was sure they would not mind her being naked soaking in their new trough.

She quickly removed the remains of her riding outfit. Easing herself into the soothing hot water. Blaine could not believe the invigorating feeling of bathing in the night air.

She loved the smell of the shampoo and soap Seth gave her. When she completed her luxurious moonlit bath, Blaine's hair and skin felt like silk.

Blaine said to the horses, "I am going to ask your man Seth if he has any spare bottles of this heavenly potion. You are spoiled I hope you know that."

Blaine rubbed her skin with the oil and began singing an Irish ditty.

As Ashton rode toward the stable, he heard a beautiful womanly voice singing.

He dismounted and slowly walked to the stable.

Ashton stood behind the bales of hay peering around them he caught sight of a beautiful vision bathing in **his** stable! He kept quiet and stayed behind the hay bales so she could not see him.

She was fascinating, with her vibrant hair, her glistening fair skin and especially her lack of inhabitations.

On the other hand, this bathing beauty did look a might young, could it be she was just naïve.

Who was this enchantress? He had never known a young woman or any woman for that matter who would bathe out in the open! She was incredible. He had to find out who she was.

Watching her started a fire burning deep within his sole.

Blaine knew it was getting late; she stood and reached for her towel. Looking at the horses, "Alright fellas you need to turn your heads. I do not want you gettin any funny ideas."

Ashton's breath hitched in his throat. She was a vision of intoxicating beauty he wanted to memorize every curve.

Ashton's pleasure was cut short when Aggie retuned to help his new obsession get dressed, Aggie brought back a new beautiful pale yellow taffeta gown with a somewhat low cut neckline but still modest.

Slowly Ashton slid out of sight; He decided to spend the night away from the house.

However, tomorrow... He planned to find out just who the bathing beauty was. Aggie said excitedly, "Oh Miss Blaine, you are not going to believe this but your room has been all changed about!"

"Changed? How?" Blaine asked as she wiggled into her under garments. "What I mean Miss Blaine, is Mrs. Rossi didn't just get you all new gowns but all new furniture too! And it's real pretty Miss, you just wait till you see,"

Shaking her head in disbelief Blaine said, "I do swear Aunt Anna is just too generous." Aggie looked at Blaine puzzled, "Miss, who is Aunt Anna?"

"Oh, I am sorry Aggie; Aunt Anna is what Mrs. Rossi has asked me to call her. She has become my dear friend and my tutor."

"Well imagine that, I always thought the Missus wanted a girl to pamper. I guess she found her one to pamper in you."

"Now don't get me wrong Miss Blaine, I like you them other little snooty pigeons can go roost someplace else. I have no notion of listen to their wining every day! I would rather have to scrub these horses' backsides by hand."

Both Blaine and Aggie started laughing.

When Blaine finished dressing, Aggie and Blaine snuck up the servant's stairwell to her room giggling quietly the whole way.

Blaine said. "Aggie, this is something me and my cousin Roslyn would do. Isn't this fun?"

"Oh yes Miss Blaine, I just hope we don't get caught!"

"Don't worry Aggie, my room is right here."

"Alright Miss Blaine, I am going back to the kitchen. You wait in your room; I will bring you something for dinner."

"That will be fine Aggie, I'll wait." Aggie ran down the hallway to the servant's stairs and disappeared.

Slowly Blaine opened her door hoping on one would hear. As she slowly closed, the door behind her, her Mama said in a firm voice.

"Where have you been girl, you missed dinner?"

Blaine whirled around startled. "Mama you just about scared the whit's out of me." Blaine stood there holding her chest.

47

"Answer my question child, where have you been?"
"Well, Mama I had a horse riding lesson today."

"Nonsense you know how to ride a horse, and it would not have taken all day! So what is this all about? And where is that ridiculous outfit you had on earlier? And do not bother trying to lie to me Blaine and say you changed up here because I have been sitting here ever since they brought this fancy furniture in."

Blaine could tell her Mama was very angry she wished her Da' would come thru the door right now to save her.

Blaine was sure her Mama's wrath had to do with the new things Aunt Anna had bought her.

She remembered what Aunt Anna said about being calm Blaine knew she had to choose her words carefully.

She took a deep breath, "Mama, I will never lie to you. I will tell you anything you want to know.

First, I did go riding something called sidesaddle. It is supposed to be the way society ladies ride it is very difficult. Anyway, my horse was spooked by lightning. I ended up being thrown in a watering hole with some rawhide horseman standing by watching laughing his head off. The ridiculous outfit was totally ruined so I ask Aggie to help me to get cleaned up in the stable, Mama that is the truth."

"Oh I believe you Blaine; even you would not make up a story embarrassing yourself that much.

But now I want to know about this furniture and all the fancy things in them." Blaine took a moment and looked around, this being her first time seeing all of her new beautiful things.

The furniture was truly the most beautiful Blaine had ever seen.

"Aunt, I mean Mrs. Rossi and Da' wanted me to go to some social affairs with Mrs.

Rossi, so she took me to the gown shop. I guess she just went a little crazy." Carlin eyed Blaine as if she knew her daughter was still keeping a secret from her.

"I think this is more than a little crazy. But since you say your Da' approved of this, I will be taken this up with him. Because I do not abide my daughter, wearing dresses and makeup that make her look like a wanton woman! And since your new friend has found it in her heart to be so generous, you can share with Roslyn when she comes to visit." After her Mama said her peace, she stormed out the door.

Blaine felt stunned by her Mama's reaction; it took a few seconds for it register in her head that her Mama had just said Roslyn was coming.

Everything else Blaine's Mama said that could have hurt her just flew away, she was so excited, she thought she could fly.

Blaine wanted to run out of her room to tell Aunt Anna Roslyn was coming. However, it was late she decided it would be best to wait until the morning.

Later, Aggie came up the servant's stairs to bring Blaine something to eat.

"I would have come sooner Miss Blaine, but when I came up the hall I heard your Mum.

I wasn't trying to listen in, I promise I wasn't but she was talking so loud and she sounded frightfully angry so I left till now."

Blaine gave her friend a reassuring smile, and then she decided to share her exciting news with her new friend.

"Aggie, do not fret over what you heard. Actually, I am in a wonderful mood. I just found out my cousin Roslyn is coming to visit."

"That is wonderful news Miss Blaine, when will she be arriving?"

"Well, I am not really sure, Mama did not tell me exactly. I think she thought telling me Roslyn was coming to visit was supposed to upset me somehow but I am happy." Aggie hugged Blaine. "And I am happy for you."

The next morning Blaine woke up early, she was so excited; she did not wait for Aggie to come help her dress.

Blaine dressed quickly; she brushed her hair bringing it to a bright shine.

Blaine picked up her mirror to give herself one final glance before going to find Anna. Again, she saw the beautiful stranger looking back at her. Shaking her head in disbelief, she put her mirror down. She slipped on her new shoes and hurried out the door, not being use to the height of the heel, Blaine stumbled as she went down the hall, and so she slowed her pace, realizing her new shoes would take some getting use to.

Blaine felt like a princess in her new gown, she looked like one too, with the pale yellow flowing around her. It truly looked as if she were floating on the wings of beautiful birds.

As she reached the bottom of the stairs, she searched for Aggie. Finding Aggie in the coatroom, "Aggie, where can I find Aunt Anna?" "She is in the study Miss Blaine, but...wait! Miss...."

"Thank you Aggie."

Blaine called out as she hurried toward the study.

Aggie tried to stop her, "Oh wait Miss… I need to tell you…there is someone with her." Aggie realized Blaine had gone, leaving her there talking to herself. Aggie turned and went back to the kitchen shaking her head.

When Blaine reached the study, she was so excited she did not stop first to listen for voices. She knocked right away.

Mister Rossi answered in his firm but kind voice, "Who is it?"

"It's Blaine, Sir, I hope I am not interrupting, I am looking for Aunt Anna, is she with you?"

Anna answered. "Come in dear, you are always welcome."

Blaine opened the door quickly, paying no attention to Mister Rossi or to the man sitting in the chair next to him. Blaine caught sight of her Aunt Anna and in her excitement ran right to her.

"Aunt Anna, last night I received the most unbelievable news! Remember I told you about my cousin Roslyn?"

"Yes dear, of course I remember."

"Well, Mama told me last night that Roslyn is coming to visit!"

"That is wonderful news! I will be most interested to meet her. From what you have told me she sounds like a lovely young woman. And now my dear I have someone I would like you to meet."

Anna took Blaine by the shoulders and turned her around to face Mister Rossi and the man in the chair. "Blaine dear, this is our son, Ashton."

Ashton and Blaine stared at each other, stunned; Ashton was thinking 'she cannot be my cousin!' Blaine was thinking, 'Oh no! The rawhide is Aunt Anna's son!' No one spoke until Mister Rossi broke the silence.

"Son I know the young woman is beautiful, but please tell me that trading horses with those heathens all this time, you haven't lost all your manners."

His father's voice brought him back to reality, Ashton cleared his throat, then replied, "No Sir, I have not forgotten my manners. I beg your pardon, Miss, you just remind me of someone I met not too long ago. But I do believe you are much more beautiful." looking at his mother, "mother I do not believe I have ever met my *cousin*."

Blaine blushed profusely, turning her attention to Anna.

Anna could see this possible attraction between her son and Blaine, so she decided not to make him suffer any longer.

"Darling, may I introduce to you Miss Blaine Ewen, she is not your cousin dear, her family is from Ireland, her father and mother work for us. I have asked Blaine to call me Aunt Anna as a term of affection, Blaine and I have become quite close since her familys arrival.

Ashton reached out taking Blaine's hand; he raised it to his lips kissing it gently. Ashton's parents were shocked, not ever knowing their son to act in such a gentlemanly manner. They looked at each other with wonder.

Blaine felt an unfamiliar jolt go thru her body leaving heat in its wake. Blaine's face turned flush.

This was the first time a man's lips had ever touched her skin, except for her Da' and he did not count.

Her heart was racing out of control Blaine thought she might faint!

Seeing her reaction, his question was answered. His bathing beauty was naive. Feisty, but naive and this young Irish beauty excited his sole.

The heat of passion rose inside of him.

Ashton asked softly, "Miss Blaine do you need some air?"

Blaine was breathless, she could not respond with words she looked into Ashton's eyes nodding her head in agreement. Ashton escorted Blaine to the garden.

It was a beautiful breezy morning so Blaine was able to catch her breath quickly. Finally, Blaine regained her ability to speak. "Thank you for not telling of our first meeting. I do apologize for being so rude to you when you offered to help me at the pond. My temper gets the best of me at times."

"That's alright Miss Blaine; my pride can take it from someone as beautiful as you." As Ashton and Blaine sat in the garden, talking, enjoying the sun and fresh air, Carlin and Shamus came walking up from behind, Carlin could not contain her self, before Shamus could stop her, and Carlin ran up to Ashton and Blaine.

"So young lady who might this be? Is this the rawhide from the water hole? That is what you called him isn't it?"

Blaine was devastated, she pleaded with her Mama. "Mama please don't!" Unshaken, Ashton stood, extending his hand, "Hello, Ma'am, my name is Ashton Rossi; my parents are Joseph and Anna Rossi."

Carlin was taken by surprise, not realizing the Rossi's son had returned from his travels. Carlin softened her voice, "Oh please! Pardon, me I have not been myself lately and I do not normally act so abruptly. Please forgive me Mister Rossi." Carlin turned quickly heading for the house.

Ashton rubbed his chin watching her leave he turned and sat next to Blaine, "I noticed there wasn't an apology in there for you Miss Blaine."

Blaine replied meekly, "No, and I doubt there ever will be."

Shamus realized what had just happened between his wife and daughter, he felt bad that he had not stopped his wife from making a scene in front of a stranger.

"Blaine Darlin', I am so sorry. Your Mama is just not herself. I apologize to you to Sir that was not somethin' to be displayed in public. Despite what she said, she just hasn't been feeling well.

Shamus thought a change of subject might smooth the matter over. "My name is Shamus Ewen, I am Blaine's Da'."

Ashton stood again to shake his hand, "it is a pleasure to meet you Sir, and my name is Ashton Rossi."

Shaking Ashton hand with vigor, "Oh, you must be Mister Rossi's boy; I have heard fine things about you Ashton."

Ashton smiled, "Well, it makes me feel good that my folks speak highly of me, even if it is only when I am not around."

Shamus turned his attention to his daughter; he could see she was disconcerted. "Blaine darlin, I really have no idea what has gotten into your Mama, she's been acting so strange of late and I can't get her to talk to me. But, she has been keeping in touch with Aunt Shannon and Roslyn, which seems to help her downtrodden mood."

Blaine looked at her Da' extremely surprised, "Do you mean Roslyn has been writing Mama?"

"Yes she has darlin, usually once a week sometimes more."

Shamus looked at Blaine and could tell she was upset. "Blaine, what is troubling you darlin?"

Blaine replied with tears in her eyes and tightness in her throat. "Da', I have written Roslyn almost every day for months now, and I have not received one letter! Not one, from Roslyn. Now you tell me Mama has been receiving letters from her this entire time. Why Da'? Why would Mama be so cruel to me? Keeping her letters from me. She knows how much I love Roslyn; she knows how much I have missed her. Why Da'?

Blaine started crying harder. Why dose Mama hate me?"

Blaine jumped up and ran toward the stable. Ashton jumped up to go after her. Shamus took hold of his shoulder. "Just let her go son, she will be alright, my Blaine is strong, and she has had to be. Your Mama has been very nice to my Blaine. And right now she needs her kindness with her Mama acting in such strange ways."

"Forgive me for sticking my nose into your family business Sir, but, from what I can see, Blaine is a wonderful young lady and I do not understand your Wife."

Shamus replied, "Neither do I Ashton, neither do I." Both men left the garden and went toward the kitchen.

Blaine fell into the hay sobbing. She could not understand why her Mama would keep Roslyn's letters from her. She lay there for hours thinking, crying, and trying to understand why.... Finally, she cried herself to sleep.

Later that evening at dinner, two seats sat conspicuously empty.

Anna was very concerned; it was not like them to miss dinner. "Shamus, is your family feeling under the weather?"

Shamus thought for a moment, and then replied, "Yes Mrs. Rossi, you could say that." Shamus glanced over at Ashton; Ashton gave Shamus a brief smile.

Dinner that evening was very quiet.

After everyone excused themselves, Ashton took Shamus aside, "Sir, if it would be alright by you, I would like to go and check on Miss Blaine." "That would be fine son; I need to be checkin' on her Mama."

Shamus headed for the stairs and Ashton headed out toward the kitchen. Anna turned to her husband "Honey, do you feel like we are missing something?"

Mister Rossi replied, "Anna dear, I am so tired they can leave me out of this one. Now, I am going to bed Anna, before I am too tired to climb all of those dadburn stairs." Anna giggled, "Alright sweetheart I will come with you."

Ashton quietly entered the stable, lighting a lantern. He found Blaine fast asleep in the hay.

Her bright shiny red hair spread out like flickers of a flame dancing across gold.

Her porcelain skin was so delicate, so perfect. Ashton thought if he touched her, she would break.

For a moment, all he wanted to do was just sit and study her, so he could dream of her in every detail.

Before he realized what he was doing, he leaned over and kissed Blaine softly on her delicate young lips.

Blaine stretched and yawned wiping her eyes she looked up and said sleepily, "Oh, it is you again. Are you going to follow me everywhere?"

Ashton replied, "Well that all depends on where you plan on going." Blaine sat up and started picking hay out of her hair.

"Here let me help you," offered Ashton.

"Thank you again Mister Ashton, you always seem to be around when I need help." "I am always happy to assist a beautiful lady."

Ashton's voice deepened revealing a hint of the desire he was feeling.

He found just sitting near Blaine set a fire ablaze in him.

Ashton could not remove the vision of Blaine's glistening naked wet body from his mind.

He desperately wanted to kiss her, to show her the passion he felt for her.

A smile came across Ashton's face at the possibilities…

"Mister Ashton, you seem lost in thought, may I ask what you are thinking about?" "Miss Blaine, I was just having a wonderful daydream. Maybe I will tell you about it sometime. I need to get you in the house before something does happen."

Blaine had no idea as to what he was talking about. However, her stomach had begun to let her know she had gone to long without food.

From the loud protest coming from her stomach they, both knew she was hungry. "Well, I hope there is some food left because I am starving."

"I believe the cupboards are never bare at the Rossi estate." Ashton proudly stated. "So if you will follow me Miss Blaine, we will make our way to the kitchen and rustle up some grub."

Blaine took Ashton's hand and said. "You lead the way dear Sir I am not sure what a grub is but I am hungry enough to eat it if you will."

Ashton started laughing and said. "Blaine, you make me want to kiss you."

Blaine's heart started beating fast.

Ashton noticed her hand began to shake, which made him smile. However, Blaine did not reply to his comment.

Ashton and Blaine ate to their hearts content, they talked, laughed, and completely avoided Ashton's kissing comment.

As they finished eating, they decided to clean up the evidence, so Blaine washed the dishes and Ashton dried.

After they had finished cleaning up, Ashton turned serious, "Blaine, I know this is none of my business but about your mother?"

Blaine looked down at the floor and interrupted softly, "Ashton, please I cannot talk about this. I hope you will understand."

Ashton gently placed his strong hand on Blaine's porcelain cheek. "Yes, I do understand and I hope you can understand this."

Lowering his lips to hers, gently caressing his moist lips against hers.

Blaine's breath was caught in her throat she could not breathe she nor could she move.

Ashton's arms slipped around her waist pulling her closer.

As Blaine opened her eyes, he lifted his head to look deep into her eyes.

The pools of deep emerald held Ashton captive, smoldering with the beginning of passion, looking back at him.

For a moment, he was speechless.

Blaine's voice broke the silence. "Ashton, I have never been kissed before." Ashton smiled, replying in a deep hypnotic voice, "I would like to kiss you again Blaine." Blaine's heart was pounding so hard she thought it would burst. Heat flooded thru her body her cheeks flushed.

Breathlessly she replied, "I...I think that would be nice."

Ashton took Blaine's arms and placed them around his neck, then he slowly he lowered his head, first, lightly brushing his lips over hers.

Blaine let out a small moan, which made the fire burning inside of Ashton harder for him to contain. However, he knew he had to control himself less he would scare his little Irish rose away. So he slowly traced her lips with his tongue, she willingly parted her lips, not wanting him to stop, He was the masterful teacher she was his willing student.

His tongue flirted with hers.

Following his lead, her tongue played with his sending him over the precipice of his desire.

Pulling her into his body he kissed her deeper with much more passion than he indented.

Blaine's mind was whirling, Ashton pressed in closer. Ashton's hands slowly slid down Blaine's back to her waist lifting her closer to his body.

He boldly moved his hands lower brazenly pressing his body to hers. He wanted more!

Blaine tried to protest. Ashton smothered her objection deepening his kiss. Blaine pulled away slightly gasping breathlessly, "Oh… Ashton, please we just met…" Ashton drew her back and began tracing her neck with gentle kisses sending another wave of heat flooding thru her body. Blaine felt Ashton was going to consume her. For a brief moment, she thought she might want him to.

Blaine was finally able to regain some of her senses. Realizing this was wrong breathlessly she spoke, "Ashton, please stop. We… We do not… I mean we just met.." Ashton was overcome with passion, his body rigid with desire.

He knew if he pressed her, he could win. Oh! How he wanted to claim this young temptress, his body said **Yes**! His mind said **No**!

He buried his head in Blaine's hair and took a deep breath, attempting to regain control of himself.

He wanted Blaine so desperately; his head swam with the intoxicating smell of her hair.

How this inexperienced young woman could confuse his mind so? Even the sent of her hair set his mind in a whirl of desire for her.

Ashton embraced Blaine for several minutes before he was able to speak.

Finally Ashton said, "I am sorry Blaine, I did not mean to…no woman has ever made me feel this way. Honey, from the first time, I saw you sitting in the…. Ashton stopped himself for he was thinking of Blaine bathing in the stable, pond you have consumed my thoughts."

Blaine gently pushed away from Ashton.

"Ashton, this is moving much too quickly we do not really know each other. My head is swimming I need time to think. And when you…"

Blaine looked into Ashton's blue eyes.

Ashton moved quickly toward Blaine, "All I know is that I want you Blaine!" Blaine turned quickly so as to not be caught in his amorous hold again, for fear she would be lost to the new arousing emotions he had brought to life within her. She hurried thru the kitchen door; raced up the stairs as fast as her legs could carry her. When she reached her bedroom, she turned to see if Ashton had followed her.

The hallway was quiet no one was following her. Blaine entered her room and locked her door quickly behind her.

As Blaine lay in her bed, she felt a thrilling sensation like none she had ever felt going thru her mind and body.

She thought, 'This is what it feels like to be desired by a man! Could he be falling in love with me so quickly? I just met him and yet he consumes me.'

Blaine hugged her pillow tight; she closed her eyes touching her lips, thinking of Ashton's handsome face, his passionate kisses.

Thrill shot thru her body at the thought of his hands… his hands were so bold on her body.

She wondered, what would have happened if… dismissing the thought knowing it to be wrong. Blaine fell asleep smiling.

CHAPTER 4

As the morning sun peeked thru the window there was a knock at Blaine's door and a quiet voice saying, "Miss Blaine, are you alright Miss?"

Blaine was startled awake then she realized the voice at her door was… Aggie.

Realizing she had locked the door, She jumped up nervously fumbling with the lock. "Oh Aggie, I am so sorry." Aggie looked at Blaine suspiciously, "why are you acting all jumpy Miss, like you're expecting some giant monster to jump thru the door!"

Blaine gave a nervous giggle, "Aggie, you do not know how close you are to the truth." Aggie looked at Blaine very confused. "Miss Blaine, what in the world are you talkin' about?"

"Aggie, maybe I will tell you later."

"Yes Miss, later would be good cause Mrs. Rossi is waiting for you." Blaine looked at Aggie wide eyed and said anxiously, "What for?"

"Well, for your lessons of course Miss Blaine, I swear somethin' has got you jumpier' than a cat in a room full of rocking chairs!"

Blaine had chosen a pink satin gown, which accented her green eyes and red hair perfectly she just knew Ashton would love it.

Aggie and Blaine finished quickly.

Blaine was hoping to see Ashton before her lessons with Aunt Anna began. Blaine remembered to walk slowly down the stairs and she kept her head held up she was now accustomed to her new shoes so she did not have to guard her pace any longer.

As Blaine entered the dining room, only the women were there eating breakfast.

Blaine looked at Anna, "um, where is Da' and Mister Rossi?" "Good morning dear, they went out in the field early this morning." "And Ashton, did he go with them?"

"No child, he and Seth had some more trading business in the city he will be most likely be gone for several weeks."

Carlin asked, "Why the sudden interest in the men's where about Blaine?" Blaine's heart sank, knowing she would not see Ashton for weeks. Her mind raced. 'Oh how ill I stand to be away from him so long!' realizing her mama was speaking to her she quickly answered.

"Oh, it is nothing Mama, I just wanted Da' to see my new gown. Do you think it is pretty Mama?"

"Yes Blaine, it is lovely." Carlin replied without looking up. "Now, sit down and eat your breakfast."

After breakfast Blaine's lessons on etiquette and social standards continued.

Anna could tell Blaine was a bit distracted.

She was sure she had a good idea *who* the distraction was however; she did not say anything to Blaine, at first.

Anna wanted to see if Blaine would talk to her about Ashton on her own.

At the end of their lesson, Anna said to Blaine "I was thinking I would show you the Rossi family library when Roslyn comes. I thought this would be a great way for all of us to spend a quiet day getting to know each other. Do you agree?"

"I think that would be wonderful Aunt Anna, I was afraid you had forgotten." Anna smiled, "I know a lot has happened to you in such a short time, but I have a surprise for you Blaine dear, first I want you to open this."

Anna went behind Mister Rossi's desk and brought out a large box.

Blaine's eyes widened. "What is it?" "Open it and see." Anna said with a smile.

Blaine quickly opened the box. She pulled out a long deep green velvet gown trimmed in black lace.

In the bottom of the box was an emerald necklace and matching earrings.

Blaine looked at Anna and asked with surprise. "For me?"

"Yes, but this gown is for a special occasion, we are holding a Ball here at the estate in two months. I had this gown made for you just for this occasion."

"But Aunt Anna, you have already given me so many beautiful gowns. Mama thinks it would be a good idea for me to share with Roslyn; I mean I was going to ask you first.

But Mama said it is not right for me to have so much and Roslyn to have so little." Anna sat for a few moments silent and then she calmly replied, "Blaine, the gifts I give to you are for you.

If poor Roslyn should be in need when she arrives here, we will see to that need then. If your mother should choose to give her clothing to someone in need that is hers to give. However, not with your belongings, she has no claim on things I have given you. Now, if your mother should wish to discuss this I will be happy to talk to her about Roslyn's needs. However, just to be safe I will keep this gown with me until the Ball. Is this alright with you?"

Blaine hugged Anna, "Oh! Yes, Aunt Anna, thank you so much."

The many days Ashton was away past painfully slow for Blaine. It seemed time had frozen. She feared Ashton would never return. When he did would he still feel the same. Blaine spent much of her time in the library reading, or in her studies with Anna. She had only known Ashton for a short time but he consumed her thoughts. She could not wait for his return.

That day finally arrived; Blaine and Anna had been having their lesson when Anna decided to tell her of Ashton's return. Anna looked at Blaine and smiled. "You might want to freshen up before dinner dear, because I think there may be a young man interested in seeing you tonight.

Blaine's blushed she could not believe Anna knew about them!

Blaine sheepishly smiled, then said politely, "Thank you Aunt Anna, I think I will." Blaine left the study and ascended the stairs light as a feather. All she could think about was seeing Ashton.

In her room, Blaine brushed her hair and applied the oil Seth gave her. Her hair shined liked the sun.

She smoothed her pink gown, took a deep breath then headed for the door.

As she opened the door, her Mama stood at the door about to knock. "Mama, I was just going down stairs for dinner."

Carlin said softly. "Blaine girl, Mrs. Rossi had a talk with me today, and even though I do not abide the idea of you sharing our private conversations with strangers, I owe you an apology. I had no right to try to take the gifts Mrs. Rossi gave you. Also, I am sorry for speaking to you the way I did in front of young Mister Rossi. I hope you were able to explain to him that I have been under the weather lately."

"Do not fret Mama, Da' explained everything to Ashton.

From what I know of him, Ashton does not seem to be the kind of man to go around telling tales."

"Oh, so its Ashton now is it? The two of you are on first name basis already?" Carlin was not really expecting a reply. However, Blaine had a reply for her. "Yes Mama, I guess you could say we seemed to have started off that way."

Just then, Shamus came up the hallway. "Are my two beautiful ladies coming to dinner?"

Not wanting this conversation to continue, Blaine said quickly. "Yes, Da', I was just coming, are you coming Mama?"

"I will be along in a moment I want to speak with your Da' first." Shamus kissed Blaine on the cheek, and then she went toward the stairs.

"Go along Blaine darlin, and by the way, you are just breath takin' in that pink gown. You look like a princess."

Blaine was curious to know what her Da' and Mama were talking about, but not enough to stay upstairs and listen.

Blaine figured she had heard all she wanted to hear of their conversations at her window.

Blaine was deep in thought as she descended the stairs.

She had practiced so much, without realizing it; she now walked lightly down the stairs with her head up, she no longer had to think about it.

At the bottom of the stairs Mister Rossi and Ashton stood talking about the horse trade Ashton had made and his trip into the city.

Both men stopped talking when they noticed Blaine coming down the stairs.

Mister Rossi elbowed his son, "Now, she is a vision."

"I know father, I know." Ashton could not take his eyes off this beauty in front of him. He went to the bottom of the stairs and offered his arm to escort Blaine to the dining room.

Anna came out from the sitting room, seeing her son's expression and his courteous action brought a wide smile to her face.

Anna came up and taking her husband's hand in hers, "Joseph, I do believe the boy just may be ready to settle down."

"If he lets this little one get away I am gonna' take him out back and horse whip him." Ashton made sure he sat across from Blaine he kept smiling at her and she would smile back. The only one who seem to be disturbed by Ashton's attention toward Blaine was Blaine's Mama.

Mister Rossi cleared his throat and said. "Miss Blaine, your father tells me you know horses pretty good, is that true?"

"Yes, Mister Rossi, I have been around horses since I was five. My Uncle trained them in Ireland and he taught me a bit before he died."

Mister Rossi continued. "Ashton, why don't you take Miss Blaine out to the stable and show her the new horses. I doubt she has seen the kind you brought in today."

Ashton turned to Shamus, "Would you approve Mister Ewen?"

Carlin went to open her mouth in protest, Shamus gave her hand a firm squeeze, and she closed her mouth tight giving him a look of disapproval.

Then Shamus said. "I have no problem with Ashton showin' Blaine the new horses. Just as long as you Mister Ashton, give me your word to be a gentleman."

Ashton shook Shamus's hand, "I give you my word Sir, to be the perfect gentleman." Ashton and Blaine walked out the kitchen toward the new stable.

Blaine quietly asked. "Ashton what kind of horses are they?" Ashton did not answer he reached down and took Blaine's hand. Blaine smiled and said. "You gave your word to be a gentleman."

Ashton leaned over and whispered softly in Blaine's ear, sending a chill of excitement racing thru her. "I am always a gentleman. And about the horses, we traded for two Arabians and one Spanish stallion."

"Oh, Ashton I cannot wait to see them."

Ashton quickly pulled Blaine behind a tree just before the stables. "First, I have something I want to give you."

"What is it Ashton?" "A kiss."

Before Blaine could think to protest, Ashton claimed her mouth with his. His tongue franticly sought to tease her, to bring her pleasure.

If the thought to protest had existed in Blaine's mind, Ashton had caused it to vanish in an instant.

Blaine melted into Ashton's arms surrendering to his mouth.

Ashton's ardor grew at an eager pace.

He had to have this woman, the stables; he would make love to her there.

Ashton reined in the firestorm of passion slowing the ardor of his kiss. Blaine was weak with this new intoxicating feeling, Ashton held Blaine to him.

His voice deep with passion. "Woman, I missed you, you consume my thoughts. I can hardly breathe when I get close to you; I want to make love to you."

Blaine looked at Ashton wide eyed. "This is love? This feeling between us. I hoped so much you felt it too."

Suddenly it was as if cold water hit Ashton in the face. Until this moment, he had not realized just how innocent Blaine really was.

He knew he wanted to make love to her. However, being in love, now, that was a different story all together.

Ashton quickly changed the subject. "Blaine, honey maybe we should go see the horses now."

Blaine was floating on air. All she could think about was being in love and Ashton had called her a woman. He made her feel like a woman.

Slowly they walked on to the stable Blaine held onto Ashton's arm. At that moment, she could not be happier.

Ashton directed her attention to the horses, explaining their bloodline and how he and Seth would break them in.

The horses were a little unsteady and Blaine and Ashton could not get to close. Blaine sighed. "I wish they were just a little tamer, I really want to pet them."

Ashton shook his head. "Blaine, you go from being a temptress, to I don't know, so innocent, like a little child."

Blaine could not believe her ears one minute this man calls her a woman and professes his love, the next he takes to insulting her calling her a child!

Blaine's temper flared, "Ashton Rossi, I take offense at both of those comparisons, I am neither, some trashy temptress or a stupid child. Good evening to you Sir!"

Blaine spun around and stomped out the stable doors heading off into the darkness away from the estate.

She was in a fine Irish fit she was not quite sure why Ashton had made her so mad but she was going to keep walking until she felt like looking at his arrogant face again. Blaine must have walked at least four miles before she realized she had no idea where she was and it was late, very late.

Blaine thought to herself, 'Well, Blaine you got yourself in a fine mess this time. I guess if I stay on the road I should come to something I hope. And I hope it does not have teeth and is hungry. Oh, I wish Da' were here right now.'

Blaine kept walking. In the moon light, she saw what looked like an abandoned cabin.

As she got closer, she thought.

'I hope it is abandoned.' As Blaine got close, she yelled out. "Is any one in there? I say is anyone or anything in there?"

Blaine waited for a few minutes. Then she heard a scary noise in the woods. She ran inside the cabin closing the door behind her.

Quickly realizing it was very dark now she was scared. Blaine stood against the door. Blaine said to herself. "Now think Blaine, think, what is the best thing to do first? All right, I need light. Blaine felt around and found the windows. There were tattered coverings over the windows so she pulled the covering off.

"Well, now I have a little light."

Blaine searched around for anything else she could use.

It was obvious this was a hunting cabin. Although it seemed no one had been around for a very long time. But Blaine felt fortunate that the hunters had left so much behind. Blaine was able to start a fire using one match stick she found, along with the old window coverings and she tore part of her under garment into strips along with the broken pieces of wood that were laying around.

Blaine cleaned the cabin up the best she could.

"Lord, I promise if you will please help me get back home I will never let my temper get the best of me again. Well... at least I will try really hard, Lord, with your help."

The only thing the hunters did not leave was food.

Blaine thought. "Well, I guess I cannot have everything now can I. At least I have a safe place to spend the night."

She shook off the cot and blankets curled up in front of the fire and went to sleep. Back at the Rossi estate, Ashton had tried to find Blaine on his own without any success. So he back to the house to get help. He found Seth stacking feed in the stable both decided not to alarm Blaine's folks and set out to find her on their own.

"Ashton did you happen to see which way she went."

"No I thought she stepped out to cool off she was mad as a hornet." Seth shook his head, "what did you do this time?"

"I guess I offended her you know my big mouth guess I stuck my foot in good this time."

"We need to split up I'll head out for the pond. You head for the cabin we'll meet up there." "good idea Seth we have to find her. Her father will kill me for sure." the two men split Ashton rode hard in the direction of the cabin.

It was not very long when he saw smoke in the moon light coming from his old hunting cabin that he and Seth used when they were young boys.

Ashton had not used the cabin now for at least eight years.

Seth and Ashton stopped coming to the cabin when they both turned eighteen and had to give up being boys and start being responsible as Ashton's father put it.

Ashton headed for the cabin hoping it would be Blaine he would find and not some squatter.

Ashton reached the cabin and noticed the windows uncovered so he decided to look in before making his presence known just in case there might be trouble.

Ashton saw a vision of red hair glowing in the fire light.

He went to the door and slowly opened it not wanting to wake her.

As Ashton approached, there she lay on his old cot covered in a dirty blanket.

He thought to himself. 'I can say one thing she is not afraid to take care of herself. I have never met a lady like her.'

Ashton went out to his saddle and brought back a clean blanket.

As he removed the old dirty blanket, his breath caught in his throat, Blaine had pulled her gown up to use as a pillow exposing her legs.

She had torn parts of her under garments to use to start the fire, so her legs were bare up to her upper thigh.

Ashton quickly covered Blaine with the blanket. Blaine moaned and moved around a little.

"I want to kiss you my Irish beauty. Even your temper makes my blood boil." As if feeling his presence, slowly Blaine opened her eyes.

Blaine sat up with the blanket around her she threw her arms around Ashton's neck and started to cry. "Ashton, I am so sorry, please forgive me. I got lost. I did not think anyone would find me. It was so dark and I heard this terrible noise. Oh, you are here, you are really here."

Blaine broke down into a sob. Ashton held her in his arms reassuring her she was safe.

Blaine looked up at Ashton with a dirt-streaked face and tear filled emerald eyes. "Are you upset with me Ashton?"

"Upset with you? Darlin, I am the clod who does not know when to keep my mouth shut."

"Ashton, are my Da' and Mama real upset?"

Ashton sat quite for a moment then he said, "Well, they don't know you ran off Seth and I thought it would be best not to upset them.

I know enough about your Da', he would skin my hide if one hair of your head is harmed."

Blaine smiled and tried to hide it by covering her mouth with her hand. "What is so funny Miss Blaine Ewen? I am very fond of my hide!"

Blaine started to giggle aloud and said, "I believe Da' would too, what I cannot believe is how you were so afraid for your hide that you would go runnin around in the middle of the night looking for **Me**."

Ashton's face tuned very serious. He looked deep into her eyes. "Blaine, it is not my hide nor your Da' that made come out here in the middle of the night looking for you. I searched all over for you myself before I went to get Seth to help me. After you were gone so long, I just kept thinking I have to get her back. Oh please, let me get her back." Ashton took Blaine's face in his hands. Slowly lowering his lips to hers; softly, pleadingly moving his lips over her.

Blaine gently parted her lips. Feeling her forgiveness, Ashton's eager tongue traced the outline of her mouth.

Blaine let out a soft moan setting Ashton's sole afire. With blazing passion Ashton claimed Blaine's mouth.

The wild passion he felt inside he desperately needed to share this magical feeling with Blaine.

Ashton knew Blaine had never felt passion, would she be willing to let him teach her....

Blaine's body felt the fire, her head was swimming, and her heart was pounding. "I believe I love You Blaine."

Blaine's heart was beating so fast she could hardly breathe.

Breathlessly she said "I love you too Ashton."

Ashton pulled Blaine closer. "I want to make love to you Blaine, right now." Blaine could not speak she felt as though she was in a dream. She closed her eyes as he softly kissed her.

Ashton left Blaine's lips and began kissing her neck.

He kissed her in a way that made her forget reality, for a moment... Suddenly Blaine's eyes flew open this was not a dream!

"Oh, please stop Ashton we cannot! This is wrong!"

Ashton looked at Blaine with a heat in his eyes she had never seen before... Like a wild animal.

"This can't be wrong! Blaine I love you. You love me."

Just then, the door came open and Seth stood in the doorway of the cabin as an angel sent to protect the Lords straying sheep.

Blaine jumped first and hurried to sit back on the cot covering herself with the blanket.

Ashton just sat there as if nothing was wrong.

Seth was stunned, for a few moments he could not speak. When he finally found his voice, he said, "Ashton you and me we been mates since we were young. I have always looked out for you, and even covered for you when you have gone and done somethin stupid. Now, I am ashamed of you. Now, you have gone and disgraced Miss Blaine, she aint like them women at the docks. How could you Ashton? You know what; I do not even want to hear what you have to say. Because there aint nothin you could say right now that I would believe. Please come with me Miss Blaine, I will take you to your Papa."

Ashton angrily turned on Seth. "you self-righteous son of a gun. How dare you come barging in here telling me what I can and cannot do! Blaine and I happen to want to be together. Isn't that right Blaine?"

Blaine took a deep breath and looked at both men hoping she could defuse this situation.

"First, Seth, thanks to your arrival there has been no disgracing, as you put it, and I do not want to come between two lifelong friends. But, yes Ashton, I do want to be with you, in the proper way. Whatever the women from the docks are like Ashton, I can only guess I am the complete opposite. Now I would hope we could all go back to the house together."

They closed up the cabin. Ashton and Seth silently mounted their horses; both men offered their arm for Blaine.

Blaine reached for Ashton, choosing to ride with him Ashton tuned giving Seth a smug smile.

Seth looked away shaking his head.

When they reached the stable, Seth grabbed Ashton's arm "Ashton I'd like a word with you."

"Seth I think you said plenty back at the cabin, so if you do not mind I am taking Blaine in the house so her father can see she is back safe."

Seth took the horses to their stalls and said to himself. "She's back safe no thanks to you, Ashton Rossi. …. That man is going to break Miss Blaine's heart. I love him but he's no good for her."

It was early afternoon when Blaine and Ashton entered the study, Mister Rossi had just handed Shamus a glass of Whiskey.

Anna was sitting on the sofa with Carlin.

As soon as Blaine caught sight of her Da, she ran to him embracing him. Shamus was stunned not knowing why Blaine was so emotional.

He pet her hair, "Now darlin what is this all about. "Please don't be upset with me." Blaine pleaded. "Now settle down and tell me what this is all about."

"My temper got the best of me again and I stormed off into the dark and found myself lost. I wondered upon Ashton's hunting cabin that is where Ashton found me." Shamus gave Ashton a wary glance, "what happened to stir your temper."

"Da it was a misunderstanding Ashton did not mean it the way I took it," Ashton chimed in, "Sir, I have a bad habit of putting my foot in my mouth. I said something stupid telling Blaine she reminded me of a child, but I didn't mean it the way it sounded." Shamus let out a sigh of relief, "well no harm is done I thank you for bringing Blaine home safe. You are a good man."

"Thank you Mister Ewen, I would have gone to the ends of the earth to find her Sir." Carlin stood hugging briefly Blaine. "Yes, Blaine, your Da' is right we are just glad you are home now."

Anna sat watching how cold Carlin was toward Blaine.

She felt troubled in her heart that a mother would act this way.

Anna stood and hugged Blaine. "I think you have had enough excitement to last quite a while. Would you like to get cleaned up my dear?"

"Oh, yes Ma'am, more than anything." Blaine said with a sigh.

Anna took Blaine by the hand, "I have a nice tub with your name written all over it." Anna had Seth fill the tub with hot water she added drops of lilac in the water for Blaine to soak in.

Blaine felt like she was floating on a cloud, the fragrance of lilac engrossed her senses. As Blaine lay back and thought of what it would be like to be Mrs. Ashton Rossi. She wondered if he would ask her to be his wife.

The hot water and sent of lilac washed all the dirt and grime away but Blaine could still feel the heat of Ashton's lips on her flesh she could still see the hungry look in his eyes...

Anna came in to help Blaine dress for bed.

As Anna helped Blaine dry her hair, she noticed a bruise on Blaine's neck.

She did not say anything to Blaine. Anna kissed her forehead, wished her a good night, sending her off to bed.

CHAPTER 5

Anna brought some coffee into the study. Ashton was sitting by himself lost deep in thought.

"I brought you some coffee, dear; you look like you could use some."

Anna poured a cup for Ashton and one for herself. She walked to the study doors closing them. Picking up her cup, she sat next to her son.

Both sat silent drinking their coffee.

Finally, Anna could no longer wait for her son to speak. "Ashton, is there something troubling you?"

"Nothing I cannot handle myself mother." Replied Ashton without looking away from his cup.

"Son, I think you better look at me, because I know more than you think." Ashton blurted out, "I swear Seth has got the biggest mouth I have ever seen. Just because he does not agree does not give him the right to go telling tails to you!"

Anna sat her cup down and looked at Ashton for a moment, and then she calmly said, "Ashton, you are almost twenty-six years old, but at the moment, you are acting about twelve. Moreover, that just will not do for what you have gotten yourself into. Now, you listen to me and you had better listen well. No one has come running to me, so you can put that one to rest. Whatever silly quarrel you and Seth have is between the two of you work it out! Now, my concern is much more serious. Tell me what has happened between you and Blaine."

Ashton sat quietly trying to think of what to say.

Getting a bit frustrated Anna said, "Since you seem to have lost your ability to speak I will help you out. I was helping Blaine with her hair and I found a love bite on Blaine's neck. Now, who found Blaine last night, you or Seth?"

"Alright, mother it was me. I found Blaine last night. I am the one who left the mark on Blaine's neck. But it is not what you think!" Ashton was trying to defend himself. Anna was trying to stay calm, taking a deep breath, "Alright, now, I know who is responsible for the mark. I need to know how far you have pushed yourself upon the young child."

"Mother, I never pushed myself on her and she is not a young child! For your information, we happen to be in love. And we want to be together despite what others think."

"Oh, this is wonderful, so when do you plan to ask her father for her hand?" Ashton looked at his mother with shock on his face.

He had not given thought to purposing to Blaine so soon. "I guess, just as soon as I get up enough courage to ask."

"Son, under the circumstances I would not wait too long. If either of Blaine's parents sees that love bite, we will be having a shotgun wedding." Warned Anna.

The next evening at dinner, Blaine stayed in her room. Ashton asked if he could take her dinner to her.

Anna smiled; she had an idea what he was up to. She had Aggie make up a tray for Ashton to take to Blaine.

Ashton carried the tray up the servants' staircase. When he came to Blaine's room, he knocked lightly.

Blaine assumed it was Aggie. "Come in Aggie." Ashton entered without saying a word.

Blaine was in her robe and nightgown sitting at her window looking out at the star filled sky.

"It is a beautiful night tonight."

Ashton replied. "Not as beautiful as you love." Startled, Blaine stood up quickly and closed her robe. "Ashton! I thought you were Aggie."

Ashton sat the tray on the bedside table. Slowly he walked toward Blaine.

"I wish I were, and then I could dress and undress you every day. But then again if you were my wife, I could undress you and Aggie could dress you. I think I like that better." "Ashton Rossi what are you saying?"

Ashton took her by the hand.

"Blaine, I have not asked your father yet, but I wanted to ask you first."

Ashton bent down on one knee. Blaine's heart began beating fast she could not believe this was happening tears started welling up in her eyes.

"Blaine Ewen, will you make me the happiest man in the world and be my wife?" "Ashton, nothing would make me happier than to be your wife."

Ashton stood up and kissed Blaine very softly then he picked her up and spun her around. Both of them were laughing. With tears of joy streaming down her cheeks, Blaine looked down into Ashton's blue eyes.

"I love you Ashton Rossi, with all my heart."

Ashton slid Blaine down his body sending a thrill thru her, since she was only wearing a thin nightgown heat rushed thru her body as, Blaine felt the heat of Ashton's hands. Ashton pulled Blaine close without words he claimed her mouth with his.

His kiss was demanding, passionate, possessive.

Blaine was consumed, swept away by a rush of emotion. Wanting Ashton to possess her. Wanting to be his wife.

The moment was broken by a light knock at the door.

Anna softly said. "Ashton, Blaine's father is in the study with your father. I think this might be a good time to ask. But of course that would be up to you, son, I am only trying to help."

Blaine looked up at Ashton and said quietly. "Aunt Anna knows about us?"

"You could say my mother is very observant. Usually nothing escapes her attention." "Well, I know that much, but I did not think we were that transparent."

"Blaine my love, with my mother, even hidden things are not safe. Now, I better go have a talk with your father while I still have the wind in my sail to do it."

"Ashton, should I go with you?"

"No, not that I have experience or anything, but I believe the man is to do the asking alone."

Ashton descended the stairs milling over in his mind what he would say. He only hoped Blaine's father was in a good Irish mood and still found him on the favorable side of life.

Ashton enter the study, both men were sitting smoking their pipes.

Ashton cleared his throat and said, "Mister Ewen, Sir, I have something important I would like to talk over with you."

Shamus turned his attention to Ashton, "Well son, the Irish don't talk over anything of importance until they share a glass of Irish whiskey."

Mister Rossi replied, "I just happen to have an unopened bottle in my desk."

"I loved your father from our first meetin and I know now he has the Irish in his veins somewhere."

Mister Rossi broke out three glasses and one big bottle of fine Irish whiskey.

He poured three stout glasses and the men sat down.

After they took, a drink or two, Shamus noticed Ashton was taking large drinks. "Son, with the way you be drinkin the whiskey there won't be any talkin comin out of your mouth tonight if you don't slow down. So why don't we get to the reason you called this little meeting."

Ashton had hoped drinking the whiskey fast would have calmed his nerves but now he was nervous and dizzy. He took a deep breath, first, he looked at his father then he looked at Shamus.

"Well Sir, this is about Blaine."

Shamus sat there looking at Ashton waiting for him to continue. "Alright Ashton, you've gotten that far now, what about my Blaine?"

Ashton took another drink of whiskey. Ashton's father was watching his son's behavior and he was beginning to get tickled. Mister Rossi said, "Son, I do not believe I have ever seen you so nervous."

Shamus looked back and forth between the two men and finally said, "Now Ashton, let us get back to why we are sitting here. What is it about my Blaine that is so important for you to speak to me about?"

"Mister Ewen, I know Blaine is young but she is very smart." Ashton paused for a moment.

Shamus was getting slightly impatient, "So far you haven't told me anything I don't already know."

Ashton continued. "Blaine and I have spent a lot of time together Sir, and I have become very fond of Blaine. Well, I should say more than fond of her Sir." Shamus calmly set his glass down and looked at Ashton.

"Explain to me what you mean by more than fond."

Ashton sat his glass down, and took a deep breath. "What I mean Sir, is I have fallen in love with your daughter and I want to ask you for her hand in marriage."

Mister Rossi started laughing. "Ashton that was probably the most drug out way of asking a father for a girl's hand I have ever heard!"

Mister Rossi was the only one laughing. When he realized neither Ashton nor Shamus found it amusing, he cleared his throat stifling his laughter.

He looked at Shamus and Ashton. "What is the matter with you two?" Shamus cleared his throat, "Pardon me, but would you mind if I had I word alone with Ashton?"

Mister Rossi stood and walked to the study door, "No problem Shamus, he is all yours but please take it easy on him. Try to remember what it was like when you fell in love with Carlin." Mister Rossi left closing the study doors behind him.

Shamus lifted his glass and drained the remaining whiskey. Ashton took a deep breath and waited for what Mister Ewen had to say.

Shamus finally turned to Ashton "Ashton, what you are asking of me is no small matter, Blaine is my only child. I have come to accept she would be finding a nice man, some day, settling down with a family of her own. And I know sixteen ain't all that young for marriage. Her Mama was sixteen when we got married over thirty years ago. The problem I have Ashton is you have only known my Blaine for a short time. I knew her Mama a year before I asked her Da' for her hand. So, is there some reason you might be in a rush?"

Ashton's mind went back to his mother's words about a shotgun wedding. Then he lifted his glass of whiskey and drained it.

"No Sir, I love her and she loves me and we want to get married. With your blessing of course."

Shamus slapped Ashton on the back, "Well, if my Blaine has already chosen you, there's nothin' left to say, but, welcome to the family, son!"

Shamus grabbed Ashton in a tight hug and said, "Now! We have something to celebrate."

As he filled their glasses to the top with more whiskey, the two men drank repeatedly to the coming wedding.

The next morning, Aggie went to the study to open the curtains.

She quickly closed the door for fear she would be knocked over by the smell of stale cigar and whiskey.

Slowly opening the doors again, Aggie had not noticed Mister Ewen and Ashton passed out in the room.

Mister Ewen was lying on the sofa and Ashton was passed out on the floor. Anna and Mister Rossi had just come down stairs to see Aggie's expression as she closed the study doors again.

Anna asked. "Aggie what in heavens name is the matter?"

Aggie looked wide-eyed and replied, "Oh, Mrs. Rossi, I have only smelt something so foul once in my life Mum, when I passed a seedy pub in England.

I have no idea what's happened in there Mrs. Rossi."

Anna looked at Mister Rossi and said with a questioning tone, "Might Mister Rossi have any idea what has defiled our study?"

Mister Rossi smiled, "Yes, my love, I will take care of this unpleasant odor myself. None of you women need worry about it. However, I will need as much black coffee and dry toast as you can supply. Just leave it at the door. Oh, and try real hard not to make any noise today."

Anna looked at him puzzled and asked. "Why?"

"Because my dear, your son asked for Blaine's hand last night. And they are either stone blasted drunk or they killed each other."

Aggie gasped in horror.

Mister Rossi looked at Aggie and smiled. "Don't worry yourself Aggie, from the smell you described those two drank themselves into a fine Irish stooper last night. I am just sorry I missed it."

Anna scolded him, "Well I am not, you men like to get yourselves all pickled, and one of you should have to stay sober to do the unpickleing." With that, Anna and Aggie left for the kitchen to fill Mister Rossi's order.

Mister Rossi opened the study doors. Aggie was right; the smell was like a back alley pub.

Mister Rossi almost could not contain himself when he saw his son passed out on the study floor hugging the whiskey bottle.

He quietly opened the curtains and the windows. Ashton moaned and turned away from the light.

Nothing seemed to affect Shamus.

Mister Rossi was worried, thinking Shamus may have drank too much. He went to the sofa where Shamus was laid to see if he was still breathing.

Shamus opened one eye, "Rossi, I know I am getting' old, but I am not ready for the undertaker just yet."

Mister Rossi stepped back. "Shamus you just about took ten year off my life. I opened the window and you didn't move."

Shamus sat up. "Well, if I took ten years off your life you better start hiding from the undertaker. And as far as me not moving. I've been awake for a while now listening to our son here dreamin about our daughter. Did you know the boy talks in his sleep?" Mister Rossi thought for a minute, finally realizing what Shamus said, "So you gave your approval."

"What else could I do, it's obvious they both love each other. I still think it's too soon. But Blaine, she needs someone to love her, someone to really care for her. Ashton promised he would give her that. And I believe him."

"Shamus I really think this is what both of them need. Ashton needs Blaine as much if not more."

Ashton rolled over moaning. "Do you have two talk so loud?"

Shamus laughed, "Son, I have to teach you not to drink quite so much. You do better huggin your whiskey than you do holdin' your whiskey."

"Sir, I am not sure what you are talking about."

Mister Rossi started laughing too. "Son, I think Shamus is referring to how quickly you past out on the floor last night. And to the way we found you, laying there hugging the empty whiskey bottle."

As Shamus and Mister Rossi laughed, Ashton moaned again. "You know this is just not funny."

A light knock came at the door. Mister Rossi said. "Here is our remedy for the glorious hangover."

Ashton sat up rubbing his head, "Father, there is nothing glorious about the way I feel right now."

Mister Rossi handed Ashton a cup of black coffee and a plate of dry toast.

Then Mister Rossi turned to Shamus. "Shamus, I realize you probably don't have a hangover. But would you like a cup of coffee."

Shamus answered with a proud voice. "Yes Sir, I will have a cup of coffee. But let it be known, there is no Ewen not here in America or back in lovely Ireland that has ever tested the bottle and could not hold his own nor has ever awoke with the bite of the snake called a hangover."

Shamus turned to Ashton, "And now, my boy, that you are coming into the Ewen clan I will have to teach you some of the Irish. Realizing you won't be able to learn everything. You not really being Irish, but we'll do the best we can."

All three men started laughing. Ashton was holding his head as he laughed felling as if his head was going to explode but he could not stop laughing.

Shamus stood up, stretched, and then said. "I better be getting' myself upstairs and give my darlin wife the good news before she hears it from someone else."

As Shamus left the room, Mister Rossi tuned to Ashton, "Son, I think there is a young lady that is probably very anxious to see you this morning.

After you get cleaned up of course."

Ashton forgot all about his headache and headed for the door, only to be stopped by his mother.

"Ashton, I heard the good news! And I am sure you want to talk to Blaine right away, or at least after you get cleaned up." Anna waved her hand in front of her face. "But before you do, I have something I want to give you."

Anna and Ashton went upstairs to Anna's room.

Anna went to her vanity and took out a black velvet pouch.

She took out a beautiful antique emerald ring. "Ashton, this ring has been in my family for nine generations. I would like you to give it to Blaine as an engagement ring."

Ashton held the ring in his hand. "Mother, I couldn't have chosen a more perfect ring. It's the same color as Blaine's eyes! I know she will cherish it forever."

Shamus entered his room very boisterous. "Carlin my love where are you?" Carlin answered sleepily, "Shamus Ewen, I am right here what in heavens name are you yelling about?"

"I have news! But first, I want a good morning kiss from my beautiful wife." Carlin climbed out of bed, as she came close to Shamus she cried. "Mercy, Shamus, you smell like you bathed in whiskey and dried off with a stale cigar. You stink!"

"I'll have you know my dear Carlin, it was fine Irish whiskey and as far as the cigar goes, I have no idea. But we were celebrating so I guess it really doesn't matter."

"And just what were you celebrating?"

"I'll tell you after I get my good morning kiss. I don't care if you have to hold your nose to do it!"

Carlin started laughing; it was the first time Shamus had seen her laugh in a very long time.

Shamus grabbed her and pulled her close tenderly kissing her. Shamus looked into Carlin's eyes. "Carlin my love, I fell in love with you the first time I saw you. I love you more today than I did then; you are my one true love, Carlin."

Carlin had tears streaming down her cheek.

Shamus kissed her gently once more.

As they sat on the edge of the bed holding hands, Shamus spoke softly.

"Carlin, I have news for you, and before I tell you I want you to know I feel this is for the best. I've made up my mind on the matter, so I don't want any fuss."

Carlin looked at Shamus, it was rare to see him so serious and when he was, she knew he meant what he said.

"Alright Shamus, whatever you say."

Shamus continued, "Ashton came to me last night and asked for our Blaine's hand in marriage."

Carlin asked quietly. "What did you say?" "Darlin, I gave him my blessing."

"But Shamus, they hardly know each other. And Blaine is only sixteen."

"Now, Carlin, don't you remember how old you were when we got married?" Carlin sat silent for a moment then she replied, "I was sixteen."

"I mean no offense my love, but I know why you have been trying to bring Roslyn here." "Shamus, I don't have any idea what you are talking about."

"Carlin, there is one thing you have never been able to pass by me, and that is a lie. You have been trying to get Roslyn here to meet Ashton for some time now. And now she coming and now Ashton's engaged to our Blaine."

"I know, and Roslyn is coming today. Oh, Shamus, what have I done?"

Carlin leaned her head on Shamus's shoulder and he put his arm around her. "Maybe things won't be too bad. After Roslyn gets here, we will just have to explain things to her, I am sure after she sees Ashton and Blaine together it will be all right. It is best if we get ready to go get our niece.

I wouldn't want her sittin at the station all alone."

After Ashton cleaned up, he hurried down the servant's staircase. In the kitchen, he saw Aggie.

"Aggie, have you seen Blaine this morning?"

"Oh, I am so happy to see you Mister Ashton I was scared out of my whit's this morning thinkin Mister Ewen had taken yer life! The way Mister Rossi was talkin about you two killin each other."

Ashton interrupted, "Aggie, calm down. Nobody killed anyone. Everyone is still very much alive except for a raging headache. So have you seen Blaine this morning?" "Yes Sir, she's in the dining room having breakfast."

"Thank you Aggie."

Ashton disappeared toward the dining room.

Blaine sat trying to eat but she was so worried about what happened last night between Ashton and her Da'.

She was deep in thought when Ashton walked into the room.

He stood there watching at her, as she stirred her coffee peering off somewhere else.

Ashton thought 'she is a vision and she is mine.'

Then he said aloud, "good morning beautiful where are you?" Blaine realized someone was talking to her she looked up. "Ashton!"

Blaine jumped up and ran over to Ashton throwing her arms around his neck. "I was so worried. Are you alright?"

Ashton put his arms around her waist and held her close. "Blaine, honey, I had a talk with your father. I didn't go out and wrestle a bear."

Blaine rose up on her toes lightly kissing Ashton on the lips.

Ashton wanted to explore her kiss further, but there was a lot of commotion and no privacy due to preparations for the Ball.

Ashton took Blaine by the hand, "come with me we need to talk."

Ashton walked with Blaine out into the garden away from the noise of the house. Under a big tree he turned to Blaine," your father is a good man. He has given his blessing for us to marry."

Ashton took his mother's ring out of his pocket.

"Blaine, this ring has been in my family for nine generations, on my mother's side. I would be honored if you would wear it for the rest of your life as my wife." Blaine had tears of joy streaming down her face.

"Ashton, I would be honored to wear your mothers ring for the rest of my life." Ashton placed the emerald ring on Blaine's finger.

They kissed a kiss of joy and happiness tender and full of promise.

Blaine thought 'My life is truly complete.'

They carved a romantic moment in time, holding one another, promising to love one another forever, dreaming about their life together.

They sat under the tree secluded from the world just the two of them.

After some time Blaine said, "Ashton, I think we should go back in the house and share our good news with the rest of the family."

Ashton pulled Blaine closer and whispered softly in her ear, sending chills down Blaine spine.

"My love let's stay here. And celebrate our good news alone."

Blaine started giggling. She played as if she were struggling to get away from him.

Ashton gently pushed Blaine to the ground and lay on top of her. "Now, Blaine dear, I have you were I want you!"

Blaine played as if she were scared. "Oh, no! Sir, just what do you plan to do to me?" Ashton's eyes turned serious. The look of the wild animal she had seen in Ashton eyes at the cabin was there in his eyes again., it frightend her a little. "Ashton, why do you look at me that way? It frightens me."

Ashton's voice was deep, filled with passion. "When I am close to you my blood boils. I desire you, I want to taste you, and I need to feel you. Blaine, I feel so strongly for you I can barely control myself. I want to be with you every second of the day. Do you understand you are mine? You are in my heart and I want to make you mine in every way." Ashton started to kiss Blaine's neck.

Blaine lay there on the grass next to Ashton. Softly, she stopped him taking his face in her hands.

"Oh, Ashton, my love, soon we will be married. Then we can be together as much as we want. But we must do thing right. I do understand how you feel. I feel the same way I want to be with you in body too. But not before we are married."

Ashton's demeanor changed, he was frustrated. He pulled away from Blaine. Ashton would not tell Blaine, but he liked the situation much better when their relationship was a secret and marriage was not an issue.

"I suppose your right we better get back to the house before they send a search party out for us."

Blaine was not sure what caused Ashton's sudden mood change. They walked back to the house holding hands but neither one said a word.

When they entered, the house there was so much going on. Decorators were arriving for the Ball now five days away. Anna, Carlin, and Aggie were in a tizzy.

Shamus and Mister Rossi seemed to be the only two with any sanity. The two men were quietly eating a late breakfast in the dining room.

Ashton decided to bypass the craziness and talk to the only two calm people in the house.

Blaine ran up to her Da' kissing him on the cheek. "Thank you Da'."

"Your welcome darlin, just promise me you will always make each other happy the best you can."

"I love Ashton, Da', I promise I will do my best."

Shamus looked at Ashton. "And what about you my boy? You look a little down in the mouth for a young man who just caught himself a bride."

"It's nothing I cannot handle Mister Ewen."

Mister Rossi eyed up his son,"It could be Ashton. Son you need to get some sleep. You look worn out."

"That's probably all it is father."

Blaine looked at Ashton with concern she wanted to talk to him but thought it was not the right time.

Ashton sat down and started talking to his father about the horses.

Blaine felt it would be rude of her to interfere.

She turned to her Da before she could say anything, he said, "Blaine, my girl, go and find your Mama she has exciting news for you."

"Da', does she know about me and Ashton?" "Yes, dear, and she is tickled pink!"

"Are you sure we are talkin' about *my* Mama?"

"Yes, Blaine, the only Mama you have, I told her the good news this morning. Now, go find her and see what she has to say."

Finding her Mama along with Anna and Aggie franticly cleaning a bedroom upstairs. "Mama, what is happening? It's like the whole house has gone mad!"

"First, let me congratulate you my dear." Carlin threw her arms around Blaine. I am truly happy for you and Ashton. I hope you will find the joy your Da' and I have had in our life together."

Blaine was shocked. Her Mama had been so cold toward her lately; Blaine was not prepared for her Mama's response.

Blaine held her Mama tight with tears of joy flowing down her cheeks.

"Mama, I wanted your approval most of all. I cannot tell you how happy it makes me to hear you say that you are happy for me. I love you so much Mama."

"I love you too Blaine dear."

By the time Carlin and Blaine, stopped embracing there was not a dry eye in the room.

All the women were hugging and congratulating Blaine. Everyone was laughing and wiping each other's tears.

All of a sudden, Carlin became panicked asking. "Mercy me! What time is it?" Anna pulled a chain watch out of her apron and said, "It is half past eleven Carlin." "How long does it take to get to the train station?" Asked Carlin.

"About one hour and a half." replied Anna.

Carlin became very excited. "Oh! Great merciful heavens! We have to leave right now!

Her train will be here in an hour!"

Blaine was very confused. She looked at her Mama. "Mama, please calm down. Whos train will be here in an hour?"

Carlin answered quickly not realizing Blaine was the only one in the room that did not know Roslyn was coming today.

"Roslyn of course. Honey her train arrives at half past noon!" Blaine's eye's widened, as she looked at her Mama in total shock. "Are you saying Roslyn is coming today and no one told me?"

Carlin replied. "Blaine, darlin, it was to be a surprise, for you. I...I was planning to tell you on our way to pick her up from the station. Your Da' and I thought Ashton could come with us and you two could give her your good news."

Anna didn't want the excitement spoiled with family feuding so she decided she would add her two cents in too.

"Now, Blaine, we do not want to spoil the moment, dear. Roslyn is coming today and that is what you have wanted. Regardless if you knew of her arrival or her visit is a surprise you should be over joy either way."

Blaine remained silent for a moment. Then looking at her Mama, "Mama, I am sorry, Aunt Anna is right. I am very happy you have arranged for Roslyn to visit."

Carlin was a little bothered by Blaine calling Mrs. Rossi Aunt Anna but she figured it could be worse Blaine could be calling her mother.

Carlin smiled at Blaine. "Darlin, you've had so much happen in the last few days I should expect you to be a little on edge. I am sure once you and Roslyn are together again it will be as if you two were never apart. Now we need go before she thinks we have forgotten all about her."

Blaine and Carlin ran down the stairs as if something was chasing after them.

Blaine yelled for Ashton. "Ashton! Come quick!" Ashton had never heard such excitement in Blaine's voice.

He thought for sure something must be terribly wrong for her to act in this way. Ashton sprang from the dining table and ran to find Blaine. Shamus and Mister Rossi were not far behind.

Ashton found Blaine, taking her by the shoulders. "Blaine honey, what is happening?

Are you alright?"

"Oh, yes Ashton, I am fine! But we have to leave right now!"

Ashton took hold of Blaine's shoulders and said. "Blaine, please calm down and tell me what you are talking about."

"We have to leave for the train station right away because my cousin Roslyn's train arrives in less than an hour."

Ashton and his father stood looking stunned not having any idea Roslyn would be arriving today and in such a short time.

Mister Rossi said. "When was anyone going to let us know we had a guest coming?

After she arrived?"

Anna could tell her husband was slightly upset. Mister Rossi was not a man who dealt well with last minute surprises, especially the ones staying in his house.

"Dear, this was a surprise for Blaine from her mother. It slipped my mind to tell you. However, I promise all of Roslyn's rooming arrangements have been taken care of; all we have to do is pick her up. Carlin even assures me that Roslyn has a gown for the Ball. So you see dear, everything is cared for. And I do apologize for not telling you sooner."

"Oh alright, I certainly don't want to be the one to cause a problem. But if anyone is going to fetch our house guest they better get moving."

At that Shamus, Carlin, Blaine, Ashton and Anna left for the station by carriage.

They made it to the train station in record time an hour and ten minutes. Shamus was concerned. "We need to spread out and look for her. The poor darlin, she is probably scared to death.

The words barely left his lips when this overdressed young woman started walking their way.

CHAPTER 6

Roslyn was wearing a periwinkle blue velvet gown trimmed in black. She was carrying a matching parasol and purse.

The neckline of her gown plummeted much too low for Anna or Carlin liking.

Anna thought, 'Please tell me this piece of fluff is not Blaine's Roslyn.'

Much to Anna's dismay Blaine ran up to this young woman and threw her arms around her.

Roslyn hugged Blaine as if she was afraid to wrinkle her own gown, and then quickly turned to Carlin.

Roslyn spoke, forcing an English accent. "Oh, Aunt Carlin, I am so thrilled to finally be here. You were right the trip was simply dreadful. Nevertheless, I am so happy to see every one. And I see two faces I do not recognize."

Blaine walked up beside Ashton taking his hand in hers.

Roslyn did not notice she was much too busy strutting about like a peacock. Carlin said. "Roslyn, I would like you to meet Mrs. Rossi she has graciously allowed you to stay in her beautiful home with us. And this is her son, Mister Ashton Rossi." Carlin did not get another word out.

Roslyn had set her site on Ashton. "Oh my, Mister Ashton, aren't you a handsome fellow. I do believe many women have swooned over you."

Ashton was smiling enjoying Roslyn's brazen flirtation.

His mother was not impressed with her son and his lack of fidelity. This strumpet turned his head the very day of his engagement to Blaine.

Anna nudged Ashton a whispered. "Remember son you are spoken for" Ashton whispered back. "I know mother but you have to admit she is something." Anna quietly replied. "No I do not. All I see is trouble."

Roslyn stepped in closer. "I just love secrets. It is not nice to whisper Ashton darlin, how is a young lady going to get to know you if you go around whispering."

"I was speaking to my mother I am positive etiquette will allow me to speak quietly to my own mother Miss Roslyn."

Roslyn realized she was coming on a bit too strong. Therefore, she steeped back. "Blaine, I am so sorry I have offended your friends."

Blaine looked up at Ashton; he smiled at her squeezing her hand.

"Do not fret Roslyn; I do not believe you offended Ashton. Did she darling?" "No Blaine dear, I am not offended; actually I am a bit flattered." Roslyn looked at the two of them very confused.

Finally, Shamus could not stand it any longer. "Roslyn, I'd like you to meet Blaine's betrothed, Ashton

Rossi. They were engaged formally sometime last night."
Roslyn looked like someone had just slapped her across
the face.

She turned to her Aunt Carlin. "Aunt Carlin, their
engaged!" Roslyn said with an angry inflection in her
voice.

Carlin took Roslyn by the arm. And said in a quiet
tone, "Roslyn, things have changed and there is nothing
that can be done. Now be happy for your cousin and enjoy
your trip, or, Shamus and I will have to send you home
right now."

Quickly Roslyn changed her tone. "I am sorry; I
was just so excited about meeting him…. I will try Aunt
Carlin. Please, don't send me home."

Roslyn went over to Blaine and Ashton. "Please, I beg
your pardon, I am happy for both of you."

Roslyn embraced Blaine as she did when they were
younger. "I love you Blaine, you know me, always acting
foolish. But I don't mean no harm really I don't."

Blaine kissed Roslyn on the cheek. "Roslyn, you
have always been this way. I will explain it to Aunt Anna.
However, you have to remember these people are not use
to Irish antics and they do not always find the amusement
in our play. So please, while you are here behave yourself."

Roslyn replied in a winning tone. "I will try, for you
Blaine. Can I at least hug your fiancé?"

Blaine shook her head at how childish Roslyn was
acting.

Blaine noticed Roslyn had not matured at all. Roslyn
still wanted to play games all the time.

Blaine felt sorry for her. Blaine said. "Yes, of course you can hug Ashton." Roslyn's expression changed when she faced Ashton. Making sure no one else could see her but him.

Now, she looked at him like a wild animal after its prey.

Ashton was no stranger to this look. "And just what are you after Miss Roslyn?" Roslyn smiled and winked at Ashton, "just a hug. I promise I have permission from your wife to be."

As Roslyn hugged Ashton, she whispered. "But, I find you terribly attractive. So if you ever need a break from playing house I can help you out."

Roslyn kissed Ashton's ear sending a chill down his spine. She stepped away leaving Ashton flustered.

Blaine was speaking to Ashton and he did not hear a word she said. Anna watched Ashton's reaction to Roslyn and felt a dread inside her heart. This girl was going to be trouble. She would have to do her best to keep that girl away from her son.

Shamus was not pleased with what he had seen out of his niece so far. Nevertheless, he wanted to give her the benefit of the doubt.

On the way back to the estate, Anna asked Roslyn questions about her schooling. Roslyn answered Anna's questions but did not offer any added information about herself.

When Roslyn would not answer, Carlin would answer for her.

Back at the estate, Blaine took Roslyn to her room. Roslyn had been given Blaine's old furniture and bed.

Roslyn swore it was all new, bought just for her.

Blaine did not want to upset Roslyn so she kept the truth to herself.

As Roslyn unpacked her trunks, she laid out five of the most elaborate gowns Blaine had ever seen.

All were different shades of velvet trimmed in dark lace. With very low necklines.

Much too revealing for a proper young woman.

As Blaine helped, Roslyn hang her gowns in her wardrobe she asked. "Roslyn, where did you get such elaborate gowns?"

Roslyn's reply was quite biting. "What, do you think you are the only one who deserves nice things?"

Blaine was taken aback by Roslyn's remark.

Calmly she replied, "No Roslyn, I want nice things for you. I was just wondering how you came by them. They look very expensive. I know if Aunt Anna had not bought my gowns I wouldn't have any."

Roslyn tone was still very flippant as she spoke, "I am surprised your Mama did not tell you. She has been sending me and my Mama her earnings so I could come here and be dressed in finery and not look like a house servant."

"Oh Roslyn, Aunt Anna wouldn't have let that happen. She would have made sure you had something nice to wear."

"Yes I am sure, charity for your poor cousin. Find a gown for poor Roslyn, **No** thank you Blaine. *My* Aunt Carlin made sure I have what I need."

Blaine laid the last gown down. Turning toward the door, "Roslyn, it is obvious you have had a very hard trip.

In addition, I am sorry you are in such a foul mood. I am going down stairs now. I hope when I see you later you will be more pleasant to be around." Blaine left the room and went to find her Mama. She had some questions she wanted to ask.

Roslyn was livid. She thought, 'How dare that little snipe come in here and chastise me for being in a bad mood. She acts as if she is the woman of the house already. I have news for her she is not married yet.'

Just then, Roslyn noticed Ashton and Seth headed for the new stable.

Roslyn adjusted her gown and fixed her hair a little. Smiling to herself, she went to the door.

Roslyn looked up and down the hallway, everything was very quiet.

She could hear noise coming from the main staircase.

She thought. 'I can't go that way someone will see me. There has to be another way out of here.'

Roslyn crept down the hallway and noticed a back staircase.

She stood and listened for a few minutes there were no sounds so she slowly went down the stairs.

She stopped suddenly Aggie came thru the kitchen doors to pick up something for the decorators.

Roslyn held her breath. Aggie never caught sight of her. Roslyn quickly made it out the door toward the new stable.

As Roslyn sauntered into the stable, she did not make her presences known at first.

Roslyn wanted to be sure that the only two in the stable were Ashton and Seth. She was sure they were all alone and just for her. Roslyn walked around the hay bail and said, "Oh, my! Look at the studs in this stable!"

Both men turned around staring at Roslyn she being very beautiful and dressed to catch any man's eye.

Seth cleared his throat and said. "Actually Miss, these are mares not stud horse." Roslyn seductively eyed Seth up and down then replied, "oh you, beautiful man who said I was referring to the horses."

Seth's eyes widened he was speechless.

Ashton smiled and said, "Seth, I would like to introduce you to Roslyn, Blaine's cousin."

Seth came to his senses and held out his hand to shake hers.

"It's nice to meet you Miss Roslyn, Blaine talks about you all the time." Roslyn raised one eyebrow and looked at Ashton. "Does she now"

Seth turned to Ashton. "Ashton, I have to go take care of the horses in the other stable.

Will you be able to handle this on your own?"

"You go ahead Seth, this won't take long. And we can both be done before dinner." Seth tipped his hat at Roslyn and left the stable. Roslyn stood quiet for a while watching Ashton work.

Finally, she said. "Are you almost done cowboy?"

Ashton was tiring very hard to not pay attention to Roslyn but he found her pushy behavior somewhat enticing.

"Listen Roslyn, I don't want to be rude but I really have to get my work done before dark."

"Alright Ashton, I can take a hint but answer one question for me before I go. At the station did you feel anything?"

Ashton stopped working he did not say a word and he refused to look at Roslyn.

Roslyn whispered in his ear before she walked away, "Me too sweetheart." Roslyn snuck back in thru the kitchen and up the back staircase down the hallway and into her room.

Roslyn closed her door; flung herself onto the bed and giggled aloud as she felt her plan to take Ashton was working. As she lay there, plotting her next move a knock came at the door. Roslyn went to the door and opened it.

"Aunt Carlin, how are you?"

"I am fine Roslyn dear, would you mind if we had a chat?" "No not at all Aunt Carlin, I always have time for you."

"Roslyn child, I have done both you and Blaine a terrible injustice. I wrote you and your Mama those letters not just to get you here to meet Ashton. I am ashamed to say it, but I have been bitterly jealous of the attention Blaine has received from Mrs. Rossi. I have always had a special place in my heart for you Roslyn, and I wanted better for you. Not that I didn't want better for my Blaine too. I just wanted it for the both of you. When I met young Mister Ashton, all I thought about was you. I had no idea Blaine and Ashton were falling in love. Can you see Roslyn everything has changed? Ashton and Blaine, they belong to each other. I know there will be a nice man for you Roslyn, you wait and see. But love is something we cannot force. It happens when it happens child. Mister

Ashton is not the one for you. He belongs with Blaine. Can you be alright with that?" "Aunt Carlin, is this because Blaine and I got in a spat earlier?"

"Yes Roslyn, it is."

"I will have a talk with Blaine and put her mind at rest. To be honest with you Aunt Carlin, I have several beaus myself back home. so I am not worried. I was hoping to live in New York. And I hope to see some of it before I have to go back."

"Roslyn, I am sure someone will show you around before you leave." Carlin kissed Roslyn on the forehead.

As Carlin stood to walk to the door, she continued. "Roslyn dear, I hope you bought something a little more modest than what you are wearing right now. Your Uncle Shamus almost past out at the sight of how much flesh you are showing. I hope you did not spend the money I sent you on such immodest attire."

Roslyn's face was turning red, not with embarrassment but with anger. Roslyn could not believe how her Aunt would turn on her.

Carlin turned to her and smiled acting as if she did not notice Roslyn's ire.

"No matter dear, we can adjust your gowns. After dinner I will come up and see what I can do to fix them."

Carlin left the room not allowing Roslyn to object to her offer. Roslyn buried her head in her pillow and screamed as loud as she could.

Then she jumped up and ran to her wardrobe threw the doors open and looked at her gowns.

She thought. 'Well, Aunt Carlin may get her hands on some of my gowns, but she won't get the one I had made for the Ball.'

Roslyn removed one gown and one pair of matching gown boots out of her wardrobe.

Roslyn wrapped them gingerly in a sheet and placed them behind her nightstand. She walked around her room to make sure no one would be able see her secret place. Then she went to her vanity, and took out a black lace handkerchief and placed it in the front of her gown covering her cleavage.

Roslyn turned and went down stairs to join the others for dinner. Roslyn entered the dining room with a commanding entrance. Everyone stopped talking as she came thru the doors.

Roslyn carried herself as if she was a queen and everyone around her was her subjects. This did not set well with most especially Mister Rossi.

This was his first time meeting Miss Roslyn, now she enters his dining room as if she owns the place.

He was not impressed and he did not think he was going to be very fond of Blaine's cousin.

Mister Rossi sat quiet all thru dinner. Roslyn did most of the talking; everyone was amazed at how much she talked, including Blaine. After dinner Carlin and Blaine helped Aggie clear the table and clean up.

Carlin asked Roslyn. Roslyn dear, do you mind giving us a hand?"

"Oh, heavens Aunt Carlin, I cannot! I would hate to ruin the beautiful gown you bought me. I could never replace it."

Roslyn turned and walked toward the study where Ashton and the others had retired.

Carlin did not say anything to Blaine about Roslyn's attitude.

Once Carlin and Blaine finished assisting Aggie, Blaine went to find Ashton.

Carlin went to find Roslyn to help her with her gowns.

Ashton and Roslyn were in the same place, sitting on the sofa talking.

Carlin felt Ashton and Roslyn were sitting much to close.

Blaine did not seem to take any notice to Roslyn's closeness to Ashton.

Blaine came up to Ashton kissed him on the cheek. "I missed you. But I see Roslyn has kept you entertained."

Ashton stood up quickly as if he had been caught doing something wrong. Excitedly Ashton said. "Why don't we go for a walk in the garden honey, we have not had any time together all day."

Shamus had been engrossed in conversation with Mister Rossi until he heard Ashton ask Blaine to go into the garden.

"Ashton my boy, you and Blaine keep close to the house. I need to be keepin an eye on the two of you."

Ashton was becoming more frustrated by the minute. He desperately wanted to steal Blaine away all to himself, he wanted to feel her flesh against his to taste her lips, to kiss her young breasts. She belonged to him and he wanted her.

Blaine followed Ashton out into the garden. They sat on a bench were her Da' could see them.

Carlin said to Roslyn. "Now, we can go and adjust your gowns my dear." Roslyn protested. "Aunt Carlin, I can do what I did tonight and place a handkerchief where need be. You do not need to go to the trouble to sew a lace in all my gowns." "Roslyn, I sent money for you to have decent gowns made. I realize you being young you picked very, shall we say, lively colors. However, Roslyn, I insist that you be dressed modest. Now, we will go to your room and see what we can do."

Roslyn knew she was not going to win with her Aunt Carlin. Reluctantly she submitted and followed her upstairs.

Ashton and Blaine held hands out in the garden. Ashton kept looking toward the house.

Blaine placed her hand on Ashton's face and turned his attention back to her. "What is so interesting in the house Ashton Rossi?"

Ashton closed his eyes, feeling the warmth as Blaine caressed his face with her hand. He took a deep breath and said. "There is nothing more interesting than you. I am just waiting for your father to stop looking out here so I can take you off to myself."

Blaine sat closer to Ashton caressed his face with her noise. "Please kiss me now Ashton. I have missed you so. I have been miserable all day."

Ashton lowered his lips to hers pleasantly surprised at meeting her ardent kiss. They kissed with matching desire. Ashton pulled Blaine closer holding her tight. Wishing to have nothing between them, Ashton left

Blaine's lips trailing light kisses down her neck, then back up to her ear.

He whispered. "Blaine I cannot wait six months."

Blaine did not say a word. Ashton's kisses had sent her into another world of amazing sensations she only wanted to share with him.

Blaine found Ashton's lips.

She traced Ashton's lips with her tongue making him moan.

Leaving his lips, she kisses his neck sending chills thru his body setting him on fire.

When she reached his ear, Ashton stopped her. "Blaine! Do you have any idea what this is doing to me?"

Blaine looked at Ashton confused. "Ashton I... thought this is what you wanted."

"It is, except I need more. Don't you understand? I desire you but I cannot have you!

And when we get this close, I cannot bear not to just take you! "I am sorry this is so hard for you Ashton."

Blaine put her arms around Ashton and held him hoping she could find a way to make things better.

Roslyn stood at her window watching the two lovers in the garden, while her Aunt Carlin adjusted her gowns.

Roslyn did not know which was worse, watching her beautiful gowns being destroyed or watching her cousin Blaine kissing on the man she wanted.

Then Roslyn had a fiendish thought that brought a smile to her face.

'To get Ashton she would simply have to dispose of Blaine. All right, she thought, this might not be simple, but it is not impossible. I just have to find a way to get rid of her.' Roslyn turned from the window with a smile and said. "Aunt Carlin, thank you so much for fixing my gowns. I do not know what I was thinking.

Ashton and Blaine waked toward the house, holding hands. Blaine had her head resting on Ashton's shoulder.

As they entered the study, Blaine said. "Da' I have something I want to ask you please." Shamus turned to Blaine and Ashton and replied. "And what do you two have up yer sleeve this time?"

"Da' this is something I need to ask you, privately, Ashton does not want to ask anything."

Both Mister Rossi and Ashton said their good nights and left the study. Shamus and Blaine sat down on the sofa together. "Da' I am naive in the ways of a man. But I can tell the idea of a long courtship is taking its toll on Ashton.

I know he has not, um…, saved himself for a wife. I don't know how many women he's been with Da" and I don't want to know. But I am guessing that once a man has, um…, been with a woman it's not easy to just to um…."

Shamus could tell Blaine was not comfortable talking about the subject so he stepped in. "Blaine darlin, I suppose for some men they may have trouble controlling their emotions, we'll call it, is that what yer saying about Ashton?"

"Yes Da,' he says he loves me so much that he cannot stand being away from me but when we are together the situation makes him crazy because of his, um…Emotions, like you called it."

Shamus thought for a moment then asked. "Blaine darlin, has anything happened between you and Ashton I should know about?"

"No Da,' I just wanted to talk to you."

Shamus was rubbing his chin, something Blaine knew he did when he was deep in thought. "Darlin, how would you remedy the problem for poor Ashton and his... emotions?"

"I want to ask you if we can be married sooner than six months." "How soon were you thinkin child?"

"Three months."

Shamus sat, silently rubbing his chin, for what seemed to Blaine an eternity. Then he asked.

"Are you sure this came from your own thinking?"

"Yes Da', Ashton doesn't have any idea I planned to speak to you about this. No one else knows just me and you."

"Alright, here is what I'll do. Speak of this to no one. I'll give it some thought. Then, I'll let you know my decision when I come to it."

Blaine leaned and kissed her Da'. "I love you Da'."

Shamus smiled. "I love you too Blaine darlin, now get yer self to bed."

Blaine left the study knowing her father would think hard on what they had talked about and make his decision. She ascended the stairs down the hall to her room.

Shamus sat in the study for a while thinking about what his daughter just asked him.

Wondering what kind of man Ashton really was.

CHAPTER 7

It was late in the evening when Shamus decided to head off to bed. As he came up the staircase, he startled Roslyn who was coming down the hall away from her room. "Roslyn child, where on earth are you goin this late and in your night gown?"

"Uncle Shamus I heard someone, and I couldn't sleep so I thought I would see who was still awake."

Shamus put his arm around Roslyn and said. "Roslyn dear, Carlin, Blaine and myself, we're your kin and walkin around in your under clothes is no mind to us. But the Rossi's they aint your kin child, and you can't go showin your flesh in such a way. They might question your decency. Now, please go back to your room and get some sleep." Shamus waited until Roslyn went to her room and closed the door.

Then he retired to his.

Roslyn waited silently by the door for an hour. She kept thinking to herself.

'If I am going too really get Ashton's attention I have to do something very daring, something sweet innocent Blaine would never do.'

The same twisted smile came to Roslyn beautiful face. Then she opened the door to see if anyone was stirring. All was silent. Roslyn laid a towel down so her door would not make any noise closing.

She slowly tip toed down the hall past the staircase to the next wing of the house. Roslyn came to Ashton's door, she tried to see if there was a light on but she could not tell.

Roslyn reached for the doorknob and slowly turned it. 'Thank heavens' she thought. 'It's not locked.'

Roslyn opened the door and there was a light on but Ashton was not in the room.

Roslyn decided to wait for him.

Ashton was in the sitting room with his mother and father talking around his feelings but never getting to the point.

Finally, Anna retired to her room. Then Ashton asked, "Father, you don't happen to have more whiskey hidden anywhere do you?'"

Ashton's father left for a moment then returned with another bottle of whiskey. Ashton still tried to drink his frustration way and much to his pleasure, at the moment, it was working.

Mister Rossi took note of how much his son was drinking. "Son, I think you might want to take it easy there. Remember what happened to you the last time you hit the bottle hard."

He stood up wobbling somewhat, looking at his father he said, "Father, it just so happens the drink has fixed my problem. So I plan to take the stairs to my room and finally get some sleep."

Mister Rossi was laughing; his son was drunk, again. "Son, I am glad you plan to take the stairs because the only other way up there would be to fly. And I realize you're as high as a mast in full wind. But you cannot fly."

"Father, I am fine, good night." Ashton staggered up the stairs, down the hallway to his room.

When Ashton walked in his room, he did not notice Roslyn standing in a shaded corner of the room. Ashton flopped down in a chair by the fireplace and removed his boots. Then he removed his shirt. He bent over to remove is socks and let out a moan. "Ooohhh my head!"

Roslyn stepped out of the shadow and purred seductively, "you need some help cowboy?"

Ashton sprang to his feet. "What in Sam-hill are you doing in here woman! You just took ten years off my life. Didn't any one ever tell that sneaking up on a man like that could get you killed?"

"Ashton honey, you wouldn't harm a little sweet girl like me, now would you?" Roslyn purred.

"I didn't think so. Now, Mister jumpy sit down and let me help you."

Ashton did not know what else to say his mind was so muddled from whiskey he just sat down and stuck up his foot for Roslyn to pull off his sock.

Roslyn was not prepared for the fact Ashton had been wearing work boots in the field all day. She did not find as much pleasure in this undertaking as she thought she would. Roslyn was feeling nauseated after she was finished. Vowing to herself never to offer to remove a man's socks again!

Ashton soaked his feet in hot water Aggie had brought him earlier. Roslyn dismissed her sick feeling and decided to try something else.

While Ashton's feet were soaking, Roslyn went behind him and messaged his shoulders and upper back, she whispered. "How does that feel Ashton?" Ashton had his eyes closed and said. "So, so good."

Roslyn had him right where she wanted him she loosening the string of her night gown. Roslyn came around sat in front of him, making sure he had full view of her voluptuous breasts. Roslyn took a towel and slowly dried his feet.

Ashton closed his eyes and took a deep breath. In his mind, he could see Blaine's loving face.

Ashton opened his eyes to see Roslyn kneeling in front of him.

Ashton placed his hands on Roslyn's arm to stop her. "Roslyn, I honestly find you very attractive, if I had met you first maybe things would be different. But I am engaged to Blaine. I can't hurt her like this no matter how I feel right at this moment. This just cannot happen please go back to your room Roslyn."

Roslyn was irate! She jumped up and stormed from his room.

She could not believe it! She even touched Ashton's nasty socks and now he was sending her away like some barmaid he was thru with. 'Well we'll just see about all of this.' She thought to herself.

Roslyn made it back to her room without incident and reluctantly went to sleep.

The next morning Blaine knocked lightly at Roslyn's door. "Roslyn, its Blaine. Can I come in?"

The first thought that ran thru Roslyn's mind was that Ashton had told Blaine her scheme. Roslyn braced herself and said. "Come in Blaine."

Blaine entered Roslyn's room; Roslyn was putting on her robe.

"Blaine dear, what do I owe such an early visit?"

"Roslyn, I want to show you a place special. It is not far from here and Aggie and I have been working on it for the last couple of weeks. We have to go early and I brought you one of my older dresses so you wouldn't ruin your gown."

"Oh you, are just so thoughtful Blaine, this place must be very important. So I must go with you! Will we be going alone?"

"No Roslyn, Aggie and Seth will be with us."

"Oh yes, Seth, he is a handsome fella isn't he, and what an accent, where on earth is he from?"

Blaine thought for a moment. "Seth told me he is from some place called Australia. I have no idea where it is, all I know is Seth said it is very far away."

"How interesting, it will be delightful to find out more about this handsome foreigner, now, wont it. I'll get dressed and be down in just a few minutes."

"Alright Roslyn, we will wait for you in the kitchen." It was taking Roslyn a long time.

Aggie finally asked. "Good heavens Miss Blaine, is she getting ready to come with us?

Or is she fixin to go to a social?"

Blaine shook her head. "I am sorry Aggie; this is why I told her so early. I hoped that way she wouldn't make us wait so long."

Seth tried to make Aggie feel better but only managed to make matters worse. "Aggie, some women like you don't see the need for all that finery. And some like Miss Roslyn; well they can't be seen without it. I am sure she'll be down soon."

Aggie wanted to hit Seth over the head with a fry pan. She turned to Blaine and in an irritated voice, "I'll be waiting outside, to wait for Miss Finery to decide to grace us with her presence!" With that, Aggie turned on her heels and went out the door.

Seth looked bewildered. "Miss Blaine, did I say something wrong?"

Blaine put her hand on Seth's shoulder. "Unfortunately, you did Seth, you hurt Aggie's feelings."

Seth rubbed his head and asked. "How did I do that?"

Just then, Roslyn walked into the room. Blaine whispered to Seth. "I will have to tell you late★r."

Roslyn chimed in. "Tell what later?"

Blaine sighed, "Nothing Roslyn, We need to go it is getting late."

As they went out Aggie was already in the wagon ready to go. Blaine climbed up in the passengers' side next to Aggie. Seth came around to take the reins Aggie looked at him. "This simple woman can drive a couple of horses without any help from you. But I am sure you can find a fancy piece of fluff that would be in need of help."

Seth walked away from Aggie not ever knowing her to be so upset with him.

As Seth rounded the back of the wagon to climb in, there was the fancy piece of fluff Aggie was talking about. Roslyn, waiting for Seth to help her into the wagon. Seth helped her up then climbed up himself.

Aggie and Blaine talked between themselves. Seth swore Aggie was hitting every rock, bump, and hole in the road. Roslyn was taking advantage of the situation, making sure to fall into Seth's arms at every opportunity.

Seth being a gentleman, and thinking her to be the gentle sort, tried his best to protect Roslyn.

The whole situation was making Aggie as mad as a red hornet. Every time she looked at Roslyn, she saw the she-devil after her man.

Roslyn asked Seth questions about his homeland and how he came to America.

Seth told her about his life. How the Rossi's became his family.

He told her how he and Ashton traded horses in the city, explaining how dangerous the city docks could be, especially at night.

This sparked Roslyn's curiosity. But by this time, they had reached their destination.

Blaine turned to Roslyn smiling. "We're here."

Roslyn looked around; all she could see was an old cabin and woods. "We are where?

Blaine dear."

Seth climbed out of the wagon. He made a point to go around to help Aggie first. However, Aggie was so upset she could not look him in the eyes. Pushing his hands away, Aggie jumped from the wagon, and walked away.

Seth was shocked. "Aggie wait."

Aggie had tears welling up in her eyes and she did not want Seth to see so she hurried into the cabin.

Seth turned back to the wagon to find Roslyn waiting for him.

Dusting off her dress Roslyn complained "Blaine dear what did you drag me out here for?"

Blaine came and took Roslyn's hand. "Come on I will show you."

They entered the cabin. Blaine and Aggie had cleaned the cabin and hung new curtains.

Seth had repaired the fireplace a few days back. So as to avoid Aggie's temper Seth decided to work on the roof.

Blaine smiled at Roslyn. "This is where Ashton and I are going to spend our honeymoon."

"Roslyn rolled her eyes. "You have to be kidding Blaine! You are about to marry into the richest family in New York. Why, you could spend your honeymoon at a beautiful inn. Or at the ocean, anywhere but in this old smelly cabin. What on earth makes you think Ashton will like this?"

Blaine sighed. "Roslyn, this is not some smelly old cabin. This cabin is Ashton and Seth's childhood hunting cabin. It is also where Ashton and I fell in love. I think it's the perfect place for us to be together for the first time."

Roslyn forced a smile and looked out the window.

"Well, I had no idea this place is so sentimental for you and Ashton. I can see why you like it here so much. You said you two fell in love here what happened?"

Blaine gave a laugh. "When I think about it now it was kind of silly but, Ashton said something to offend me and my temper flared. I was irate with him. I started walking in the dark and I got lost. I ended up here at this cabin. Ashton was so worried about me he rode all over looking for me he found me sleeping here. He woke me up and we were so happy to see each other we finally realized how we felt for each other."

Roslyn looked at Blaine and lifted her eyebrow. "How did you realize your feelings for each other?"

Blaine blushed she was not comfortable talking about this with Roslyn so she gave her the simplest reply she could think of.

"Well, Roslyn, the situation between Ashton and me became somewhat passionate." "Oh come now Blaine, do tell more. I just have to hear the details!"

Aggie interrupted. "And there's nothin else to tell Miss Busybody. *My* Seth came and interrupted the two lovers so now they can come back here and continue what they started with the blessing of everyone who matters."

Seth finished the roof. Hoping things had settled down with Aggie, Seth interred the cabin.

As the two worked franticly to get the final touches done, Roslyn decided to perch herself in a chair by the window. Aggie sighed, "Why we are in such a hurry to get the cabin finished Miss Blaine?"

Blaine smiled at Aggie. "Let's just say this could be the shortest six months in history." Aggie shook her head. "Miss Blaine, you confuse the daylight out of me. But I am happy we've finished."

They closed up the cabin and everyone took their same places back in the wagon.

Aggie was still miffed at Seth so he thought it better to keep his distance.

In the back of the wagon, Roslyn decided to question Seth about the city and the dock. When they arrived, back at the estate, Aggie said nothing to no one. She went around to the side entrance and in thru the kitchen.

Roslyn, Blaine and Seth entered the front entrance. Ashton was waiting for them. Roslyn caught sight of him first. She gave him a sideways smile and winked. "How are you feeling this morning Ashton?"

Ashton looked past Roslyn to Blaine and smiled. "Just wonderful thank you. And how is my beautiful bride this morning?"

Blaine went to answer but Ashton did not give her a chance he picked her up by her waist whirled her around setting her lightly to the floor. Taking her face in his hands, he kissed her passionately. Blaine was taken by surprise. Ashton had never displayed his affection toward her so openly. With a smile of satisfaction, Ashton glanced at Roslyn. Once Blaine's mind stopped swimming with the intoxication of Ashton's embrace, she realized they were not alone. Her cheeks were set a fire from embracement. Stepping back, Blaine worked to regain her composure.

Ashton had a wide grin on his face. "Now my dear tell me where you've been sneaking off to?"

Blaine was still trying to regain her composure.

Softly she replied, "You'll find out soon enough. It's a surprise to you from me." Ashton caressed Blaine's face. Well in that case I can wait. I like surprises." Roslyn could stand no more of this sickening display. "Well Mister Ashton, if my memory serves me correctly, you made it pretty clear the other night you were not especially fond of surprises."

Ashton's grin faded. "Roslyn some peoples idea of a surprise is a snake in your bed. And someone else's is a bed of roses. One is pleasant the other is not, now, if you ladies don't mind I need to talk to Seth."

Ashton turned to Seth, with slight excitement in his voice.

"Seth my man, the runner came this morning from the dock the pirate trader ship made it back with the horses we wanted. The only problem is we have to leave right now. Or we will lose the trade. You know those scoundrels won't wait."

Roslyn had been eavesdropping; she came around the corner full of excitement. "Oh! Seth, can I go with you please!"

Seth looked as if he was staring in the face of a mad buffalo.

"Uh well uh, Miss Roslyn, you will have to ask Ashton this is his deal not mine." Ashton rolled his eyes and thought, 'Way to go Seth just pass this off on me.'

"Please, Please, Please, Ashton, Aunt Carlin said someone would take me to the city and you two are the only ones going."

Blaine came out of the kitchen and asked. "Ashton, what is going on?" "Miss Roslyn wants to go to the docks with Seth and me."

"Oh Roslyn, **No**! It's much too dangerous down there!"

"I will be fine Blaine dear; look, I am with the two strongest men I have ever met." Anna heard all the commotion and came out of her sitting room. "Oh good you young ladies are back. I thought we could do the Rossi library today. Wouldn't that be nice Blaine?"

"Yes it would. Wouldn't you like to join us Roslyn? Aunt Anna saved this for us to do together."

Roslyn was slightly flippant. "Blaine, please, I have the chance to see something exciting or look at photographs of dead people that I do not even know. I am sorry, Aunt Anna, I think I will go to the city with Ashton and Seth."

Anna calmly addressed Roslyn. "Roslyn that is completely your choice but as to you calling me Aunt Anna that is reserved for my close friends which I do not conceder you to be one. Now, if you are planning to take this trip please inform your Aunt and Uncle. You will find them in the main hall."

Roslyn turned on her heels and headed for the main hall.

Anna turned to Blaine. "Blaine, my dear, are you still up to our tour or would you rather cancel due to Roslyn's behavior."

"Aunt Anna, I would love to take the tour with you. I have no idea what has gotten into Roslyn, she has not been herself since she arrived. I am sorry for the way she is behaving."

Anna put her arm around Blaine. "Blaine, people change. Some for the better and some not. Even though we may love a person, we can't control their behavior. Their choices may affect us but their actions are completely up to them."

"I know, I just wish thing could have stayed the way they use to be. I don't know who Roslyn is any more, she is so hateful."

"And that is a shame Blaine, It truly is. Let us try to think of better things. Come with me we will get started."

Roslyn hurried into the main hall. Roslyn found her Aunt Carlin and Uncle Shamus helping the decorators.

Roslyn pulled her Aunt Carlin aside, "Aunt Carlin, I get to go to the city today! Ashton and Seth are taking me. We are leavening right away. So I wanted to ask you for a little money in case I find something I like."

Carlin looked concerned. "Why are Ashton and Seth going into the city Roslyn?"

"I really have no idea Aunt Carlin; they said something about a horse. All I know is I intend on going. Can I have a little money please?"

"Roslyn, I have no money to give you. I spent every cent I had on your train ticket. Roslyn dear, Ashton and Seth go to a very shifty area to trade. I don't think it would be safe for a young lady."

Roslyn straightened her back and spoke in a very demanding tone. "Aunt Carlin, you told me I would defiantly get to see some of New York City. Now with this Ball coming and me leaving a few days after, this will be my only opportunity and I want to take it." With that, Roslyn turned and hurried out of the main hall to find Seth and Ashton. Shamus came over to Carlin and asked. "What was all that fuss about?"

Carlin rubbed her forehead. "Shamus, I swear that girl is going to be my end before we get her back on that train and back to her Mama."

"Well Carlin, my love, that can't happen soon enough for me that child is a pain in my neither region!"

"Shamus Ewen! You shouldn't be talkin like that!" They both laughed and went back to work.

Mister Rossi came in from the field to eat. Aggie approached him. "Mister Rossi, if ye don't mind me askin Sir, where did Seth get off to today."

"Aggie, I never mind you asking me questions dear. Seth and Ashton went to the docks to trade for a couple of stud horses we have been waiting for. Oh, and they took Miss Roslyn with them. Which between you and me they could leave her there. That girl drives me crazy. However, I guess I should not say that. Anyway, thank you again Aggie your cooking is wonderful as usual."

Mister Rossi left without noticing the expression on Aggie's face. She went back into the kitchen all alone. She sat down at her bread-making table and wept.

Anna and Blaine were enjoying each others company Anna was explaining each photograph, each person and their life. Blaine was enthralled.

CHAPTER 8

Ashton drove the horses; Roslyn sat in the middle holding on to Seth arm. "My, Seth, you have enormous arms. You must be incredibly strong."

Roslyn's compliment made Seth blush at first. After a while, Roslyn began to noticed, she was losing her charm over him.

Therefore, she started asking Seth questions about what went on at the docks. Seth being a gentleman did not mention the dark underside of the shipping docks. He only mentioned the horse-trading and merchant trading.

Ashton was becoming irritated over all the attention Roslyn was showing Seth.

So he thought he would scare Roslyn, maybe he would even shock her.

"Seth, you forgot to tell Miss Roslyn about the real interesting things that take place on the docks."

"No I didn't Ashton I told her all a lady needs to know."

"But there is so much more Roslyn, do you think you can handle hearing about it?" Ashton knew enough about Roslyn that she would take the bait.

"Yes! Do tell more." Roslyn said with a wicked little smile on her face.

Seth interrupted. "Ashton, I really don't think this is something to be said in front of a lady."

Ashton laughed. "Relax my friend. She wants to hear. Anyhow, if it gets to be too much for her she can tell me to stop. Can't you Roslyn?"

"Of course I can. Seth, don't worry so much I am not a child."

Ashton continued. "The traders don't just trade for horses or merchandise. They also trade for humans, Mostly woman."

Roslyn acted shocked but truly, this was what she wanted to hear. "Oh, my lands, Ashton why?"

Ashton looked at Roslyn and said in a deep voice. "They take them overseas and sell them for sex slaves."

Roslyn gasped.

"Were do they find these women?"

"I don't really know. I guess people make deals with the ship Captains and somehow they get the women. I am certainly not into that. so I have never asked too many questions. Roslyn, you are something else I thought for sure that would scare you." Roslyn placed her hand on her chest. "Ashton, just because I did not faint does not mean I am not afraid."

Seth put his arm around Roslyn for support. "Miss Roslyn, Ashton and I ain't real sure what the women are sold for. We were told once the women were sold for that purpose." As they reached, the docks there were people everywhere.

Roslyn notice the men from the ships were much darker skinned and most were barely dressed.

The woman around the docks she gathered must be prostitutes or something like it. Which made her wonder why the ship captains wanted to buy woman when they had willing ones right here.

Ashton stopped the wagon in front of one particular ship. This was a large ship with ornamental carvings all around it.

Roslyn thought. 'This is owned by a very wealthy man.'

As Ashton and Seth climbed out of the wagon. Ashton turned to Roslyn and in a stern voice said. "Roslyn, this is not a joke you are in a very dangerous place. I am telling you for your safety stay in this wagon. If any men want to talk to you ignore them, if any women ask you to go with them ignore them or tell them no. Seth and I will be on this ship for a while."

Roslyn obeyed Ashton and stayed on the wagon for a little while. Meanwhile, Ashton was right, many men tried to talk to her and many women tried to get her to come with them. Some even climbed up in the wagon to talk to her. Which Roslyn did not like at all for it was obvious these people had forgotten what soap and water was for.

Roslyn had been sitting in the wagon for a long time and she knew she would have to find a ship Captain soon.

The likelihood of one just walking by was not going to happen. The later it got the stranger the people started to become around her.

Roslyn decided to take a chance. She jumped off the wagon and raced up the gangway of the ship that Ashton and Seth had gone aboard.

She was not looking where she was going, she ran right into a massive half-dressed dark man wearing a large hoop earring in his left ear.

Startled Roslyn looked up. "Oh my gracious you are a big man now aren't you." The large man had a stern menacing look about him "Why you on this ship golden hair?"

Roslyn's mind was racing. remembering her reason for coming to this nasty place she straightened herself. In a demanding tone, she said. "I want to see your Captain about a trade."

The large ominous man pointed. "Captain is below with other traders you must meet below."

Roslyn held her head up and said. "No, my large fella you go tell your Captain I have a special trade and I will only trade alone."

"I will tell the Captain, golden hair, he will not be happy."

The large man was gone only for a moment but to Roslyn it felt as if he were gone for an hour.

The large man reappeared seemingly out of nowhere startling Roslyn. "Captain said you wait he be here soon." Roslyn stood by herself again.

She thought. 'Alright Roslyn, this is it, do not back out now. Do not let this man see fear no matter what he looks like no matter what he says.'

Just then, Roslyn saw the large man coming with a smaller dark man, this man had a scar on his right cheek. He was not an ugly man but as he came closer, Roslyn could see in his eyes he was a cruel man. Roslyn straightened her back and put on her queenly air.

He said. "What do we have here Sobbo, a beauty wanting to trade alone with me? And what wares might you be offering that you could not come down below my beauty?" Roslyn lifted her chin looking the man in the eyes. "Are you the Captain, Sir?"

Her air took him aback. "I am the Captain of this ship, my beauty." "Well, Captain, I am Mrs. Rossi **Not** your beauty! Do I make myself clear?"

"I beg your pardon Mistress Rossi Master Rossi is my best trader I had no idea you belong to him."

The man bowed. Roslyn noticed he spoke with a strange accent and his English was properly spoken not like the other people she had encountered on the docks. "Captain, I need to keep our meeting discreet. Mister Rossi must never hear of our meeting."

"Yes Mistress, now you said you had a special trade."

"Yes I have a young red head in my house I need to dispose of. Can you assist me?" Rubbing his chin, the Captain eyed Roslyn with curiosity. "I will need to know what sort of red head you are speaking of Mistress Rossi."

"The young sort that has turned my husband's head. Moreover, I want her to vanish I was told men of your, shall we say, business dealings could handle such a problem for me."

"Now Mistress, it would depend on how experienced and how beautiful the young red head is."

"Captain, that is why I want her gone, I assure you at this point she is untouched and very beautiful."

The Captain paced the floor considering the Mistress' offer. "Where can we find this red head? And what price will you demand for her?"

Holding out a map to Ashton's cabin. Roslyn did her best to keep her hand steady. "You will be able to find her at this location on the twentieth of this month. Here is the map. As far as the price, my dear Captain, I leave that to you. Leave it in the back of the place you get the girl."

Shocked the Captain turned to Roslyn "You trust me to set the price?" Realizing her mistake Roslyn waved her hand at the Captain as if royalty dismissing a peasant and replied, "Of course, that way if you like what you get you will not feel cheated. Now do we have a deal Captain?"

Eyeing her with slight suspicion, "Yes we have a deal." Motioning to Sobo, he took the map from Roslyn.

Without another word, the Captain turned and walked away.

Sobo waited for his Captain to leave then turning to this woman, he spoke, "You come with me now." Roslyn followed this massive man to the gangway.

Roslyn took a deep breath.

She raced down the gangway turning to make sure the large man had not followed.

Roslyn quickly made her way back to the wagon and climbed in.

Not long after Roslyn made it back from the ship, Ashton and Seth came down the gangway with the two stud horses they had come for.

Both men were in a very good mood. "Seth this is the best deal we have ever gotten." "Yea and we didn't even have to barter on the price any."

As they tied the horses to the back of the wagon, Roslyn pretended to be aggravated with them.

Ashton was grinning. "Why Miss Roslyn did you not enjoy your experience with New York dock side?"

Roslyn looked at Ashton with disgust. "I will have you know Mister Rossi, I was not only talked to by the nastiest men I have ever met, the women who climbed up here to speak to me smelled so bad, if I had any money, I would have given it to them for a good scrubbing. I have never smelt such vile people in my life! Seth, you keep the stables smelling cleaner than any of these people. How on earth can you stand coming down here to deal with such filthy heathens?"

"Miss Roslyn, maybe next time you will listen. Seth and I only deal with the ones we have too. And it is only for horses. Now let's get out of here this place can get pretty wild after dark."

Ashton turned the wagon around and headed for home.

Roslyn was exhausted with all that happened. She had fallen asleep on Seth's shoulder. When they reached the estate, everyone was asleep except Aggie who waited in the kitchen. And Roslyn's Uncle.

Ashton told Seth he would care for the horses if Seth would carry Miss Roslyn into the house.

Seth agreed. Seth carried Roslyn in gently turning her over to her Uncle.

Seth whispered, "Mister Ewen, I don't think Miss Roslyn will ever want to go back to the city again. She held on to me like a frightened child all the way home and she hasn't woke up once."

Shamus smiled at Seth and carried Roslyn upstairs to her room.

Aggie overheard Seth and thought for sure she had lost him she was completely broken hearted.

Aggie made it back to her room and cried herself to sleep.

CHAPTER 9

All was quiet in the Rossi house the night before the Ball. Chef Reon and kitchen staff would be in early in the morning. Anna had given Aggie the day off.

Mister Rossi hired help of every other kind to arrive by noon.

The housekeeping staff had been hired earlier in the week to clean the extra rooms for the guests coming to the Ball.

The decorators had put the final changes on the night before.

Everything was beautiful and ready for the nights event.

The morning came and Blaine was up first. She was excited about the Ball. She did not want to wake anyone else so she went down the servant's staircase.

On her way down, she heard someone crying when she entered the kitchen, she found Aggie sitting at the bread-making table with a cup of coffee sobbing by herself. Blaine did not want to startle Aggie so she tried to act as if she did not notice Aggie's emotional state.

"Good morning Aggie."

Aggie tried her best to stop crying. "Oh Miss Blaine, it's you. I am sorry for my state.

Please forgive me." Then Aggie burst into tears again.

Blaine came to Aggie and held her in her arms. Both of them sat on the floor as Aggie sobbed with tears of heartbreaking pain.

"Oh, Aggie it is obvious something has you torn to pieces. Do not apologize for crying." Blaine held Aggie for a while. Finally, Aggie sat up and dried her eyes.

Blaine took a towel and wiped Aggie's face. "Aggie, do you want to talk about it?" Aggie was still sniffling "I have lost my Seth to that fancy piece of fluff, Roslyn." "Aggie, what makes you think Seth has fallen for Roslyn?"

"She has been following him around. Swooning over him he even took her with him to trade yesterday. He has never asked me to go trade. I watched him carry her in last night she was all curled up in his arms. I just do not know what to do Miss Blaine. I cannot compete with her. Look at me I am no beauty. That one falls out of bed ready for a social."

"Aggie, Seth is in love with you, not Roslyn. He told me you are the one who hung his moon and stars. Now, how could he let some fancy piece of fluff like Roslyn take the place of the one who hung his moon and stars?"

"She is persistent that one."

As the two young, ladies sat on the floor holding each other and talking. Aunt Anna walked into the kitchen. "Well my goodness my dears, could you have found something better to sit on than that cold floor?"

Blaine looked up and said. "Good morning Aunt Anna, Aggie is having a problem." Anna replied. "Aggie,

I would love to help you. But I insist you both get up off that cold floor before you catch your death of a cold."

Aggie and Blaine got up off the floor; Anna had them go into her sitting room to talk. Anna brought in coffee and three cups. "Now my sweet, Aggie tell your Aunt Anna what is upsetting you."

"Well Mum, Miss Roslyn has set her sights on my Seth, and it seems he is attracted to her fancy ways. I watched him carry her in last night. After askin her to go to trade with him yesterday. She has been persistent in thrown herself in his way. I just cannot compete with her. She is so beautiful."

Anna took in all the information although silently she was relieved because she had feared, Roslyn had been throwing herself at Ashton.

Anna knew Seth and knew Roslyn was not his type.

"Aggie, first you need to know Roslyn invited herself to go with Seth and Ashton. So please put that fear to rest. And you are a very beautiful young woman and what is more you do not have to hide behind all the frills and lace. However, if Seth seems to wonder about the frills and lace, then my child, we will give it to him tonight at the Ball. I will dress you like a princess Aggie my dear, and you will have the time of your life." Aggie was completely speechless.

Blaine nudged Aggie and said. "Well what do you say Aggie? Are you ready to stand your man on his ear?"

"Yes Mum."

Anna placed her hand on Aggie's knee. "From now on Aggie, I want you to call me Aunt Anna."

Aggie smiled as she realized the privilege and said. "If you really want me to." "I insist my dear."

The three ladies were in a frenzy of fun going thru gowns and ribbons. Things Aggie had only helped others put on but never thought she would be wearing.

Anna finally found one she thought perfect for Aggie. It was rose pink with opal trim and red roses along the neckline and bottom.

"Aggie, this is a perfectly beautiful gown, Seth could make no mistake about you being feminine. Do you like it?"

Aggie stood there staring at it. "Yes, Aunt Anna, I doubt a wedding gown could be more beautiful."

"Well our goal is to catch Seth's eye. If we happen to catch you a husband that would be good to."

Blaine chimed in. "Then we can have two weddings this year!"

Aunt Anna shook her head. "Hold on girls let us get to the Ball before we start planning another wedding. All three started laughing.

Mister Rossi had come down stairs and followed the noise and the smell of coffee. "Alright ladies I can see you have started the party without me. Did you happen to save me any coffee?"

"Yes dear." said Anna. "You can have my cup."

Mister Rossi took a seat and Anna poured him a cup of coffee.

Mister Rossi was trying to make heads or tales out of what the women were all chattering about.

Finally, he interrupted. "Would someone please tell me what is going on. I have been sitting here nearly ten minute and I still don't know."

Aggie, in all her excitement, spoke up first. "Aunt Anna gave me this beautiful gown to wear tonight so Seth will finally see me as a real lady and hopefully start treating me like one. Doesn't that sound wonderful Uncle Rossi?"

Aggie just assumed if Mrs. Rossi was now Aunt Anna then Mister Rossi would be Uncle.

Nevertheless, since all she knew was his last name, she called him Uncle Rossi. Everyone was Quiet; Mister Rossi took a drink of his coffee. Anna was afraid of what he might say because he had always insisted on being called Mister Rossi by most people. He sat his cup down and said. "Aggie, dear, it is a very beautiful gown and if you are going to call me Uncle please call me Uncle Joseph. And as for you little Blaine, you better start calling me Papa Joseph."

Anna had tears well up into her eyes. She had never seen her husband reach out to his family like this. Anna would cherish this as one of her happy moments. Turning to the girls.

"You two need to get upstairs your help will be here in one hour."

Blaine came to Anna and took her hands." "Aunt Anna, would it offend you if Aggie and I helped each other get ready."

"Blaine are you saying you want no other help?" "Yes Aunt Anna, I just wanted to share this with Aggie."

"Alright, but you do not have much time so I suggest the two of you be busy getting ready and not playing."

Aggie winked at Aunt Anna. "No worries I won't let her be playing no Irish games today Aunt Anna, I promise."

Aggie and Blaine grabbed the gown and raced upstairs to Blaine's room.

Anna looked at her husband. He was headed for the door. "And where do you think you are going Mister Joseph Rossi?"

"I thought I would take care of something outside before our guests started arriving." Anna walked up to Joseph she put her arms around his neck. "You are an amazing man Mister Rossi. And you just changed the lives of two very special young ladies. I love you so much."

Anna kissed Joseph. With such warmth, caring, and love that two people share when they have lived a life together. Joseph held Anna for a moment then he said.

"Anna I love you. I know I have not been the easiest man at times. But you are my Anna. I could not have done any of this without you. He kissed her on the forehead and said I am the luckiest man in the world. I have my beautiful wife."

Anna was fighting tears, "My dear, I think you better take care of your business outside now."

"Your right I better, before I forget."

Anna watched him walk out the door. She thought. 'I am the luckiest woman in the world because I have you Joseph Rossi.

Shamus woke Carlin by pulling back the curtains while singing an Irish love song.

Carlin slowly sat up.

"Oh, Shamus please tell me you were not out drinking again."

"No my love. I needed to wake you early because your personal helper for tonight's festivities will be arriving soon."

Carlin rubbed her eyes and stretched. "Shamus we are the help we were not invited." "That where your wrong Carlin my love. Mrs. Anna spoke to me about four weeks ago.

She told me we'd be goin."

Carlin was upset. "But Shamus I spent all my money on Roslyn. And nothing I have is fittin for a fancy Ball." Carlin fell back into the bed felling terrible for herself.

Shamus went to his closet and took out a large box laid it next to his troubled wife. "I would not say nothing you have would be fittin for a Ball."

Carlin sat up quick. Her eyes wide with excitement quickly she opened the box. Inside Carlin found a beautiful ball gown the bodice was solid red velvet the sleeves were red and puffy but shimmered as if they had gold in them the skirt was full, with red with gold swirls all around. She also found matching shoes in the bottom of the box. Carlin was so happy she was speechless. Then Shamus took out his Irish green silk shirt with its black ruffle down the front. Carlin burst into laughter. "Shamus, my love, I believe we are going to be wearing the brightest colors in the room tonight everyone is going to think we belong in the circus!" Shamus and Carlin fell on the bed laughing and talking about how they would be tonight's entertainment.

Mister Rossi went out to the stable he knew that even though he had given Seth the day off. Seth would still care for the horses.

He was right.

Mister Rossi found Seth brushing the new stud horse they had just traded for. Seth said without even turning around. "He's a beauty isn't he Mister Rossi?"

Mister Rossi shook his head. "Son I do not know how you do that but I' m sure it is a useful talent."

"Well Sir, it's saved my life a few times in the past."
"Seth, I thought I told you no working to day."

"I know but whose gonna take care of them. I figure their like havin little ones they gotta have attention every day. No time off from what I've heard."

"Well Seth, I never thought about it like that and you're right. I sure wish Ashton felt the same way you do. Have you told him how you feel about the horses Seth?"

"Mister Rossi, Sir, Ashton does not see me the way he used to. I'm just your hired help and he is not inclined to listen to anything much I have to say."

Mister Rossi was very upset at what Seth said, not at Seth but at Ashton, after growing up with Seth, them practically being brothers, now for Ashton to treat him as a hired hand.

Then Mister Rossi realized that is exactly what he had done to Aggie and Seth. "Seth, my boy I have done you an injustice that I am determined to remedy right now! First, I no longer want you calling me Mister Rossi."

Seth looked very confused "Then what might I call you Sir?"

"Seth I want you to call me Uncle Joseph. Will that set alright with you?" "Uncle Joseph yes sir."

"Second, I have this satin shirt it's too big for me so it should fit you. I want you to wear it and escort Miss Aggie to the Ball tonight.

Third, after the Ball you are to move all your belongings into the house. The new house staff I am hiring will show you where to put your things."

"New house staff? Uncle Joseph, where is Aggie going?"

Mister Rossi smiled. "Oh I forgot to tell you, I have informally adopted both you and Aggie as my niece and nephew. Therefore, she will no longer be working in the house. She will be our charge and tutored by her Aunt Anna and you are no longer a stable hand. You will work under me."

"Thank you so much Uncle Joseph!"

"You're welcome Seth; I just wish I had done this sooner."

Joseph walked back to the house. Seth sat with the horses thinking about what his new Uncle just told him, wondered how Ashton was going to react.

Ashton awoke to someone knocking at his door he did not feel like getting out of bed so he raised his voice. "Its not locked come in!"

In came this tiny little man. Ashton had never seen him before but the little man reminded him of a mouse as he scurried around starting a fire, and moving furniture. Ashton watched in amazement, this little man really did not look like he was physically capable of doing any of this.

Then the little man disappeared into the hallway a few seconds later, he came pushing a wooden tub.

Ashton was truly amazed now, as he watched this little man push the tub right up next to the fireplace.

Now he had a roaring fire and an empty wooden tub.

Ashton just had to ask "Alright little man how are you going to fill the tub with water?" The little man took a deep breath. He turned and walked over to the side of Ashton's bed. "I beg your pardon Sir, for not introducing myself. [He bows] my name in Nigel and I am your personal manservant for the Ball. I noticed you called me little man. Since you now know my name please use it Sir. And as to how I will acquire water please let me show you."

Nigel took out a strange metal object, placed it in his mouth, and blew. It made a very loud noise. Within five minute, there was a line of more little men in black and white suite caring buckets of hot water and dumping them into the tub.

Nigel turned to Ashton handed him a robe.

"Do you have any more questions for me at this time Sir?" "No Nigel, I really cannot think of any."

"Good, Sir, then I will return in one hour to assist you in your dress and grooming." Before Ashton could say, anything Nigel and all his helpers were gone. Ashton took a long soak in the hot tub.

A knock came at Roslyn's door just as she had removed her gown from its secret place. Realizing her door was not locked she nervously clutched her gown close to her chest.

Roslyn asked "Who is it?" Roslyn watched the door with bated anticipation.

"My name is Doris I am your personal servant to assist you to get ready for the Ball, Miss."

Roslyn was overcome with joy. Now she could really turn Ashton's head.

Come in please, come in. We must get started right away. I am a dreadful mess this morning. I am so glad you are here. I will need a hot bath and my hair washed. I need scented oils. Do not just stand there, hurry?"

Doris went as fast as she could. She had help with the tub and all the other extras Roslyn demanded.

Mister Rossi happened by and overheard Doris complaining to Nigel he stopped. "Would you mind me asking who is giving this young lady such a fit?"

Nigel did not want any trouble. "Mister Rossi, I explained to Doris that sometimes young women are hard to please and she should not let it upset her."

"Sir, I understand what your trying to do but please tell me which young lady is hard to please."

Nigel bowed his head and said. "That would be lady Roslyn, Sir."

"And am I to assume that all this frilly stuff is about to go to lady Roslyn's room." Nigel never looked up "You would assume correctly Sir."

"Nigel, do not fear my good man I am not upset with you. However, I do not want any of this to go to Miss Roslyn's room. I want Doris to take it to Miss Blaine's room and to stay in that room all day and help my niece and my daughter in law look and smell as beautiful as possible."

Nigel laid his small hand on Mister Rossi's arm. "Sir, whom shall I send back to Lady Roslyn?"

"Nigel, do not send anyone. That little peacock can get herself dressed." Mister Rossi headed for his room to get ready.

Roslyn waited for an hour. She was fit to be tied she stomped around her room talking to herself. "'Even rich people can't get good help. I asked for a few things a she just disappears. She is probably out chasing the cook or something. I guess I am going to have to do this myself."

Roslyn's window was open and she heard laughter coming from Blaine's room. She wanted to find out what was going on and why she had not been included.

Roslyn put on her robe and went to Blaine's door.

She was just going to walk in on them but she found the door locked. Therefore, she had to knock. Blaine was still laughing when she said, "Who is it?" "It's your poor lonely cousin Roslyn, can I come in?"

Doris panicked, nervously She whispered. "I was supposed to be in her room. Mister Rossi said no, he sent me here. She will have a fine fit if she sees me here!" Aggie thought fast. "Doris, get under the bed and do not make a sound."

"Alright." Doris quickly crawled under Blaine's bed Blaine dropped her blankets so Doris could not be seen.

Then Blaine opened the door. Roslyn look around the room.

She instantly noticed the table of oils and lotions she had wanted for herself." "My lands Blaine, with as long as it took you to open that door someone who did not know you better would think you two are hiding a man up here."

"Miss Roslyn, you could learn a few things from Miss Blaine. She is a decent, respectable lady. No man can respect a woman who goes about throwin themselves at everything that catches her eye."

"Now Aggie, who on earth could you be talking about."

Aggie shot a look of disgust at Roslyn. "Oh I wonder who it could be Roslyn."

Roslyn noticed a table with all the things she had ordered her servant to bring to her room. Only the good for nothing girl never retuned "Just how did you come by these wonderful things?"

Aggie answered. "Uncle Joseph sent them up for Blaine and myself. To help us get ready for the Ball."

Roslyn stopped turned around and asked. "Who is Uncle Joseph?"

Blaine spoke up. "Mister Rossi's first name is Joseph and he has asked Aggie to call him Uncle Joseph and Anna, Aunt Anna."

Sarcastically Roslyn spoke with her hand on her chest. "Well, are we not just one big happy family? Did I hear correctly, Aggie, you have been invited to the Ball? I suppose there is no accounting for taste. I must go now, my help disappeared so I have to do everything all by myself."

Just as Roslyn went to open the door, someone knocked.

Roslyn said in a very trite manner "Why, let us we see who this is, everyone is decent, right? I certainly would not want to be responsible for someone's character being marred."

Aggie rolled her eyes. "Open the door Roslyn, the only character in this room you need worry about is your own. And when you open it, step thru it and keep goin!"

"Well, I can tell when I am not wanted. Blaine you really should be choosier about your friends."

"I am Roslyn and I have the best."

Roslyn opened the door and Seth was standing in the doorway.

Roslyn spoke as if honey dripped from her mouth. "Why my goodness Seth you get more handsome every time I see you."

"I am sorry Roslyn; I don't have time to talk right now. I need to speak to Aggie." Roslyn stood in Seth's way "I just wanted to ask you one question."

Seth was becoming impatient. "Alright what is your question?" "Are you going to attend the Ball tonight?"

"Yes Uncle Joseph asked me to come. I will be there. I am really sorry Roslyn; I do not have time to talk with you."

Seth lifted Roslyn and moved her out of his way, and went into Blaine's room. He was so excited he forgot to ask if it was all right to enter.

"Ladies please excuse me, Aggie darlin, Mister Rossi he came to see me today! He gave me a beautiful shirt. He wants me to call him Uncle Joseph. He asked me to move into the house. He told me I would be workin under him, Aggie! No more stable hand! I will be able to make something for... us Aggie.

151

So we can get married! If you think you would have me."

Aggie looked at Seth with surprise. "Seth are you askin me to marry you while I am standin here in my robe?"

"Yes Aggie, I am proposing to you, not to your robe."

Aggie squealed throwing her arms around Seth's neck and started kissing his face all over.

"Darlin, does that mean yes?" "Yes! Seth yes, yes, yes!"

"Oh and I want to know if I can escort you to the Ball tonight."

Aggie stopped kissing his face "You better not even dance with anyone else especially that fancy piece of fluff Roslyn!"

"Aggie darlin, you are not jealous of her are you?" Aggie looked at the floor "I might have been a little."

"Love, you should have never been jealous of her. She has a pretty wrapper but she is empty on the inside. You are my love. You are beautiful on the outside and inside. With you, I get the whole package. I love you so much."

"I love you to Seth."

Doris crawled from under the bed. "Forgive me for breaking up your lovely celebration but we do have a Ball to prepare for. Shewing Seth toward the door you Mister Seth need to be finding your way out and we need to be closing this door and getting you ladies ready." Reluctantly Seth followed Doris' order.

Aggie and Blaine were crying and hugging each other.

What they did not know was Roslyn had been standing outside the door listening for most of the conversation.

After hearing what she thought was information she Could use, she hurried herself to Ashton's room. She knocked lightly. Nigel opened the door. "May I tell Master Ashton whose calling?"

Roslyn looked down at the little man and said in an irritated tone. "Tell him it is Roslyn and it is very important!"

Ashton came to the door with his robe on. "Well Roslyn, I can see we are dressing alike. What is so important that you have come to my room wearing your robe in the middle of the day?"

"Ashton this is no time for joking. I have come to you with serious news. I just over heard Seth say to Aggie and Blaine that your father has asked him to call him Uncle Joseph, and he is no longer to work in the stables. Your father is actually going to bring Seth in the house to live. And give him part of the family business."

"Roslyn you are trying to cause trouble again."

"I certainly am not. Since do not believe me, you can go ask him yourself Ashton Rossi. You ask Seth if your father has asked him to call him Uncle Joseph and if he asked him to move into the house and if he told him he would be working under your father from now on."

"Alright after I get dressed I will."

"Good! I cannot believe this, Ashton I came here to share, what I thought, was important information with you and you assume I am trying to cause trouble.

Information, mind you, no one else will share. Not even, you're sweet Blaine. Who knows all about this? I came to share it because of how much I care for you."

Roslyn acted as if Ashton had crushed her. She turned and walked slowly down the hallway.

Ashton called after her, "Roslyn wait."

Roslyn replied in a slightly sad tone "Just get dressed cowboy." That night everyone was ready and the guests started arriving.

The orchestra was playing enchanting music.

The women in all their elegance, with their stunning Ball gowns, the gentlemen dressed in their finery standing by their ladies.

With all the excitement, Anna had not seen her husband yet. Quietly Joseph he came up behind her and gave her a little squeeze. He startled her, she turned around and noticed Joseph was not wearing the shirt and coat she had bought him.

She smiled and whispered. "Joseph, what are you wearing?"

"I am wearing my new smoking jacket Ashton got for me at trade. And look Anna it matches your gown. Plus that shirt was too big so I gave it to our new nephew." "Joseph Rossi what on earth are you taking about. Our new nephew?"

"You know darling, Seth, our nephew. He did not have a shirt for the Ball. So, since the one you bought me was too big I gave it to him. I didn't think you would mind, him being family and all."

Anna started laughing. "You're right dear I do not mind. Seth being family and all." "My love, I guess I better tell you. I picked out a new house staff this week, they have been working with you, let me know if you want to keep them. I'll not have my niece working as a house servant. Oh and I have asked Seth to move into the house with us." "Joseph, you are full of surprises! You said Seth be moving in?"

"He will be moving into the house after the Ball tonight. And he'll be working under me from now on."

"My goodness Joseph is there anything else?"

"Only that I love you and I thank you for opening my eyes. Now, I had better go find Ashton and talk to him before he hears all this from someone else. He might get the wrong idea."

Joseph kissed Anna on the forehead and he disappeared.

Anna stood at the bottom of the staircase facing the doors greeting guests as they came in.

Blaine descended the stairs in her emerald green gown.

She looked like an Irish princess with her flame red hair piled in loose curls on top of her head like a crown and emerald eyes glistening with joy.

Everyone in the main Fourier stopped to watch her come down the staircase.

Anna turned and said to all those present.

"This is Blaine Ewen, my future daughter in-law. Isn't she beautiful?"

People came around Blaine to congratulate her and to ask where she and Ashton met.

Finally, Blaine was able to get away and try to find Ashton.

Carlin and Shamus were already down stairs.

Blaine finally found Ashton. As he caught sight of her, his breath caught in his throat. "You are the most beautiful woman here tonight Blaine. That is the perfect gown for you."

Blaine was feeling Ashton's shirt. "You look quite handsome yourself Ashton. I cannot say I have ever seen fabric like this before."

Ashton looked down at Blaine she lovingly smiled up at him.

His mind shifted to what Roslyn said earlier, he could not imagine Blaine would keep secrets from him.

Blaine brought him back to their conversation "Ashton, the fabric, where did it come from?"

"I was able to get it in trade along with a smoking jacket for my father. It comes from overseas. I am going to get a drink, would you like anything?"

"No thank you Ashton but I would love to dance."

"Maybe later darlin I am not up to it yet." Ashton went off to find a glass of whiskey.

CHAPTER 10

D own the staircase, descended Roslyn in her black velvet gown with the corset bodice laced so tightly and cut so provocatively her breasts were barely covered. Roslyn held herself in queenly air as she entered the main hall.

As she past the other guests, their conversations stopped as they stared.

Roslyn smiled provocatively, enjoying the attention.

When her Aunt and Uncle caught sight of her they were both mortified at the sight of Roslyn's boldness and brazenness to dress in such an immodest fashion. Shamus was red in the face and ready to give Roslyn a good thrashing when Joseph caught him by the arm.

"Shamus my friend, do not feed into her little game. She wants people to look at her.

And she wants you and Carlin to be upset and have your evening ruined."

"Well, my blood is boilin and I would like to ring her neck so I can say, in truth, Joseph my night is ruined!"

"Come with me Shamus I have a detraction set for the gentlemen in the study I am sure after a while you may even sing us an Irish tune or two tonight."

Anna went to Carlin. "Oh Mrs. Rossi that girl is a black mark on our family name.

Please I beg your pardon for her crassness"

"Carlin you and Shamus have done all you can for Roslyn. She is making her own misery. The kind of attention she is seeking will only bring her heartache and trouble. I say tonight that we ignore her. Let her make a fool out of herself. Then let her go home. Now come with me I have something called chocolate I think you will love."

Seth and Aggie came in together holding hands both were smiling and they looked beautiful.

Another young man asked Blaine to dance. "No thank you I am waiting for someone." She went to find Ashton. She found him with another glass of whiskey.

Blaine was disheartened when she found him drinking. She could not imagine why Ashton was in such a peculiar mood on such a festive night. Blaine decided she would do her best to bring him out of his stupor. "Ashton, darlin, do you feel up to dancing now?"

Ashton drained his glass and said. "Alright my love let's dance." Blaine could tell Ashton had already been drinking a considerable amount.

They went to the dance floor Ashton whirled Blaine around the floor so fast she became dizzy. At the end of a waltz, Blaine's Da' came up behind Ashton and asked if he could cut in. Ashton excused himself in search of another glass of whisky to drown his mounting bad mood.

Blaine caught sight of Roslyn mortified to see her cousin dressed in such revealing attire she stopped dancing Blaine was visibly horrified; she could not contain her shock. Roslyn took notice making a point to walk up to flaunt herself even more.

"Good evening Uncle. Oh and to you too Blaine of course." Shamus decided to take his friends advice and ignore Roslyn.

Blaine on the other hand had made no such agreement. "I would like to say good evening to you also Roslyn but I think you forgot part of your gown upstairs in your room!"

"Blaine you are such a child. This gown is the latest design from Paris France. It is my personal creation."

"You mean you made the gown yourself?"

"Yes, you probably had no idea I had any talent. Well, surprise I made all my gowns." Blaine looked at Roslyn with concern. "Roslyn I have never doubted you for talent. What I cannot believe is that you think dressing like this is attractive or even decent. I cannot even look at you dressed like this. Roslyn, I could not care less who in Paris wear such revealing clothing or if they say that it is fashion, it is not befitting."

"Blaine dear I cannot expect you to appreciate my designs. You have lived such a sheltered life. But you might be surprised at the people who have taken a fancy to them, even in this very room."

"Roslyn I highly doubt that, Da' let's go please I cannot talk to her anymore."

"It will be my pleasure Blaine dear to move us where the sights are better improved." Ashton found another glass of whiskey drained it quickly, and then he ran into Seth. "There you are my *friend.*" Ashton said loudly. "I would like a word with you Seth if you have the time."

Aggie was holding Seth's hand she whispered to him, "Seth luv, Ashton has been drinkin and he ain't any too pleasant. Please be careful."

"Do not worry Aggie."

Seth smiled at Ashton and said. "Alright Ashton where do you wanna go talk?" "Outside in the stable no one will bother us there."

Seth followed Ashton outside into the stable.

Roslyn had seen them go out. Quickly she went out into the garden hoping Seth would leave Ashton alone in the stable.

"Now Ashton what is so important we have to come all the way out here to talk." Ashton started pointing his finger at Seth. "You, you cannot stand living within your station. You have to start playing games with my father's head."

"Ashton your drunk and you're not making any since." "Alright Seth. Did my father ask you to move into the house?"

"Yes' Ashton he came and told me I was moving in the day after the Ball." "Did he tell you he considered you family now?"

"He did, Ashton I have always looked at your family as mine, seein I did not have one. Your father told me to consider him my uncle. And I will be workin under him now." Ashton I thought you would be alright with this, what is this all about?"

"It is about nothing being run by me, the son! Even my darling fiancé knows all about this!"

"Ashton you're taken this all wrong. Go find your father. I know he will straighten it out for you."

"Why not, he has made your life a whole lot better now hasn't he?"

"You know Ashton I don't like you much when you're drunk. I'll talk to you later, when you're sober."

Seth left Ashton there and walked away from the estate he needed a chance to cool off before he went back to Aggie.

Once Roslyn realized Seth was gone, she made her move.

She walked slowly into the stable. She found Ashton lying in a pile of hay holding an empty glass.

She purred. "Hey cowboy you got room down there for one more?"

Ashton half sat up and seeing Roslyn for the first time in her risqué gown. Drunken lust surged through his veins. "I might have room for one more depending on what Miss Roslyn's hunting tonight."

Roslyn replied with a seductive tone. "Well I am not hunting much Master Ashton, maybe a kiss or two."

"Well Miss Roslyn, sit yourself down and puckers up! If all you have been wantin is a couple of kisses we could have handled this some time ago."

Roslyn pretended to trip and fell on Ashton. Ashton was quite drunk so he fell over with her on top.

Roslyn kissed Ashton wildly. She ran her lips around his neck.

She bit him and licked his ear brazenly.

Ashton moaned.

Roslyn reached down taking Ashton's hands she placed them on her bodice.

Ashton lost all control of himself. Roslyn tore at Ashton's shirt tearing it open.

Roslyn whispered. "I would be your love slave Ashton."

Taken over by hot blind lust Ashton grabbed Roslyn as a wild animal seeking to devour its prey.

Roslyn kissed and touched Ashton in ways he had only dreamed of. Ashton and Roslyn were out of control nothing to stop them...

Anna gathered the women together to sample Chef Rheon's decadent French chocolate. After one taste Carlin quickly went and found Blaine, she just had to introduce her to chocolate. All the women were praising the chef.

Anna did not know it yet but Joseph had already hired him and his staff permanently. Aggie came to Blaine and before Aggie said a word, Blaine slid a piece of chocolate into her mouth.

They went on raving about this divine candy.

Shamus, Joseph, and most of the other men had found their way to the whiskey and cigars.

After a few drinks, Shamus had finally made a decision about Blaine's request.

Shamus gathered everyone around.

"I have an announcement. I would have liked to have made it to both Ashton and Blaine but since Ashton cannot be found at the moment I will be given it to Blaine and all you fine people. Blaine, darlin, you will have to tell your man when you find him. Now, to the point of me announcement. Carlin and I will give our blessing to our two lovebirds to set their wedding date whenever they see fit. They will not have to wait no six months." Blaine was so excited she grabbed her Da' and hugged and kissed him.

She hugged and kissed her Mama. She spun around to hug Anna. "I have to go find Ashton has any one seen him?"

Blaine went toward the kitchen; Seth was coming in the back kitchen door. "Seth, have you seen Ashton?"

"Yes Miss Blaine, I left him in the stable about an hour ago. Miss Blaine, he is not himself tonight. He has been drinkin heavy." "Thank you Seth."

Blaine hurried to the stable she could still see light coming from the stable so she knew Ashton was still in there.

As Blaine got closer, she heard laughter and talking. She slowed her pace.

A sick dread came into Blaine's stomach. Blaine stood at the side of the stacked bales of hay.

She heard Ashton's voice and someone else's. She waited and listened. She could not believe her ears Ashton was with another woman…. Roslyn! She could hear Ashton and Roslyn giggling and talking.

With her heart in her throat Blaine, she could bear no more. She stepped around the corner. "Ashton is that you?" The sight before her sickened Blaine…

All of a sudden, Ashton's world came crashing in around him he sat up quickly.

Roslyn sat there all sprawled out in the hay. Ashton jumped up. "Blaine let me explain!"

Blaine stared at him tears streaming down her face. "There is nothing to explain! You…, you are not the man I thought you were Ashton Rossi!"

With malevolence Roslyn spoke, "Really Blaine, did you actually believe Ashton was going to wait around for a simpleton like you."

Blaine's temper blazed. "You shut your mouth you two-bit harlot. You have spent your entire time here flaunting yourself like some she-cat in heat! Now I find that my husband prefers to be with trash. Well that is just fine Ashton, she can have you I don't want the likes of you!"

Blaine could not control the flood of tears. "I can't believe I trusted you. I thought you loved me. You! You! Are a liar Ashton Rossi you both deserve each other!" Blaine ran out into the darkness.

CHAPTER 11

Blaine ran until she was too tired to run anymore then she walked. She was not afraid she had made the trip so many times she would be at the cabin soon.

As Blaine neared the cabin she was still crying, she thought she noticed lights from the window. However, as she got closer there were no lights. Blaine opened the door and reached for the lantern.

A very large hand caught hers; she went to scream another large hand covered her mouth then the lantern was lit. Blaine could only see one man.

The other large man stood behind her holding her in his grasp.

The man she could see was dark skinned and he wore bright ornate clothing.

He looked at her as if she were a piece of property or cattle he had just purchased. This man spoke to the man holding her. "Mistress did not lie. She is very beautiful, with hair like the sun."

The large man spoke. "King Aviv will not like this Captain, King will say we not to take woman like this one for trade."

"Sobbo do not upset your self with what the King would say. Do as I tell you, now we will take this beautiful woman for our King. Not for trade."

"Now take her to the carriage and keep her from screaming. I have to take care of some other business. Hurry Sobbo they will come looking for her soon."

Blaine was in shock. Who were these men? Who was the Mistress he spoke of? How could she have told them anything about her? This had to be a mistake.

The large one named Sobbo had gagged her. But he was not harsh about it.

Then he placed a black cloth bag over Blaine head and tied her hands behind her back but not to tight. Blaine was frightened she began to cry.

Then the large man said to her.

"I will not tie your feet if you tell Sobbo you will not run."

Blaine shook her head no, that she would not try to escape. Blaine was shaking with fear.

The large man seemed as if he were trying to calm her. "Sobbo will not hurt you red hair, Sobbo will not let anyone hurt you." Blaine did not know if she could believe him but he sounded convincing. "Sobbo will take gag out if you will not scream..."

Blaine shook her head in agreement showing she would not scream. Sobbo removed the gag.

"Mister Sobbo this must be a mistake. I don't know a Mistress. This cabin belongs to my fiancé. Do you understand Sir you must have the wrong person."

"No Mister no sir just Sobbo you be quiet now." Sobbo fearing the captain might harm her for talking, he placed the gag back in her mouth.

Blaine huddled in the corner of the carriage and cried.

The Captain had done as promised. He placed what he considered a fair price for the red head behind the cabin.

The Captain climbed into the carriage and they were off.

As the approached, the ship the Captain hit Blaine over the head knocking her unconscious.

This made Sobbo angry. "Captain I say no harm come to her why do you hit the woman?"

"Sobbo this is my ship! I am Captain! Do not question me. Now take this one below with the others."

"Sobbo will take her below, I will stand watch. You are Captain, but this ship belongs to the King, you are Captain for the King."

Sobbo boarded the ship carrying Blaine, He placing her limp body below deck in a small dark room.

Ashton sat in the hay for a long while trying together his whit's. He had drunk so much his head was still spinning.

Roslyn was trying to play the jilted lover.

"Ashton, [Roslyn said with tears in her eyes] do you care for me or not?" Ashton did not answer he was trying to figure out what had just happened. His head spinning in his drunken stupor he was hoping to wake up and all this would be a bad dream.

Roslyn's tone became demanding. "Ashton Rossi look at me." Ashton turned his head and looked at Roslyn

Realizing this was not a bad dream, at least not one from hich he could wake up. "For heaven sake Roslyn cover yourself up. I think the two of us have done enough damage tonight."

"Ashton what are you saying. You do not want to be with me over Blaine?" "Roslyn let me explain something to you. You cannot go chasing a man around half- naked all the time, sneaking in a man's bedroom, throwing yourself at him at every opportunity. Then you find him stone drunk past out in the hay, you practically remove your clothes and start kissing him. That is not love Roslyn that is lust, nothing but pure heat between two people, not an emotional attachment. To know I have probably lost Blaine over what you and I have done makes me sick. Now please get your clothes on we have to get to the house and get help finding Blaine."

Ashton came thru the kitchen entrance holding his head. Aggie and Seth were in the kitchen to be alone for a moment. They could not help but notice the way Ashton looked.

Seth asked. "Ashton did Blaine find you?"

"Yes brother she found me alright. And I have just messed my whole life up Seth." "Ashton what have you done."

"I got drunk, jealous, mad and stupid. And that is a fatal combination with a woman like Roslyn around."

Aggie took a deep breath and said. "Oh my merciful heavens that she-devil took advantage of you in your drunken state and Blaine found you there together." Ashton replied," Well Aggie that is pretty much it."

Liking the sound of it being all Roslyn's fault. However, of course, Seth was not going to let that be.

"Ashton I do love you like you are my own flesh.

I had that piece of fluff chasin me about. But she held no candle to my Aggie. So no matter what she said, or what she was willing to show, I was not impressed. She finally got the hint and flittered off somewhere else. The problem with you Ashton is you liked her attention. And it disrespected Blaine.

I hope someday that you will forgive me for sayin this.

But if one fancy piece of fluff could trap ya right after you, bein engaged. What makes you think it would not happen again. Ashton there is somethin missin... When you truly love someone she is your only piece of fluff."

Ashton was quiet, he was not mad because he realized Seth was right. Seth went and found Ashton's father. Carlin and Shamus had already retired. Therefore, they let them sleep.

Aggie believed she knew where Blaine would have gone. "She would have gone to the cabin."

Seth agreed, Ashton decided they would start their search at the cabin. Joseph did not know the details but he decided not to wake Shamus. The three men rode horses Aggie and Roslyn took the wagon.

Aggie was surprised Roslyn had changed into a modest gown.

When they reached the cabin, the cabin was dark. Roslyn's heart was pounding, had her plot been carried out?

Ashton dismounted and ran to the cabin door, which was standing wide open.

Ashton yelled for Blaine there was no answer.

Ashton found a lantern and lit it.

Aggie slowly entered behind Ashton. "We fixed the place up Mister Ashton for you and Miss Blaine's honeymoon. Miss Blaine thought you would love it here." [Aggie's voice trailed off sadly]

Seth found one of Blaine's earrings lying under the table. Everyone in the room stared at each other in shock.

They knew what it meant. Blaine had been taken. But by who? And why?

Aggie spoke in a meek voice. "Seth you don't suppose it could have been Indians do you?"

Seth thought for a moment then looked at Ashton and asked. "Ashton, have you seen any Indians around lately?"

"I have seen a few but never heard of them taking white women, not like this." Joseph spoke softly. "It won't do us any good to look tonight we will have to look first thing in the morning."

Seth spoke up. Uncle Joseph I think it would be safer if the ladies were taken home.

Aggie please find Roslyn. Ashton and I will stay here." Aggie went outside "Roslyn where are you?

Roslyn came from around behind the cabin caring a lantern.

"Roslyn what in heavens name are you doin? you want the Indians to swoop out of the woods and grab you too?" come on we are getting ready to go."

Aggie and Roslyn walked into the cabin the front of Roslyn's gown was dirty.

Ashton asked "Where have you been Roslyn?" Roslyn nervously looked at the faces staring at her. "Looking for clues just like everyone else."

Ashton replied. "Outside in the dark?" Ashton rubbed his head and said. "Yes father would you please take them back. And please tell Blaine's parents Seth and I are searching for her."

Joseph agreed and took the wagon and the girls. Leaving the extra horse behind.

Joseph arrived back at the estate with Aggie and Roslyn.

Roslyn stretched and yawned. "I am tired I think I'll go to my room now." Roslyn diapered upstairs to her room as if nothing was wrong.

Joseph and Aggie talked for a little while then Aggie said she needed to go upstairs.

Aggie took a deep breath but she knew this was something she must do. Aggie stopped in front of the Ewen's bedroom she said a prayer then knocked. Mrs. Ewen answered. "Who is it?"

"It's Aggie. Mrs. Ewen and I be needin to speak to both you and Mister Ewen as soon as you're decent please."

"Alright, Aggie just give us a moment." Aggie waited outside their door. When the Ewen's were ready, Carlin opened the door. "Come in please Aggie." Aggie was every nervous she knew this was the worst news any parent could get. Carlin could see Aggie was terribly upset.

"Aggie honey, it's alright just tell us what has happened."

"First Mrs. Ewen I want to tell you how this happened. Roslyn has been throwin herself at both Mister Ashton and my Seth. Last night Mister Ashton was on a bad drunk. Past out in the hay. I know it is true because Seth left him there. Well, that half-naked she- devil Roslyn goes into the stable and takes advantage of Ashton in his bewildered drunken state. Then Miss Blaine goes out to the stable to find her man, only…. she finds her man with the she devil."

Carlin looked at Shamus both shaking their heads.

Carlin said. "Oh this is awful!"

Aggie start to cry. "No mum it gets worse"

Shamus could see the pain in her face, "Aggie dear how does this get worse?"

"I hate to tell you this sir, but I love Blaine as my sister. She ran to the cabin last night after what she saw. Well, sir, someone was at the cabin and, I do not know how else to say this…. Someone took Blaine away. They took her away. She is gone. Aggie collapsed onto the floor Carlin went to her.

Shamus was in shock he went down stairs to find Mister Rossi.

Carlin and Aggie sat on the floor sobbing together. Joseph had awoken Anna and told her what he knew.

Anna had made coffee and warm towels. She brought them to Carlin's room.

Anna sat on the floor and wept with Carlin and Aggie.

When Shamus had talked to Joseph, Shamus began to cry. Joseph put his arms around his friend and cried with him.

The chef sensed it was going to be a very stressful day so he prepared a very light breakfast.

The house staff took over seeing the guests out that had stayed.

Once Roslyn thought, it was, safe she locked her door she took out the gold purse the Captain had left behind the cabin.

She sat on her bed, the purse felt heavy she opened it and poured it out onto her bed. Roslyn could not believe her eyes. There were fifty solid gold coins lying on her bed. She rolled around laughing. She let her mind wonder to of all the ways she could spend her money.

Roslyn never gave any thought to Blaine. Nor what she had just done to her. Roslyn hid her gold coins in her suitcase, and then went down stairs for breakfast. Roslyn had a bounce in her step as she came down the stairs, as if everything was right in the world.

When she enters the dining room, she noticed only coffee and a few pastries for breakfast.

Roslyn called for the chef. "Chef Rheon where is the rest of the food?"

"Excuse me Madam, but with the trauma in the household today I did not think anyone would eat much. However, if you have an appetite, you tell Rheon and I will make you your delight, Madam." Roslyn gave chef Rheon her request.

Ashton and Seth had gotten up before sunrise.

They had found horse tracks heading up into the hills. They also found carriage tracks.

Both Seth and Ashton agreed they would follow the tracks leading into the hills.

They would not go back to the estate.

They would leave from the cabin and pick up supplies along the way. Seth turned to Ashton. "I just wish I could have said good bye to Aggie."

Ashton thought for a moment. "Let's look quick and see if there is anything you can leave a note on. I have a feeling Aggie will come back here."

Seth left his note. They saddled up and were off up into the hills hoping to find Blaine.

Roslyn was sitting at the dining table with all her dinning requests in front of her. She was so overjoyed at the sight and smell of such wonderful culinary masterpieces Roslyn found herself humming while she ate.

Mister Rossi walked into the dining room. He watched Roslyn for a moment. Then he said. "That looks like a mighty nice breakfast you have for yourself Roslyn" "Yes your chef is wonderful simply wonderful!"

"I am happy you have enjoyed our hospitality. Now, Miss Roslyn as soon as you have finished your wonderful breakfast. I have the carriage prepared to take you to the train station. So please finish as soon as you can and pack your things we need to be leavening soon."

Roslyn was stunned, "I thought I wasn't leaving for two more days."

"Let's just say your trips been cut short." With that, Mister Rossi walked out of the room.

Roslyn lost her appetite. She went upstairs and packed for the train.

The house staff carried Roslyn's bags out to the carriage.

When Roslyn opened the carriage door only Mister Rossi waited inside. "Oh, I see my early departure has been missed by everyone."

"Not really, Miss Roslyn please gets in."

Once Roslyn was seated, Mister Rossi tapped on the roof and they were off. "I am surprised that not even my Aunt and Uncle wanted to come see me off." Mister Rossi was trying to be polite but he was finding it difficult.

"Miss Roslyn your Aunt and Uncle didn't want to come. They are aware of last night's affairs as well as I am. Now before you go spouting tears and telling me how my son just took advantage of poor little ole you.

I want you to know a couple of things Miss Roslyn. I know who you are, and I know what you are. And I would bet my last dollar that somehow you know what happened to Miss Blaine."

Roslyn just looked out the window and said." You would bet your last dollar?"

"Yes Miss Roslyn I would." "You really dislike me that much?"

"Roslyn, I believe there are three types of women. Those who have no interest in marriage and like livening alone just fine. Then there's the ones who dream of marriage and hope someday they will meet a faithful, loving, hardworking, man to call their own. Then there is the other kind. Who do not really want to marry, nevertheless, does not mind fooling around with a man who is, provided he can take care of her. In addition, this type does not even care how many homes she breaks up.

How many lives she ruins. As long as she gets what she wants."

"Well, Mister Rossi please enlighten me which one am I? I am sure I can guess." "Well Miss, it's not the first two."

All Roslyn was shocked at his bluntness. "Oh I see." The rest of their trip to the station was silent.

When they reached the train station, Mister Rossi turned Roslyn's baggage over to the train Master climbed back in his carriage tapped the roof and he was gone. Roslyn stood at the train by herself to wait alone.

Shamus and Carlin sat in Anna parlor holding each other. Shamus looked at Anna "I don't blame your boy he never could hold his whiskey. I have known for some time he's been emotionally tangled."

Shamus laid his head hands and said. "I just waited too long to say something." Carlin started to cry again. "This is my fault, I wrote those letters to Roslyn about Ashton, and I sent her the money to come here. If I had not been so jealous of you Anna and how Blaine took to you. None of this would have happened."

Anna sat down between them both and said. "Nonsense both of you. Neither of you are to blame for this disaster. I do believe someone is. But not the two of you. Carlin, Blaine was having me make plans to bring Roslyn here so if you had not I would have. As far as Ashton's is concern, he is a grown man. He has known for some time now he cannot handle whiskey. That stuff is the Devils brew! Moreover, with that she-cat on the prowl, he should have been extra careful! In addition, I know about your celebrating Mister Ewen. Well his celebrating has created a world of a mess! I am sorry Mister Ewen for raising my voice but I Miss Blaine too."

Mister Rossi returned home. Everyone in the house was relieved Roslyn was gone.

CHAPTER 12

B laine woke to a horrid smell. The room she was in was rocking she realized she was on a ship.

She was not tied up anymore but she had a terrible headache and a bump on her head.

She could not see very well but she could hear others moaning in pain around her.

Blaine scooted her feet across the floor not wanting to step on any one.

She slowly moved toward the outside wall hoping to find a porthole. She was in luck, finding a small porthole Blaine felt around for a latch, she unhooked the latch and the porthole blew open.

Sea air rushed into the room the moon light lit up her surroundings. Blaine was shocked to see nine young women lying in filth in a space not much bigger than a horse stall. She looked around there were no blankets, no water to drink, not even a sanitary place to relive one's self.

Blaine's Irish temper flared, she beat on the door. Yelling for water and clean blankets.

Moments later the door flew open.

The man who called himself Captain stood glaring at her with the threat of violence written on his face. "Who is it that disrupts my dinning?"

Blaine decided to be firm. "Pardon me sir but we have no blankets and no clean water to drink not to mention any food. What kind of man are you?"

Captain Bogota's voice resonated thru the small dark cabin. "I am Captain Bogota! I do not answer to demands of slaves! You will get what I give you when I see fit! And unless you want more than a bump on your head, pretty one... keep your mouth shut!"

Captain Bogota slammed the door. Blaine had never met anyone so wicked.

She had never been dealt with in such a horrid manner, what kind of a nightmare was this.

She covered her eyes, slid to the floor praying that God would protect her from the nightmare she found herself trapped in. eventually she cried herself to sleep.

When morning came all the girls were covered with blankets and there was a small bucket with a dipper for drinking.

Blaine was not sure but she believed the big man named Sobbo had brought it for them.

Blaine opened the other two windows and the girls began waking up.

It was obvious to Blaine that several of the girls had been badly abused. From the foul smell Blaine had no doubt all were in need of a bath and clean clothes. She tried to speak to them but they would not talk, she was not sure if they could talk.

Blaine had a strong feeling the big man, Sobbo, was responsible for the drinking water and blankets. She hoped he might be willing to help her so she quietly went to the door and whispered, "Sobbo, Sobbo please, help us we need two buckets, one with water and soap."

Later that day Sobbo brought food, it looked rotten and smelt even worse.

Sobbo said. "This what the Captain send, you will not eat this dump it out the porthole." He took out fruit and Bread from his pockets. "You will eat this. And this is for you red hair."

Sobbo gave her the two buckets and three bars of horse soap.

Blaine touched Sobbo's arm, "thank you."

Sobbo bowed to Blaine not saying a word he left locking the door behind. The other girls noticed the honor Sobbo gave to the red haired woman.

Blaine first wanted to set up toilet rules. She had no idea how difficult this would be with a language barrier.

So once again, after several hours of frustration trying to explain her self Blaine surrendered. Turning to the door she whispered for Sobbo's assistance.

Sobbo opened the door quickly starling Blaine. He bowed, "Do you need Sobbo?" "Yes, yes I do. Sobbo please, I want to help these girls but they don't seem to understand me."

Sobbo did not understand. Blaine thought she would try something different.

"Sobbo do you speak the language girls speak? Sobbo bowed his head in agreement. "Sobbo, will you help me speak with girls?"

Sobbo could tell the red hair wanted to help the girls. He agreed to help too. "Sobbo will help you red hair."

"Please Sobbo, my name is Blaine. I would like you to call me Blaine not red hair." Sobbo bowed, "As you wish red hair."

Blaine explained to Sobbo the one bucket was for excrement and the other bucket she would be helping them bathe.

If their situation were not so dire Blaine would have found Sobbo manner of explaining quite amusing he acted out the use of each bucket so the girls were left with no doubt what they were to be used for.

Much to Blaine's surprise each girl lined up at the bucket to be washed.

Blaine pitched all their rags they had for clothing, scrubbed each girl, and washed her hair.

Some were so dirty she had to wash them two times. Sobbo had to bring several buckets of water before the task was through.

Blaine thought 'these poor children haven't ever seen a tub.'

Sobbo had snuck Blaine the horse oil that she used it on the girls who had extremely tight curly hair.

It changed their look completely.

These girls were beautiful.

However, the oldest could not be a day over fifteen and the youngest looked to be about five.

She was the most beautiful; she had long dark hair and big dark eyes.

Blaine had heard one of the older girls call her Lome. Blaine gathered they must be sisters.

Blaine worked hard around their small room to throw out any vile smelling thing or anything that might draw rats.

Blaine shook out and folded the blankets every morning.

She emptied the chamber pot and worked on making clothes for the girls out of layers from her gown. This went on for several weeks.

None of the others offered to help. Blaine prayed constantly, she felt these girls needed her and maybe this was what she was supposed to do. Therefore, she kept pushing herself. In addition, Sobbo was proving himself a trustworthy friend to Blaine. He always brought fresh water, bread and fruit.

After four weeks, the ship had set to port. Blaine hoped this was their destination.

Sobbo came early that morning quietly he woke Blaine. "Sobbo, is somethin wrong, are we getting off the ship now?"

"No, you must stay, Captain not happy with me, he says I make too nice with you and the others. He says I go ashore for supply I be gone all day. This no good, I believe Captain will cause trouble for you red hair. I ask you to be safe." Blaine touched Sobbo's hand. "I will do my best. Sobbo please call me by my name its Blaine not red hair." Sobbo spoke no more. He bowed to Blaine and left the cabin. Blaine busied herself waking everyone up however; she noticed Lome's sister was missing.

She hid the small water pale on a hook outside the porthole.

Blaine hurried and hung the blanket out the window closing it so they would not fly away.

She looked at the girls. "I am so sorry about this but it's for our protection."

Blaine took a small pile of hay and dumped the chamber pot into the hay near the door then hid the bucket under the bench.

She had the girl's rubbed dirt on their faces and arms. Many started to complain, not wanting to be dirty again.

Blaine told them. "Captain Bogota comes with bad men. If we look bad they will go away."

The girls seemed to understand and began rubbing dirt all over themselves. Blaine smeared her face and arms with dirt.

She had the youngest girls get in the middle so they could not be seen.

She closed the windows so the smell would be overwhelming when Bogota opened the door. The girls lay quiet.

When they heard the men's foot steeps coming, Lome started to cry.

Blaine stroked Lome's hair whispering, "shhh my dear it is going to be alright. Let's all pretend we are sleeping, quiet now."

Captain Bogota had one of his men open the door quickly he stepped back quick holding his noise with his hands. "Captain It is a foul place for sure!" Whatever this wench has been telling ya Captain it ain't true."

The Captain became angry turning his venom on the wench. "It is a dangerous thing to lie to me!"

The young woman was shaking and frightened. "I swears I be tellin you true. I no lie to you Capin."

"But you were willing turn on every wench, including your young sister. Why?" "Cuz you says me free if I, I, I, I, I tell what I see. I, I, I be hopin you'd work somethin out bout my sis."

"I do not like men or women who are easily led into betrayal! And as for your sister I will be keeping her."

Captain Bogota turned to his first mate. "Give this one to the men. Then throw her to the sharks. And in the name of the gods close that stinking door before I become sick!" Blaine and the girls were crying and shaking they could hear Lome's sister scream as she was drug away.

Lome lay in Blaine's lap silently sobbing.

The other girls opened the portholes, brought in the blankets, and pitched the defiled hay out the window.

Suddenly Blaine realized how fluent Lome's sister spoke English.

Blaine asked. "How many of you speak at least some English?" Lome patted Blaine's leg.

Then the oldest girl said. "Most do some. I means we z be from plantations." Blaine asked. "Why did no one respond when I was trying to help you?"

The same older girl spoke up. "Cuz Zeba, she be the one they took, she z tellin us you bein white we aint trustin ya. We waz scared of ya. An dat big Sobbo comes in ere a he actin like you somthin, bowin and things.

Zeba she thinkin she gettin free. Leavin her young sis in the Hans of dat beast.."

Blaine put out her hand. "My name is Blaine Ewen. What is yours?" The young woman started laughing.

Their reaction puzzled Blaine. "That wasn't meant to be funny. You do have a name?" "Yea Ma'am I gots a name. I never in me life thought a fancy white woman likes you, would wanna be touchin my hans an askin whats be my name that's all. I be Ebina. Ya knowz Lome and tis ere is Vantaa, tis be Malina. not knowin who em others be." Blaine went up to the other three girls, "Do you speak any English?"

The girls just looked at her confused.

Blaine went up to one girl placed here hand on her chest and said. "Blaine"

Then Blaine put her hand on the girl's chest. The girl thought for a moment then replied slowly.

"Zuni"

Blaine said. "My name is Blaine."

Then she pointed to Zuni. "Your name is Zuni."

Both of them became very excited because now they could communicate.

The next girl came and wanted to share her name with Blaine.

When Kenya told Blaine her name. Blaine thought these girls might be from Africa. The last girl would not share with them.

She slept alone, ate alone.

The only time she came around the others was at bath time or if there was danger. Sobbo was angry when he came back aboard and found the body of the young girl. The men left her there for Sobbo to dispose of.

One of the shipmates had been drinking staggering up to Sobbo as he put her over the side.

The seaman slapped Sobbo on the back, "It must be might bothersome to have to clean up the mess without havin any of the fun."

Sobbo was angry he turned on the man. "You one who hurt this girl?"

The man started backing away. "Now settle yourself Sobbo, Captain Bogota gave err to us cuz she was a lie'en to the Capitan. And it weren't just me. It was the whole crew, cep the Captain."

Sobbo had heard enough. He pick up the scrawny man in his rage snapped his neck. pitching the man to the deep with the body of the young girl.

As he watched the body of the man sink to the depth of the sea, he said. "Justice is done....be at peace little girl."

Slowly, Sobbo walked back to his post in front of the woman slave's door, swearing an oath to himself, he would protect the women with his life.

Weeks turned into months it seemed. Blaine had begun teaching the girls how to speak, write, and a few were learning to read.

Blaine had not noticing the young woman who had secluded herself had been listening and learning.

One day the young woman came up to Blaine and asked. "Blaine you teach Tobua to read?"

Blaine sat stunned. "Oh my you can speak English."

"Yes you good teacher. you teach Tobua to read."

Blaine was so excited because only the three girls from the plantation had started to read.

The girls from Africa had a hard time speaking.

Blaine was more than willing to teach Tobua if she wanted to learn. "Yes Tobua! Yes, I'll teach you to read."

Progress was slow and difficult, but there was progress. When the other noticed the effort Tobua was putting forth to read.

All the girls wanted to read. Blaine had a real classroom of very eager students. She decided to teach social graces and manners. And about running a household and keeping clean. She thought 'Aunt Anna would be proud.'

One night Blaine had trouble sleeping she sat at the window peering out into the night at the star filled sky, her mind drifted back to the night of the Ball.

Blaine ran her hands over the remains of the tattered gown she now wore.

She closed her eyes and she could see herself coming down the stairs in her beautiful emerald gown.

She could see her Da', with his big Irish smile and bright red hair. And her Mama, with the love she had seen in her eyes that night.

Aunt Anna had truly been her best friend honest and protective so generous and loving.

Papa Joseph, a man who could read people, could understand people, a man who loves his family.

Aggie and Seth, she hoped they would be getting married soon and have beautiful babies.'

Then Blaine's thoughts shifted to Ashton. And silently she started to cry. She thought 'And for me, there will be no marriage, no happiness, and no babies she cried until she fell asleep.

Blaine was awakened by moans of pain coming from two of the girls.

She found Tobua and Vantaa lying next to each other, Blaine touched their foreheads, and they were burning up with fever.

Blaine took the soaked blankets off them.

She went to the door and whispered. "Sobbo are you there?" The door opened Sobbo greeted Blaine with a bow.

"Sobbo I need you, two of the girls are burning up with fever. I don't know what to do.

Please help me." Sobbo did not say a word.

He entered the room and looked the girls over then quickly left the room locking the door.

He was gone for quite a while.

Blaine wiped Tobua and Vantaa off with cool rags watching the door. waiting for Sobbo to return.

Sobbo came back with herbs in his pockets. Sobbo took Blaine aside. "Many men sick s with fever. some dead. If these herbs not work, these die too. Ones not sick, need come with me."

Blaine took Sobbo by the arm. "I have to stay here and take care of the girls, they need me."

"I know, mix herbs in water make girls drink. if fever break good. fever no break. Sobbo pointed at the bible he had given Blaine.

Sobbo took all the other girls into the horse stalls with the horses.

Sobbo said. "You stay with horses they no get sick. I be back for you when all is safe." The girls had come to trust Sobbo. Blaine had told them she was to be taken to the King and she would try to get them set free.

Entered the cabin "Not safe for you my Blaine I take you to others. I care for them. I come for you if fever breaks."

"Sobbo, you are my friend just like these girls are my friends, my students, the only reason I have not gone crazy. I would never forgive myself if I didn't do all I could to save them."

"I understand. You Sobbo's friend too."

Sobbo made sure the other girls were feed and cared for.

Blaine stayed with her two sick friends for three days.

Despite the herbs and care the darkness of the fever took over for Blaine's friends. Vantaa never woke up at all Tobua chanted in her native tongue until she passed away. Blaine believed it was a prayer of some kind. she silently prayed for her two lost friends. Blaine did not cry knowing death was probably a better place than where Bogota was taking them.

Blaine's heart was broken she knocked on the door, Sobbo entered; gently he touched Blaine on the shoulder, knowing the pain she must feel.

Sobbo carried the two bodies out with their blankets over them so no one would know it was the young women.

In all the fever took the lives of half the crew and two of Blaine's friends.

Sobbo brought the other girls back in with Blaine. They hugged each other crying over their lost friends.

Malina said in a soft meek voice. "They better off I think. We need be happy for um not sad. I hear Tobua chanting for she go. She be happy now. Miss Blaine it nutin you could-a did ta save'um. They not wanna stay. I think."

Blaine put her arm around Malina and said. "I think so too." Things were quiet on the ship with so many men gone.

Blaine decided to ask Sobbo how much longer this living nightmare would take.

. "Sobbo, my friend, please tell me how long we have been on this ship?" Sobbo thought for a moment then said, "In two weeks it will be six full moons." Blaine was stunned. Had she really been at sea for nearly six months?

With the shock still in her voice Blaine asked, "Sobbo how much longer?"

"Two weeks, on fifth full moon we reach King." Sobbo left, locking the door behind him.

Blaine sat on the bench looking out at the sea wondering how far away six months had taken her from her family.

She hoped and prayed they were all alright restlessly she drifted off to sleep.

CHAPTER 13

Ashton and Seth had been in the mountains for close to five months. It was obvious no one had seen anyone who even resembled Blaine.

So the two men headed home they first stopped at the cabin.

Seth was right, Aggie had come back but it seemed Joseph and Shamus left their signature to let Seth know they were not taking any chances.

Seth and Ashton closed up the cabin, with heavy hearts not finding Blaine had broken Ashton.

The two men rode back to the estate.

Aggie was so happy to see Seth she ran out of the house and jumped in his arms. As Seth spun her around he said. "Mercy Aggie your light as a feather ain't you been eating?"

Aggie smiled. "Not much with worrying about you."

Seth held her tight. "Well I am home now, so I need to be making sure you are properly feed."

Ashton stood by watching his friends. His smile was sincere only his eyes showed his heartbreak.

Aggie noticed his expression. "Oh Ashton we do apologize."

Ashton shook his head trying to hide his emotions. "You two have absolutely nothing to apologize for. You are perfect for each other. I wish you the best. In fact, Seth, if you want it, the cabin is yours and the ten acres with it. It would be a nice place to start a family. And if you out grow it, we will build a bigger one. Well…

At least give it some thought."

The couple could not believe what they were hearing now they could marry now that they had a home of their own. Aggie whispered to Seth. "Ashton sounded like his father just then."

"Aggie, Ashton is a broken hearted man. It's a shame to have to lose your love only to realize how much you really loved her."

Ashton left the happy couple making his way back to the estate.

Ashton walked in thru the front doors. His father and Shamus were the first to see him.

Ashton looked at them both then fell to his knees. He cried.

"I couldn't find her!" "We searched everywhere, followed every trail." "Papa I lost her!" "Someone took my Blaine because of my stupidity!" Shamus got down on his knees and held Ashton. Making Ashton cry harder.

Shamus was eventually able to calm Ashton then Shamus spoke. "Your papa and I have a pretty good idea who played the devil's advocate with our Blaine. And it was not you, son. So as soon as we catch the creature red handed we may at least get some justice if we don't get Blaine back."

Ashton looked at Shamus, with tears in his eyes and Said. "I just want her back."

Joseph placed his hand on his son's head and said. "Son you are going thru a very difficult time, why don't you go upstairs and get some rest.

Ashton did not argue. He did not say a word. His heart hurt so bad he could barely breathe. He went to his room and fell into a deep sleep. Two weeks later Shamus asked Ashton to come into the study. Carlin was there along with Ashton's mother and father.

"Someone knows where Blaine is, don't they!"

Shamus opened a letter. "Son, Carlin and I felt we should read this to you all. We feel strongly this is connected somehow with Blaine's disappearance.

Shamus began to read:

'Dearest Carlin, Roslyn spoke highly of her trip with you. She is regretful things did not go better with Mister Rossi. I told her not everyone could be compatible. Some day she will meet a fine man. I do not believe it will be any time soon. Not long after her return, Roslyn came into a very large sum of money. She never has been clear just how she came by it. But you know our Roslyn she has some imagination. And so creative. She took that money, went to Paris France for two months. She has come back and opened her own very gown shop. She also hired French tailor. My girl is amazement to me. Her visit must have been an inspiration for her. Thank you so much Carlin, that trip was just what my Roslyn needed.

She is her own woman now. Thank you again Carlin. With love, Shannon'

Shamus folded up the letter and put it in his pocket.

Joseph spoke first. "It seems to me Miss Roslyn never mentioned to her Mama that Blaine is missing. Or that her stay was less than welcome." Ashton asked. "Where on earth did she get the money?"

Seth had been standing outside the door listening. He walked into the room. "Forgive me Uncle Joseph, Aunt Anna Mister and Mrs. Ewen, Ashton, I know I was not asked to this meeting. And I know it is powerfully rude to listen when you have not been invited. But I have information after hearing that letter that might help. All the time Miss Roslyn was throwing herself at me. Or so I thought. She was asking all kinds of questions about what happened at trade. Then Miss Roslyn made such a fuss about comin with us Ashton. Remember?"

Ashton thought for a few moments, "Yes, Seth, remember on the way to trade I tried to scare Roslyn by telling her those stories about women slave traders. She just wanted to know more."

Carlin let out a gasp, and said with terror in her voice. "Great merciful God in heaven are you two sayin Roslyn sold my Blaine to some low life slave trader? Roslyn is a bad girl, but that, that is evil!"

Carlin went to sand up and fainted Shamus caught her, laying her on the sofa. Anna ran and brought back a cold cloth and a cool glass of water. After a few moments, Carlin came to.

Anna gave Carlin the glass of water. "Carlin you have just had a terrible shock." Carlin sat silent for quite a while then she looked at Shamus "I must go to see if this is true Shamus."

"Carlin darlin I don't think Roslyn will be forth coming with the truth."

Then Carlin tuned to Ashton. "Ashton, I believe you may be the bate to the truth. If you think, you can play the part. I think if Roslyn believes you have come to seek her out, she will tell you at least part of what she has done. Are you up to it Ashton?"

"I am not sure Mrs. Ewen. I need to think about this."

Carlin went to Ashton put her arms around him and kissed him on the cheek. "Ashton, take your time you just let me know."

Ashton went out into the garden sitting under the tree, he and Blaine were under together when he gave her his mother's emerald ring. Ashton laid there on the grass it was a cool night. Realizing he would probably never see Blaine again.

Ashton said a prayer that Blaine's fate would not be like the stories he had been told.

Ashton's eyes filled with tears at the thought of not being able to save her.

As he laid there looking at the stars he knew there was one way he could see some justice done for Blaine's sake.

Ashton got up off the ground looked up in the sky and said, "I will do this for you Blaine my love where ever you are. I will always love you." Ashton closed his eyes for a moment then he turned with a new determination and went back into the house.

He walked back into the study with confidence. "Mrs. Ewen I will go with you. And I am ready to play my part to get Roslyn to tell the truth, if that is possible."

Carlin looked concerned as she said. "Ashton do you know what this may call for you to do?"

"Yes Ma'am I have to play the same ruse on her that she played on me. Only hopefully I'll be better at it."

Carlin could not believe his confidence. "Well I suppose we should leave tomorrow." The next morning Ashton was ready before anyone else was awake. The chef was in the kitchen starting breakfast. Ashton came down the servant's staircase.

"Good morning Rheon."

"Oh! And good morning to you Master Ashton. I was not expecting anyone up so early.

All I have ready is the coffee."

"Its alright coffee is fine. And I'll get it myself."

Ashton poured his coffee then and had a seat in his mother's parlor.

Anna came down stairs. Got her coffee add went into her parlor. She saw Ashton setting there staring at Blaine's portrait.

"Ashton are you alright son?"

Ashton never turned away, "She sure was beautiful that night wasn't she?" "Yes son she is."

Ashton took something out of his pocket, "I found this at the cabin that night. Its one of the emerald earrings you gave her."

"Do you want me to hold onto it for you son?"

Ashton half smiled at his mother. "That would probably be a good idea."

Anna was not sure Ashton was ready for this trip. To face Roslyn to be prepared for her cunning. "Ashton dear are you sure you Can handle a ruse with Roslyn after everything she's done?"

Ashton touched his mother's hand. "I have to for Blaine. Roslyn has to pay for what she has done to our family. And if I have to kiss the she devil to get some justice I will."

"I am proud of you Ashton."

After breakfast, Carlin and Ashton were off to the train station.

Now that the train ran all the way Carlin and Ashton reach Sweetwater in record time. Shannon was surprised to see Carlin and even more surprised to meet Ashton Rossi. Ashton hired a carriage to take Carlin and himself to Shannon's place. Approached her sisters place Carlin was not happy to see her sister living in the same rundown house.

Carlin asked. "Shannon I thought you said Roslyn came into some money?"

"Oh Sis not some money a whole lot of money, the pot at the end of the rainbow I tell ya."

Carlin had a serious face. "Then why may I ask are you still living in tatters?"

"Now Carlin don't go getting your dander up. You know Roslyn, she thinks of herself first and then her Mama. She keeps me in clothes and makes sure I have plenty of food." Ashton took a quick look at Shannon's house and it was in desperate need of repair before winter.

"Ma'am I am pretty good with my hands I would be more than happy to do some repair for you letting us stay here since we came unannounced."

Carlin nudged her sister and said. "Take his offer if I've learned anything it's don't argue with a Rossi, you won't win."

Shannon shook Ashton's hand and said. "That would be just fine Mister Rossi." Ashton hitched up Shannon's horse and wagon and headed to town.

He stopped at the general store to pick up supplies to work on the house. After paying for the supplies, he asked were the nearest gown shop was.

The general store owner was more than happy to point the way, but also told Ashton it was a very pricey place.

Ashton just rode by with his hat pulled over his eye, he caught sight of Roslyn in her shop dressed in one of her provocative gowns speaking to a customer, Ashton did not stop he made his way back to Shannon's house.

He was restless, concerned he might not be able to fool Roslyn, worried how he would react if his worse fears were realized. Needing to distract himself Ashton started right away on the house. Within four days, Ashton had repaired most of the problems. Ashton asked Shannon. "Mrs. Shannon I really came here to see Roslyn. And I was wondering since the house looks so nice. Do you think if you invite her over she'll come?"

"Mister Rossi I don't know, Roslyn is so busy, she does not have much free time." Ashton smiled. "Tell her a rich secret admirer has come by train to see her."

Carlin added, Shannon, since it is Ashton who wants to see Roslyn, please do not mention my arrival. I will surprise her later after she spends time with him. Shannon agreed feeling this would make a good impression on Roslyn.

The next morning Shannon went to town alone. She went to Roslyn's shop Roslyn was less than happy to se*e her Mama.

"Mother what are you doing here?"

Shannon smiled and replied. "Now does a Mama have to have a reason to see her successful beautiful daughter?"

"She does when her daughter has told her not to come to the shop."

"Well darlin I just happen to have a message from someone who want you to come out to the house tonight."

"Mother I have an engagement."

"Then young lady you just break that engagement."

"Mother who on earth are you talking about, who wants to see me?"

"Well he wanted me to play word games with you. But since you are being stubborn as usual, I will just tell you. It's your Mister Rossi from New York."

"Mother do not be cruel."

"Darlin I am not. He showed up at my place four days ago. He said he would do repairs on my place if I would let him stay. He came into town that day. Driving the wagon right past your shop, he told me. Said you were busy so he did not stop. He asked me to come here today, to get you to come tonight to see him. Child I do not know how long he plans to stay. Don't waste time!"

Roslyn began to pace she could not believe Ashton was here for her.

If she was to go tonight, she had to look her best. Not to provocative, womanly, beautiful.

For the first time in a long time, Roslyn asked her mother to help her get ready. Carlin had done the cooking. Ashton and Carlin decided it would be better if Carlin stayed out of sight for now.

Roslyn had her carriage follow her mother back home.

Ashton heard the carriage coming down the road. He went out to meet Roslyn. Ashton hurried to open Roslyn's carriage door. She truly felt nervous heart raced her breath was caught in her throat.

"Roslyn you are more beautiful than ever." Roslyn took Ashton's hand. She thought she was dreaming.

"And you Ashton are the most handsome man I have ever seen."

As she entered the house, Roslyn looked around. "Mother what you have done to this place it looks wonderful."

"Mister Ashton has worked wonders. He is a miracle worker. I feel like I have a new home."

Ashton smiled at Shannon and said. "Now Mrs. Shannon you give me way too much credit you were working as hard as I was."

"Thank you Mister Ashton and its Ms. Shannon there is no Mister around here anymore."

Ashton raised an eyebrow and said. "Oh I see."

He could tell Roslyn came by the flirting honestly., it did not seem to faze her to be flirting with the man her daughter claims to love. Ashton thought, 'Daughter like mother Roslyn knew just what her mother was up to, she took hold of Ashton's arm and asked, "Now why did you take that long dreadful trip to come see me?"

Ashton paused for a moment he knew this had to be flawless. Looking into Roslyn's eyes. "Because I missed you something awful."

Roslyn thought she was going to melt in Ashton's arms. Was he really saying this to her?

Changing the subject quickly Ashton turned to go in the dinning room. "I am hungry Roslyn let's eat."

Shannon made herself a plate and went to her room. Ashton and Roslyn ate alone he let her do the talking, which was no problem for Roslyn.

She told him about Paris, how she started her fine gown shop, and tales of her odd customers.

Ashton pretended to be completely enthralled in with Roslyn's rambling.

At the end of the evening Roslyn invited Ashton to her place in town for dinner the next night.

They said good night, Ashton kissed Roslyn's hand. She climbed into her carriage and was gone.

The next morning Ashton was up at dawn working on the last few projects.

Carlin came out to talk to him while he was alone. "Ashton how did thing go last night?"

"Mrs. Ewen they went to well. Roslyn was falling all over herself for my attention.

Although that is not the Roslyn I remember." "When are you to see her again?" "Tonight at her place in town."

"I am not sure I like that Ashton, it's too soon. When you get there see if she will go to the inn with you. We need to keep all things public as long as we can. I am going to see the constable today."

Ashton thought for a moment then said. "Maybe you should stay in town tonight and meet with me after my date with Roslyn."

Carlin agreed. "The longer a trap lays in wait, the more likely it is to be discovered. We have to work fast but not too fast."

Ashton kept working. Carlin left him to prepare to go to town. As Carlin entered the house, the aroma coming from the kitchen was delightful.

"My goodness Shannon you have enough food there to feed a small country, what has gotten into you?"

"Oh Carlin, isn't it just wonderful, havin a man around the house, and in my house! I do not live in a shack no more. Even Roslyn took notice."

"Shannon love, it was Roslyn who should have taken notice when her Mama was living in a shack. Do not be given me the rubbish about her thinking about you. I looked at yer clothes, that girl is not keeping you in good clothing. And I would wager to say she does not give you enough for food either doses she? And answer me straight I want no lying." Shannon looked at the floor, "No sis, Roslyn gives me very little. I usually run out by the middle of the month. But then I have the eggs and milk I sell to the general store. She gave me extra last night! Enough for more than a month if I am careful."

"Shannon do you hear yourself? I am ashamed of you; you are letting a child, who thinks she is all grown up run your life. What is wrong with you?"

"Carlin nothings wrong with me. Roslyn is the one with the money." "And as her Mama, did you ever find out where it came from?" "Carlin our whole family has been poor our entire life.

I am not going to look a gift horse in the mouth!"

"Shannon there is more to life than money. Like happiness. Is Roslyn happy? Do you know if she has any gentlemen callers? Any potential marriage mates?"

"Well, Carlin, being a wealthy single woman, I guess it limit's the men who might be interested. I assume it has to do with the man wanting to take care of his wife and not the other way around. Roslyn thought if she moved into town and lived on her own, suitors would call. But I am afraid she only had one or two. And when they became aware of how much money she has, I suppose that frightened them off. But now Mister Ashton is here. And my lands did my Roslyn light up when she caught sight of him. She looked like she was floating on air."

Carlin was becoming upset thinking of how Roslyn looked at Ashton.

She quickly excused herself and went outside she was trying so hard to hold back the tears.

Ashton watched Carlin head for the barn he decided to follow her.

Carlin sobbed mournful tears believing she was alone.

Ashton came up behind her and held her in his arms. Carlin wept bitterly for the loss of her daughter.

Ashton said to Carlin in a soft voice. "Carlin we are here for Blaine. Shannon is responsible for the way Roslyn has turned out. And if this turns out right, she will pay a heavy price to for Roslyn's evil ways. But we have to be each other's strength right now. Or all will be lost."

Carlin pulled herself together, dried her tears, and then asked Ashton. "What are you planning for tonight?"

"I hope to get Miss Roslyn terribly drunk and make her think something happened between us."

Carlin looked at Ashton with shock. Finally, she found her voice. "Ashton she may still be an innocent."

Ashton laughed and replied. "No Ma'am she is not, please just take my word for it." Carlin chose not to ask any more questions.

That afternoon Carlin and Ashton borrowed Shannon, wagon and rode into town, Carlin checked into the inn, then arranged to see the constable.

Chapter 14

Night came and Ashton was dressed in his finest. He met Roslyn at her Dress shop Roslyn acted as if she was surprised to see him when he walked in. "Ashton dear, would you like to see my shop before we go?"

"Yes, Roslyn I think that would be nice." She showed him all the rooms except one.

Ashton asked. "Roslyn what is in here? Your hidden secrets?"

Roslyn walked in front of the door putting herself between the door and Ashton. "Mister Rossi there is nothing in that room that would interest you but fabric and patterns."

Ashton closed in pushing Roslyn against the door.

His body against hers. Roslyn became weak. Her heart was racing.

Roslyn was dying for Ashton to kiss her.

Ashton bent and kissed her on the neck he worked his way up to her ear he softly whispered. "We better go before something happens here."

Roslyn felt like she would faint. She had wanted him before but not like this. She quietly follower him out of the store, locked it up and walked to her place. Ashton held Roslyn's hand he noticed she was not talking.

"Roslyn, dear why are you so quiet?" "Honestly, Ashton, I am afraid you're going to leave."

"Well, Roslyn, I have to go home if that's what you mean."

Roslyn stopped walking, she tuned to Ashton with desperation in her voice, "When! It will not be too soon will it?"

"It really all depends on how things go between you and me Roslyn. This is what I came here for. This visit wasn't to care for your mother's house."

Roslyn laughed nervously, although excitement to see Ashton welled up in her. She was afraid he would leave her.

As they entered Roslyn's home, Ashton was shocked it was like nothing Ashton had ever seen. Roslyn had surrounded herself with the best money could buy.

She opened her bedroom door; Roslyn had a large ornately designed brass pollster bed and the biggest closet he had seen in his life. It all started to make Ashton feel very sick. Roslyn called out from her room, "Ashton I just had a thought, why don't we celebrate and go to the inn for dinner tonight. I mean if that is alright with you of course."

"That is amazing Roslyn I was just thinking the same thing." Roslyn was dressed in one of her finest gowns.

As she came out of her bedroom, she asked. "How do I look?"

Ashton looked at Roslyn, he thought 'If this was any other woman I could honestly say beautiful.'

Closing his mind to those thoughts, Ashton smiled. "You look stunning Roslyn. Now, shall we go?"

As they entered the Inn, Roslyn entered as if she owned the place. As far as Ashton knew maybe she did. Ashton order for them both, Roslyn felt as if he treated her as a Queen.

Ashton ordered port wine, which is a strong and sweet and he never let Roslyn see the bottom of her glass Ashton purchased another bottle for later.

By dinners end Roslyn was very giddy, hanging on to Ashton and laughing aloud.

Once they made their way to Roslyn's home Ashton had to carry her inside. "Now, Mister Rossi, what do you have on your mind?"

Setting Roslyn to the floor, he pulled out the bottle of wine. Roslyn smiled at Ashton with a seductive look in her eye. She moved in closer to him.

"Would it be too forward of me to ask for a kiss?"

Ashton pulled Roslyn close and pretended he was kissing Blaine. He kissed her soft and gentle. Ashton truly felt Blaine in his arms.

When he opened his eyes there was Roslyn looking back at him.

Roslyn stared for the bedroom playfully calling back. "I will be right back and if not come and find me."

Ashton waited for some time he did not hear anything coming from the room. He was not sure what game she was playing cautiously he entered Roslyn's bedroom. Ashton found her past out in her closet partially undressed.

Ashton let out a sigh of relief. 'Well that was easy.'

He finished undressing her. Laid her on her fainting couch. Messed up the bed as if two lovers had been in it all night.

Took off his waistcoat and laid it on the floor. Then he places Roslyn's naked body in her bed. Quietly he left her bedroom.

Ashton picked up the wine took a drink, wiped his mouth to get the taste of Roslyn off his mouth. He found two glasses poured a tiny amount in each. He stepped outside and poured half the bottle out then he went back inside setting the bottle down he quietly left Roslyn's home.

Ashton headed to the Inn to find Carlin. He found her waiting for him outside the Inn. Carlin had brought Ashton a change of clothes. Ashton changed quickly behind the inn so no one would recognize him.

Carlin and Ashton entered the inn together nobody seemed to notice Ashton from before.

Carlin asked for a quiet table away for the main goings on.

The barmaid sauntered to the table. "You want a whiskey sweetie?" Ashton replied. "No Ma'am, don't touch the stuff just bring me coffee." The barmaid asked Carlin. "you want coffee too Ma'am?"

"Yes, coffee for me too please."

Carlin asked. "Ashton when did you stop drinking whiskey?"

"I took a vow the night Blaine disappeared. No more whiskey or drink of any kind." Carlin patted Ashton's arm. "Son, I am proud of you. Whiskey can be a dangerous poison for some. But maybe it was the amount of the drink not the drink its self that was the problem."

"That is the problem Carlin, so I won't drink at all."

"Well let me tell you what the constable said, he said he has always felt Roslyn's instant successes smelt bad to him. But no one knows a thing."

Ashton sat his coffee down. "Carlin, maybe there is. That little man she brought back from Paris. Why would she need a French designer if the designs were all hers? Moreover, if he doses the sewing, he is one expensive tailor, especially when you can do it yourself. Someone like Roslyn would not be eager to part with her treasure to pay for work she can do herself. Seein how she won't even help her starving mother, I cannot imagine her wasting any. I know this man is our key. We need to get to the constable and give this fella a wakeup call."

After finishing their coffee, the two made their way to the constable.

The constable was usually a friendly man but being woke up in the middle of the night puts a strain on the nicest person's disposition.

Fumbling with the lock the constable grumbled.

"Who in the world could be needing a constable a four in the morning!" He opened the door to find Carlin and Ashton.

"Listen Ma'am like I told you before we have no proof of any foul play of any kind." Ashton spoke up. "But Sir we might, and if you will listen to us, I have no doubt you will want to follow this to the end."

The constable hesitantly invited them in. He sat listening in disbelief that something this sorted and horrible would take place partly in his quiet little town.

He stood up, "I know where this Frenchman lives. Mrs. Ewen I think it better if you stay right here at my place. Mister Rossi and I will ride out right now to roust out this man and see what he might know."

As Ashton and the constable rode out, it now being early morning, they decided to handle it like a friendly stop.

As they came to the Frenchman's place. The constable said.

"I think I picked the wrong profession, look at this place! Do you believe this is on a dress makers pay."

"No Sir, maybe on a black mailers salary" "Now Mister Rossi we don't know for sure."

The Frenchman came out on to his porch to see who was coming.

He did not look like a tailor to Ashton.

The constable spoke first. "I am sorry it's my first time out. I usually like to come visit all my new residents."

The Frenchman said. "I don't consider myself new anymore. I have lived here two months now."

The constable replied. "I never caught your name sir." "That is because I never gave it."

Ashton asked. "Is there any reason you might not want to give the constable your name sir?"

The Frenchman scratched his face as he studied Ashton.

He noticed Ashton was not afraid of him were the constable was a little nervous.

The Frenchman asked. "Are you a deputy or something?"

Before Ashton had a chance to reply, the constable chimed in. "Yes he is." "Alright deputy, my name is Francis DeBow. That is all you need, yes."

Ashton dismounted. "Actually Mister DeBow we are hoping you can help us. We are investigating a missing person."

"What is this? I know nothing of people. Look where I live no one comes here. I like it this way."

"Actually it involves your employer. Miss Roslyn Ewen." "Employer? Who told you she was my employer?"

Ashton was playing the part well. "Miss Roslyn Ewen is the one who said she brought you over here as her tailor."

"Baugh! That woman is crazy. I do not work for her."

The constable had dismounted and gone around behind DeBow. Ashton asked. "Mister DeBow have you ever heard the name Blaine Ewen?"

DeBow became very agitated. "Why do you ask me this? What has that crazy woman told you? I had nothing to do with that girl! Do you hear me?"

DeBow tried to run but the constable hit him over the head with the butt end of his gun knocking him out. When DeBow came to, he was sitting behind bars. Ashton and the constable were quietly talking.

"Sir, Roslyn will be up soon and I can't take a chance of her seeing me come out of here. So, I leave our dear fellow in your capable hands. I do not think prison bars are a stranger to this man. However, maybe if we could send him back to France. He might be more than willing to talk."

"Mister Rossi you are a wise young man. Have you ever considered becoming a constable or a sheriff?"

Ashton smiled "No sir, horses are my thing and you don't have to worry about one shooting you when they had a bad day. They just throw you off their back a time or two." Ashton left the constables office and went to the wagon to get his clothes then he made his way to the Inn. Roslyn was already there waiting for him.

He waited until he was sure she was not looking his way, he quickly made it up the stairs to the room Carlin had rented. Once Ashton had cleaned up, he casually went down to greet Roslyn.

Roslyn stood up when she caught sight of him her face was beaming.

If Ashton had not known her better he would have thought this is a woman in love, but he did know her, she was not capable of love as far as he was concerned.

Taking his hand Roslyn asked. "Darling why did you leave last night. I woke up and you were gone."

Ashton thought quickly.

"For you virtue Roslyn, I don't want the towns people thinking you to be a lose woman.

So I slipped out while the town was sleeping."

Roslyn squeezed his hand. "Oh you honor me so Ashton no man has ever treated me the way you do. You make me feel… good about myself."

Avoiding any more questions Ashton redirected the conversation.

"Well, Roslyn let's eat you must be hungry I know I am. And I am sure you have work to do today."

Roslyn sighed. "Oh yes I have several gowns I am working on. But can we have dinner together tonight?"

"I will be in anticipation until then my dear."

Once they finished breakfast Roslyn left Ashton making her way to her shop. Once Ashton was sure Roslyn was deep into her work he took the back way to the constable's office.

Ashton walked in the door. "What has our fine French friend DeBow had to tell us?" The constable shook his head. "Mister DeBow will not tell me a thing. He will only tell his story to you, deputy Rossi."

Ashton said. "Fine, he talks to me you sit on the other side of the door then we have two witnesses right?"

The constable smiled. "You sure are a smart one." He opened the door speaking over his shoulder. "Rossi I hope you do better than I did."

Then he closed the door pretending to leave the constable sat in a chair behind the door so DeBow could not see him.

Ashton walked in the cell room and sat down, "From the way you acted this morning DeBow you obviously know something. So we can pin the disappearance on you." DeBow stopped Ashton. "I told you I had nothing to do with that girl!"

Ashton raised his voice. "I know that's what you said. However, here is my problem DeBow. You are the only one, a foreigner, who seems to know anything. And I am sure that is enough around here for a hanging!"

"Wait the constable said I could go back to France!"

"DeBow that offer is only good if you help us uncover the truth. You do not think we are just going to give you a free pass back home now. It doesn't work that way. You see DeBow I think you are a betting man. So you know you can't get something for nothing.

You want to go home. Start talking."

DeBow thought for several minutes then said. "I want it in writing deputy, that if I tell you, you send me back to France not to prison."

Ashton stood up went to the constable's desk, found a piece of paper and wrote…

'If Frances DeBow assist in the uncovering of the disappearance of Blaine Ewen.

He will forego prison.

Be taken to New York and be placed on the first sea vessel going to France.

He will be stripped of all assets held in America and these assets will be turned over to the missing girls' family.'

Ashton signed it, and then handed it to Mister DeBow. upon reading it, DeBow responded angrily.

"What is this deputy? I have to forfeit my assets! I will do no such thing!"

Ashton leaned into the bars and said in a firm voice, "Sign it DeBow! Because it cannot go to France. And dead men can't spend money. So either way it's not yours anymore." DeBow begrudgingly signed the affidavit.

Ashton took out a note pad. "Mister Frances DeBow do you swear to tell the truth?" "Yes, Mister Deputy I swear."

"Please Mister DeBow start at the beginning."

"I met Roslyn Ewen in Paris. She claimed to be a clothing designer with a lot of money.

She seemed young and stupid to tell people she was so wealthy."

"She asked me to dine with her. One thing lead to another we became lovers." "One night we had a fight. I told her she was weak and needed someone like me. We had been drinking."

"She turned like a wild crazy animal.

She said I had no idea how strong she was, or how far she would go to get what she wanted."

"I asked her what she was talking about. She went to a safe, pulled out a purse. She threw it on the floor and so many gold coins came out. I could not believe my eyes!" "Then she started acting like she wanted me. She came on very strong. We made love on the floor next to all that gold. Then she just rolled over and picked up her coins. She asked me if I really wanted to know how she came to have the gold. Her voice was dark. She asked, did I think I was strong enough to hear. I was thinking she had lost her mind. I had no idea where my Roslyn had gone. Then she became very docile she rolled over and laid her head on my chest and said she could not tell me and asked me to leave."

"Things were strange. Until one night, I found her inviting another man to her room. I knocked him out. I drug her back to her room I threw her on the bed. I knew then she had been using me."

Ashton interrupted. "DeBow sounds to me like you were using Miss Ewen." "Deputy I never took any money from her. Not until she played DeBow for a fool. I could have loved that stupid girl. However, she wanted someone new. She hurt me.

I demanded to know where she came by the coins, or I would go to the French police.

She told me a story my ears could not believe. She said that she had fallen for her cousin's fiancé.

And the only way she could have him was to get rid of this Blaine."

"As she put it, to her good luck, the fiancé and his stableman were going to the docks to trade horses. Roslyn said she used her charm to dupe the stableman into telling her about slave trade."

"I believe deputy she had to confess to someone this was the worst thing I had ever heard.

And I have done bad in my life."

Ashton stopped DeBow. "I'll be back in a moment please hold your thought." Ashton stood up and walked out the door.

The constable did not move but he was concern about Ashton's reaction. Ashton stepped around the building held his head in his hand and took several deep breaths.

He kept repeating to himself. "This is for Blaine, this is for Blaine."

After taking a few moments, Ashton pulled himself together and went back into the constable's office.

Ashton sat down and said. "Now where were we?" De bow said, "Nature calls eh deputy?"

Aston shook his head. "somethin like that now let's continue." "Yes deputy, oh yes now I remember."

"Roslyn begins to tell me how she gets her way to go with the stableman and the man she is after.

The men leave her on the wagon while they go to trade for horses.

They tell her to wait for them. Only Roslyn dose not wait. She boards the same ship. Now I do not know how much of this is true but I tell it the way Roslyn told this to me. Roslyn say she run into a very large man on a ship. She told this man she wants to make a trade. The big man goes down and gets another man he says he is the Captain. Roslyn tells this Capitan she is the wife of a wealthy man this Capitan knows this man. Roslyn tells this man she wants to get rid of a young woman. She tells this big man and this Capitan where to find the young woman for exchange of all the money she has. The Capitan takes the girl he leaves the money. The young woman is gone, Roslyn is rich but somehow she does not get the man. And that, deputy, is all I know."

"Did Miss Ewen ever mention the Captain's name?" "No"

"Mister DeBow did she ever mention the name of the man she claimed was her husband?"

DeBow thought for a moment then he said, "His name was Ashley or Ashton something like that."

"Mister DeBow do you know where Miss Ewen keeps the gold coins?" "In a safe in a locked office in her shop."

"And how do you know this?"

"Because she had me build the shop for her and the safe. That is what she brought me here for. I know you think I was black mailing her. But I was not. I cared for her and she used me. I was not good enough for her.

She would use me when she needed things done without anyone else knowing. I loved her and I kept her

217

ugly secret until now. Now I wish to go home and forget I ever met that demented woman!"

"Thank you Mister DeBow I'll have someone from the inn bring you some food." Ashton stood up and closed the door between the office and the cell.

The constable stood up rubbing his chin, "Ashton is it. I think there are a few details to this story you conveniently left out."

Ashton did not reply to the constables' statement. He looked at him and asked. "Can you swear me in as a temporary deputy?"

The constable was confused, "What for? We already got the information we wanted." "Because constable that promise I made isn't worth a lick of salt unless you swear me in. Also, we have to go to Roslyn's shop right now. And she is a very unstable person.

You can use a deputy right now."

The constable scratched his head, "Alright hold up your right hand and repeat after me." After the Constable swore Ashton in, the two men went to pick up Carlin. Ashton told Carlin of DeBow's confession. Carlin found herself emotionally numb, unable to cry, she stood frozen as she listened to a tale to horrible to be true...but it was true. Ashton realized Carlin was not responding. "Carlin have you heard what I said?" Carlin looked up, "yes I heard you, I'm shocked is all. I know this is what we expected but to hear it... Ashton took Carlin by the hand, we need to get this over with." Carlin took a deep ragged breath, "I know let's go." Ashton, the Constable and Carlin their way to Roslyn's gown shop. Ashton looked in to make sure Roslyn was there working. He nodded his head to let the others know she was there. The constable went around to the rear entrance. Shannon happened to see Carlin standing at the entrance of the gown shop. She yelled. "Carlin wait, I'll go visit with you."

Carlin turned around. "Shannon this is a visit I should do alone. There are too many things, sister, you do not know and I have no time to explain. Please Shannon for once in your life listen to me and go back across the street!"

Shannon was shocked that Carlin spoke to her this way but she listened and went back across the street.

Shannon stood watching, wanting to know what was happening, she watched Ashton enter first.

She thought, 'Now if he can be there why can't I.' feeling something had gone a rye she did not move from where she stood.

Roslyn she had a delightful smile when she noticed Ashton enter the shop. She stopped sewing asking sweetly, "What brings you here this afternoon Ashton my love?"

Ashton's voice was dry, emotionless, I met somebody today Roslyn. A very close friend of yours from France."

Roslyn's face dimmed. And her speech grew serious. "And what did my so called friend and you talk about?"

"How you met in Paris."

Roslyn's lips tightened. "And what else did dear Mister DeBow tell you." Ashton widened his eyes and said. "Now, Roslyn, surely you would call him Frances after all you two are lovers."

Roslyn lost her temper. "He only wishes! I took pity on him and he has tried to suck the life out of me. I hired him to build for me. Yes, we had a brief relationship.

However, then I realize all he wanted was money. I ended up building him a place bigger than mine." I have nothing to do with him anymore. Please believe me Ashton my heart belongs to you." Roslyn ran to Ashton with open arms.

Ashton caught her by the arms, "Then Roslyn my dear, I want you to prove your devotion to me."

She looked at Ashton with excitement she would do anything for him. "Tell me my love I'll do anything you ask."

"I want to see what is in that locked room."

She took Ashton by the hand leading him to the locked door.

Roslyn kept the key around her neck she unlocked the door and let Ashton in.

Ashton looked around and pointed to the safe. "What is in there Roslyn?"

"Darling I keep my money in there I don't trust banks there always being robed you know."

"Will you show me?"

"Of course I will. You're welcome to go through it if you want." Roslyn opened the safe and there lay the coins from the trader's ship.

Ashton picked up one of the coins, his heart went cold, he recognized it from the ship he and Seth traded from the day Roslyn went with them to the city.

He then remembered the Capitan leaving for some time. Then coming back in a very generous mood toward him. As he held the coin and without looking at "That day you went to the docks must have been terrifying for you. Or was it more terrifying getting on the ship?"

Roslyn did not think before answering. "Oh Ashton, when I ran into that giant man I thought he was going to kill me. But then that Capitan, he was truly frightful." Ashton slowly turned around, Roslyn then realized what she had said.

"Ashton I, I, I, was afraid I came on the ship…. He held up his hand, he was frightfully calm. "No Roslyn, I need the truth from your lips. I need to hear the truth."

Roslyn misunderstood Aston's calmness she took it to mean Ashton would understand the length she had gone to for his love. "Darling I did this for you and me." Ashton had to keep reminding himself she was completely out of her mind. Roslyn continued. "I…I did go aboard the ship to see the Capitan."

Roslyn smiled at Ashton. "I told him I was your wife and that Blaine was a servant that had turned your head and I didn't want you to act on your desire. So I wanted to sell her to him. I gave him a map to the cabin and told him she would be there. I knew that is where she would go after she caught us together."

Ashton just had to know, "Roslyn, how did you know she would find us together?" "Ashton, I knew you were attracted to me. All I needed was to get you alone long enough, to…to open your eyes. Create the opportunity for Blaine to find us." Ashton's conscious pained him knowing she was right. He had not turned away her advances he had encouraged her.

"The morning of the Ball I overheard Seth telling Aggie and Blaine all the things your father said. Moments before I came and told you. I embellished them some. Anyway, you went out to the stable that night to confront

Seth like I knew you would. I followed you and waited for him to leave you. The fact you had been drinking so much just made things easier. We seemed to connect really well for a while remember? Then Blaine came looking for you, as I knew she would. She made such a scene before running off toward the cabin. The Capitan was waiting. Now you're here and we can be together." Ashton was trying very hard to hold himself together. "Alright Roslyn there is one more thing the money what about all the money?"

"The Capitan left it behind the cabin. That's why I was out there with the lantern that night."

Ashton stood up and walked to the door Carlin was holding on to the constable crying.

Ashton reached out to Carlin and whispered "This is for Blaine, take my hand."

Carlin took his hand and walked into the room. Roslyn stood up with shock. "Aunt Carlin what are you doing here?"

"Looking for justice Roslyn, and as painful as your words were to listen, to at least Shamus and I will know that the one responsible will pay for the evil that has happened to our Blaine. Constable, I want to press charges against this woman for the kidnapping of my beautiful daughter Blaine Ewen and also for ill-gotten gain from that kidnapping." The constable handcuffed Roslyn. Not grasping what had happened Roslyn kept begging Ashton for help. "Ashton, please help me I did it for us, I love you. I thought you understood Ashton listen to me!"

Without a word Ashton turned away from Roslyn leaving her to face the horrific reality she created.

As Carlin came out of the dress shop Shannon ran to her. "What has happened?

Where are they taking Roslyn? You can't let them do this to her, Carlin."

Carlin turned to her sister. "Shannon you should have looked a gift horse in the mouth, you should have gotten control of that girl a long time ago. Because now your daughter has sold my daughter into slavery to get her dream. Now we have both lost our children.

I am going home now. Please don't write me anymore."

The next morning Carlin, Ashton and Mister DeBow, handcuffed to Ashton, climbed aboard the train headed for New York their trip went without incident Ashton managed to get DeBow on a ship destined for France. DeBow gave a written promise never to return.

After the ship cast off and Ashton was sure DeBow was gone, he and Carlin headed for home.

That hour and a half trip seemed like forever to Carlin she missed Shamus so badly.

When they reached the estate, Ashton and Carlin went in together.

Life seemed to be going on as usual. Carlin found out where Joseph and Shamus were working and asked Ashton to take her to her husband. Shamus stopped working when he caught sight of his beautiful Carlin.

She jumped from the wagon and ran to him. They held each other tight. Shamus took Carlin's face gently in his hands kissing her as she cried. Holding his wife in his arms he whispered "No more tears my love." Carlin nodded her head.

Carlin finally found her voice. "Shamus darlin, we did it. Ashton and I we got Roslyn to confess. She is going to prison now."

Shamus looked at Ashton in disbelief. "You mean to tell me Roslyn actually sold my little girl into slavery?"

Ashton took a deep breath and put his arm around Shamus. "I am afraid so." That night everyone was in morning for Blaine. Silently no one believed she would be able to survive. On the other hand, maybe it was they were hoping she would not survive living a life of torture. They all prayed and held on to each other. They were a family, they needed each other now...

CHAPTER 15

The Island of Praia
Near the Tropic of Cancer

It was now the tenth day of the sixth month.

Blaine had been counting the days closely, she was desperate to get off the ship.

However, the thought of what was to come next frightened her.

All at once, they could hear the men yelling above them. "Land ho!"

It seemed as if all chaos had broken loose. The men's voices boomed from above. The girls could hear a frenzy of footsteps running everywhere.

Then they heard a commotion coming down the stairs! Sobbo was yelling.

The wild frenzy heightened outside the door, it sounded like war!

Blaine could hear men falling to the floor. Sobbo yelled as if he were a warrior.

Then they heard Captain Bogotá's voice thunder. "Move away from the door Sobbo!"

"No! Capitan these women are for King Aviv. You will not sell women on. Capitan Bogotá pulled out a pistol.

All the while knowing if he shot Sobbo, King Aviv would hunt him down and put him to death.

However, Bogotá bargained that Sobbo did not know this. "I do not wish to shoot you Sobbo. So... I will make a deal with you, you take as many slaves as you can carry, that is how many will belong to the King. Now! Decide! How many will be important to your King…. choose carefully."

Glaring death daggers at Bogota, Sobbo unlocked the cabin door. The girls had been standing close to hear what was being said, as they heard the key

They quickly moved away from the door, all eyes fixed on Sobbo as he entered, wondering what he would do next.

Sobbo knew even with his great strength, he could not carry all seven girls.

At the most, he would be able to carry four of the smaller women.

But if he chose Blaine, he would only be able to carry three...

Without a word Sobbo grabbed Blaine and threw her over his right shoulder, then he grabbed Lome and Zuni, throwing both over his left shoulder.´

The three held on to their rescuer knowing their lives were dependent on Sobbo's strength.

The women he could not carry cried out for him, begging him not to leave them. They grabbed at Sobbo almost making him lose his balance. Sobbo made his way to the door holding fast to the ones he could save. He did not look back; it sickened him to leave these women in Bogotá's evil hands. But he had no choice if Bogotá shot him none of them stood a chance.

Sobbo swore to himself to come after the poor ones left behind. Blaine could see the young women behind holding on to each other.

They cried out for Blaine, "You promised the King would protect us!" Blaine felt sick in the pit of her stomach knowing she had made such a promise.

Sobbo kept walking until he was out of sight of the ship.

Blaine held her eyes shut tight Tears were streaming down her cheeks she could still hear the cries of her friends echoing in her ears.

Sobbo stopped for a moment to make sure no one from the ship was following. He would not set the three young women down until they were safe from Captain Bogotá. He carried them four miles to the gate of the King's palace.

Sobbo rang a large silver bell daunting ornate gates opened allowing Sobbo to enter. Once the large gates were secure, Sobbo slowly placed the young ones on the ground then gently he sat Blaine to the ground holding her to sure her footing.

Lome and Zuni reached out to Blaine for comfort. The three girls embraced, relieved to be free from Bogotá's bondage, saddened for the ones left behind, afraid of what their future might hold.... Sobbo tried his best to comfort them.

Once she was able to contain her emotions Blaine was determined to speak to Sobbo's King. She would not forget her t promise to her friends.

She had to see the King right away. Blaine turned to Sobbo. "Please Sobbo; I must see your King now!"

Sobbo shook his head. "No my friend you cannot. King Aviv will call you when he is ready."

Pleading Blaine begged. "Sobbo, what about the others, we cannot just leave them!" "Calm yourself, I will speak to King Aviv soon. I will tell him what Bogotá has done and about the others. We will see what can be done. Now come with me."

Sobbo showed Blaine to an empty bedchamber. "You need rest my Blaine, please rest here. I will speak to the King soon. Now I will take the little ones to rest."

Sobbo shut the door behind him leaving Blaine alone. As she turned from the door with a heavy heart, she appraised her surrounding She could not believe her eyes, the bed was made of gold, and even the vanity was made of gold.

The fabric around the bed was beaded with crystals. the bedding was a soft pink silk.

For a moment, Blaine was awe struck. 'This man really is a King.'

Blaine continued to investigate the room. She stepped down to a grand private bathing area decorated with the most beautiful stones Blaine had ever seen in her life. the washtub looked more like a small ornate swimming hole. Blaine laughed to herself "I have to say, this is much nicer than the swimming hole back in Wyoming, and a whole bunch better than a horse trough or a bucket.' Blaine's attention drifted to a large closet, she opened the large carved doors. To her dismay, it was full of what looked to be fancy night shifts. Most likely something a woman of ill repute would wear!

Blaine's heart sunk, she felt sick allover. Here she thought she escaped the evils Captain Bogotá had planned for her, only to find herself in the hands of another evil man. 'Oh merciful God help me! I would rather die than be abused by some heathen King!' Blaine's temper was rageing, she ran for the door only to find it locked. Quickly she turned to the window, looking for an escape. She realized she was much too high off the ground to jump; however, there was a ledge...

Talking to herself, Blaine tried to get her thoughts straight. 'Maybe I could get to the next window and escape! I cannot believe I trusted Sobbo! he called himself my friend! Why did he bring me here! Oh, don't be so foolish, he works for this man!'

Blaine climbed out onto the window ledge then slowly worked her way to the next open window, she awkwardly fumbled her way inside.

King Israel Aviv had been peacefully sitting in his chamber reading, as Blaine fell thru his window.

Startled, King Aviv stood quickly reaching for his sword realizing his intruder was only a woman; the King lowered his guard and watched her conquer his window.

After Blaine mastered the window, she attempted to regain her composure.

Once she looked up, she was startled at the sight of a half dressed, foreign, man, with black curly hair, his gold robe hung open to his waist baring his dark chest.

Blaine was speechless; this was truly the most handsome man she had ever seen in her life.

Blaine touched disheveled hair, self-consciously smoothed her tattered gown realizing she must be a frightful sight.

'This man must think me mad!' she thought to herself.

Finally, Blaine found her voice. nervously she spoke, "Please, pardon me Sir; I am so sorry for intruding on you in such a crude manner. If you would please help me, I am looking for King Aviv. I would not have had to disturb you, but for some reason men, of my recent acquaintance, seem to have taken to keeping me behind locked doors. I find this a bit dangerous seeing it leaves me to scale outside walls only to fall into stranger's windows. But if you will be so kind as to point me in the direction of the King, I will bother you no longer."

King Aviv stood, amazed by this woman. She appeared as a tattered little street mouse, but spoke with such bold refinement. He stood silent studying Blaine for a moment. never had a woman climbed thru his chamber window. never had a woman spoke to him so directly. This peevish young woman intrigued the King.

"I am King Aviv. Who are you, Madam, who climbs thru my window?"

Blaine let out a sigh of relief, "King Aviv, my name is Blaine Ewen, I am from America. Your Captain Bogotá kidnapped me. I was on your ship for six months. I was kept in a small cabin with what started with nine girls. I believe this Captain Bogotá took us to sell, trade or... worse. Sobbo swore you would not approve of such evil actions. He kept us alive the best he could. when we arrived in port this morning, Captain Bogotá would not allow all of us to leave the ship. he would only allow the ones Sobbo was able to carry. He carried myself and two of the youngest. I fear the fate of the five left behind will be worse than death. I hope Sobbo was true with me, he said you had nothing to do with Bogota's plans. He said you are a good King. He said you will help the others left behind."

King Aviv peered at her seriously, "Why do you say their fate will be worse than death?" "Because, in all the time on your ship, Capitan Bogota tried to feed us rotten meat. He gave us putrid water to drink and no blankets."

"How did any of you survive?"

Blaine's demeanor changed. "As I said before, Sobbo, he saved us. He brought us soap and water, decent food, clean water to drink and warm blankets."

"You think highly of my man Sobbo?" "Oh, yes I do, Sobbo has a gentle heart."

"Please, continue I wish for you to explain what you mean."

"Well, your highness, when two of the young women were deathly ill, Sobbo helped me care for them. He showed me how to use the herbs to try to nurse them back to health.

Unfortunately, it did not work, my friends died from the fever. along with half the crew." King Aviv grew solemn, "Madam Ewen, how many women died all together?"

Blaine looked at the floor remembering the horrible night Capitan Bogota took Lome's sister, "Three"

"Madam Ewen, you said two died of fever. Please, tell me how the third woman died." Blaine's eyes filled with tears she looked at the King and pleaded. "Please, your Highness, it is a horrible, gruesome, tale. Please ask your man Sobbo. I came to plead for the lives of the young women Bogota kept. he is an evil man. The girls are young. Please, have mercy and stop him from hurting them. And I...I beg you please do not hurt me!" tears flowed down her dirt streaked face.

King Aviv thought to comfort her but he did not come close to her. He calmly replied, "Go back to your chamber Madam Ewen; your doors will no longer be locked. Bathe and change your attire, you have my word no one will disturb you. You will find a change of clothing in your chamber."

Blaine blushed, she was embarrassed to ask but she needed to know. "Um... your Highness, the garments in the closet are they for, um... the daytime or to sleep in?" King Aviv was taken aback at her sudden shyness. The King found this change in her behavior intriguing.

The King smiled. "Madam, please, go, take your bath. I will have the dressmaker send someone to help you put the sari on correctly. This is worn by women during the day." Relieved, Blaine went back to her chamber not realizing how much danger she had put her self in by intruding on the King in his private quarters.

As a woman, speaking to the King without being called by him could have meant her life.

Blaine was completely confident Aunt Anna would have been proud of the way she spoke to the King.

Closing her door behind her, Blaine made her way to the inviting bathing pool. she went to the large window near the pool; once she opened it, the sunlight flooded the room. Blaine thought she must be dreaming she could not believe the beauty around her lit up by the sun, glistening warming the room. Blaine removed her smelly tattered gown realizing what a shock it must have been for King Aviv to see her filthy and in tatters. Touching her hair, she thought, 'King Aviv must have truly thought me a mad woman. Sighing, 'maybe I am.'

Blaine held up the gown remembering its former beauty, once upon a time. Now it looked like a tattered rag, only useful to start a fire.

Blaine felt like it was lifetime ago, that night at the Ball, the excitement, her family. Blaine remembered she felt like she was floating on air as she came down the stairs wearing her emerald green gown.

She gave what was left of her gown a weak smile then she laid the tattered gown to the side. Slowly she slid into the warm water.

Blaine could not believe the wonderful sensation of amercing herself in warm water.

On a shelf, Blaine found beautiful smelling soaps and oils.

She washed herself repeatedly, poured oil over her whole body. Until this moment, Blaine had not realized how desperately she missed bathing!

Blaine became startled by a young girl's voice.

"Madam, is that how you get your skin so white by scrubbing the color off?"

Blaine looked up to see a beautiful dark eyed girl, who looked to be about the same age as Zuni. Blaine smiled at the little girl. "No I was born with skin this white."

The little girls' eyes widened. "And were you born with that hair too, it looks like fire?" "Yes little one I was born with the hair too, and who might you be?"

The little girl smiled. "I am here to help you dress."

Blaine stepped out of the tub wrapping herself in a large bath sheet. "So you are, and what is your name?"

The girl ran to the closet and chose for Blaine a dark blue sari and dark blue slippers. She turned to Blaine and said. "My name Tiki and if you like my help.... I come to you every day."

Tiki helped Blaine dress in her new attire. Blaine still felt quite naked compared to her former way of dressing. This was going to take getting used to.

She hoped the King had been honest with her but she wanted to know for sure.

. "Now Tiki if you are to help me you must be honest. Do you know what this means?" "Oh yes, quite, Madam it means I do not steal or lie."

"Alright Tiki tell me true. Do all women here dress like this?"

"Oh no, Madam, only ones of position, important woman. Well...Some not so important they just have money."

"Tiki I have two young girls in the room next to me. Their names are Lome and Zuni I want you to do the same for them as you have for me, understood?" "Yes Madam right away."

"Oh Tiki if their bedchamber does not have baths [Blaine pointed at the tub] bring them here and let them use mine."

"Yes Madam." Tiki left to find the girls. Blaine left her chamber to find Sobbo.

As she wandered around the palace, she was marveling the beauty of such a place. Blaine started up a staircase made of marble inlayed with gold. The handrail was a work of art, detailed carvings of ships at sea. Blaine was amazed at the detail.

She walked up the stairs slowly studying every intricate picture. Tracing it with her fingers.

She collided with King Aviv. The King had not seen Blaine as he was in deep conversation with Sobbo. Blaine lost her balance almost falling backward down the stairs. King Aviv caught her by the waist and pulled her close to him.

Blaine's hand rested against the bare flesh of King Aviv's muscular chest.

From their touch, a spark of heat exchanged between them.

Blaine believed her reaction was from her near fall down the stairs. She removed her hand quickly not wanting to give this foreigner any wrong impressions. King Aviv took notice of her reaction, Not wanting to cause her anymore alarm, he steadied her, letting her go. Suddenly, as if seeing her for the first time, he noticed the fire color of her hair and the beauty of her features. How could he have missed such beauty before...? Her touch had such a potent effect upon his senses.

"Are you alright Madam Ewen?"

Blaine was embarrassed her cheeks flushing red. "I am so sorry; please forgive me your highness. I was so fascinated with the design in this railing, it is beautiful wouldn't you agree?"

King Aviv had never really paid much attention to the railing or its design. Nevertheless, he would not look foolish in front of this beautiful woman, so he replied, "Of course I find it beautiful, but everything in my palace is beautiful. Including you... Madam Ewen." Turning away without a word, Blaine hurried down the stairs, angry with herself for blushing in response to the Kings compliment. What was it about this man that befuddled her mind?

This was something that was beginning to disturb her. Now after her ridiculous display, she had to speak to this King about the other young women in Bogota's hands. She prayed it was not too late for her friends.

Regaining her composure, Blaine approached the King. "King Aviv I must speak to you about the other girls... The girls who were left with Bogota.

King Aviv was not accustomed to women speaking of important matters. Instinctively he changed the subject. "Madam Ewen, I noticed your choice of attire, this is very becoming with your beautiful hair and eyes. I would like to know, how are you enjoying your chamber?"

Blaine could see the King was going to be like every other man, except Sobbo that is. Blaine could feel her

Irish temper rising. She was going to say her peace even if it set his Royal Highness on his ear.

Blaine shot a look at the King that went straight thru him.

He could see she was angry. He was quite certain she was about to inform him as to why.

Her emerald eyes darkened holding him captive. "King Aviv. I have survived, what I conceder to be, the closest thing to hell that could be imagined at the hands of Captain Bogota. I have been ripped away from my family! Tormented on a ship for what felt like an eternity! Kept the lives and spirits of those girls going because Sobbo told me you were a good King! A just King! Sobbo and I promised them you would help. And all you want to know is if I like my room! You..., you. Sobbo said you are a good and just King... Uh!"

Blaine ran to her chamber and slammed the door. As her temper settled she heard laughter coming from her bathing pool, bubbles were everywhere.

Blaine called out with a firm voice. "Alright who is in there?" she had completely forgotten she had instructed the girls to take a bath in her room. out popped three heads Lome, Tiki, and Zuni all covered in bubbles.

Blaine couldn't help from laughing. "Have you three been playing this whole time?" Tiki blew the bubbles out of her mouth. "Honest, Madam, it started out the way you said. But the more Lome and Zuni splashed around the more bubbles they made. It looked like fun, so, I got in too. And the more all three of us splashed we made even more bubbles."

Blaine could not help but love them. And now her Lome and Zuni had been in a bathtub and obviously loved every minute. "Alright time to get out of the water you are all wrinkled. Hesitantly, the girls ended their playtime.

Blaine dried each one off as if they were her own children. Tiki helped them dress in small saris found in another closet.

Blaine even had Tiki wear a bright yellow silk sari. Tiki beam, she had never worn silk before.

Climbing up on Blaine's large bed the three begged Blaine to tell a story. Blaine chose to tell a fairytale her mama told her when she was young. Before she finished the tail the young girls were curled up together fast asleep.

Blaine held Lome close and, for the first time in six long months, drifted off into a peaceful sleep herself.

Later the King went to Blaine's chamber. He planned to address the way in which she spoke to him. Although he understood her pain, he is King; no one is permitted to speak to him with disrespect.

King Aviv knocked lightly but he heard no reply he opened the door and walked in. The King's heart was moved with what caught his sight lying upon the bed, four beautiful princesses sleeping soundly.

King Aviv quietly covered them with a blanket leaving them to sleep.

King Aviv decided to find his man Sobbo, wanting to know more about this fiery flower Sobbo had brought to his palace.

"Sobbo, what matter of a woman is this Blaine Ewen?"

Sobbo was not clear as to what his King meant. "My King, Madam Blaine, is my friend" King Aviv though for a moment. "Sobbo, you do not allow many to be your friend, why this woman?"

"She strong, my King. She stood up to Bogota for the other women. She not afraid for herself, she teaches the women to read, she bathes them, she make them stay alive.

She protected them." "How did she protect them?"

"Madam Blaine, she teaches girls to be clean, to speak, to write." "I want to know what happened on the ship Sobbo."

"I tell Bogota not to take women, that you will be angry. Bogota tells me he is Captain and I must do as he says. I choose to wait, and settle this with you my King. Madam Blaine, I know her not want to come with us to the ship. Bogota say he bring her for you to be your servant, she not for trade. I no like this, my King. We set sail, with nine women. One woman, Bogota keeps calling to him. She was willing to go so I do not say no. I think this one tells Bogota stories about Madam Blaine. He no like the good things Madam Blaine dose. I think Bogota get angry. When we dock for supplies, he make Sobbo go ashore for the day. I know there will be trouble, I tell Madam Blaine. She smart, she fool Bogota. He come to see himself, he find the women dirty. Bogota no go in, stink to bad, Bogota close door leave girls alone."

"Wait, Sobbo, there were nine women. What happened to the one woman Bogota used for information?"

Sobbo's face went hard. "Sobbo not on ship or this not happen, my King. Bogota evil man, he give young woman to crew. Tell men to use poor thing until dead."

"How do you know this Sobbo?"

"One of the crew came to me as I put the poor dead body over the side. He made fun of what he did to her said Capitan gave her to the crew."

"Sobbo where is the seaman now?"

Sobbo's eye narrowed. "I broke his neck and feed him to the sharks!"

"I assume this was for his part in what happened to the young woman?"

"Yes! my King. If I could, I would have done the same to all who touched her that night!" "I believe you my friend. Now, please tell me Sobbo how did the Capitan acquire Blaine Ewen?"

"This golden hair woman came to the ship, say she wife of Captain's biggest horse trader. She wants private trade for red hair house servant. Golden hair say husband like this servant girl and wife want her gone."

"What did you think Sobbo?"

"I tell Capitan this is bad and you not be happy. As I say before, he tell me, she is a servant, he do this is for you. When I see her I know she not house servant. She special woman."

Sobbo pulled out the emerald engagement ring, the necklace and the one earring. "No house servant wear this. And her clothes rich and heavy, weighed like three people."

"I believe you Sobbo." "Did you tell Blaine Ewen that I am a good and just King?" "Yes my King, you are a good and just King."

King Aviv thought to himself. 'If I do not try to help those young women in Bogota's possession, am I a good and just King?'

That evening Sobbo brought dinner to Blaine's chamber.

Enough food for all, for a while, she forgot her pain and enjoyed her small friends who seemed to light up about everything. Blaine sat back with a smile on her face and watched the girls tell about where they had lived.

Lome crawled up next to Blaine, she knew Lome needed her and she needed Lome.

It was getting late and Blaine told the girls they needed to go to bed.

Tiki stood and asked. "Do you wish me to leave you Madam?"

Blaine was slightly puzzled. "Well, Tiki won't your parent worry about you if you don't go home?"

"I do not have parents or a home. I live with the dressmaker she not nice like you. I...I could stay with you Madam."

Blaine was shocked to think children were kept in a storehouse and sent out as workers hoping to find some resemblance of a home.

"Tiki dear, how many more children are at the dress makers shop?"

"I do not know the number Madam. But I know there are many. Some have to sleep on the floor. Are you going to keep me Madam?"

Blaine put her arms around Tiki. "Well, I most certainly am. Now and always, Tiki now where to put you to sleep."

"Madam I will sleep on the floor right outside your door!" "Tiki you absolutely will not! You are a young lady not a dog."

Zuni asked. "Miss Blaine can Tiki share my bedchamber with me please?"

"Well, that settles it, now you have a place to sleep. That will be perfect. Now, is this all right with you Lome? Because you will still have a bed chamber but you will be by yourself."

"I want to stay here with you my Blaine."

"how wonderful, we all have roommates now don't we. You two go to your bedchamber it is getting late. Lome and I will be here if you need us."

Zuni and Tiki went off to their bedchamber chattering and laughing. Blaine tucked Lome in kissing her good night.

For the first time, in what felt to be an eternity, Blaine relaxed, she sat down to read the bible Sobbo had given her.

Lome was deep in sleep and Blaine was nodding off herself when a knock came at her door.

She opened the door to find King Aviv standing on the other side., "Madam Blaine, may I please have a word with you."

Blaine left her chamber following King Aviv; he escorted her to a small sitting room. "Please, have a seat, "I spoke with my man Sobbo, he speaks as highly of you as you do of him. He also gave me some of your things he kept safe for you. He wanted you to have them back now." King Aviv handed Blaine the jewelry.

Blaine was over taken with emotion. She just sat staring at the beautiful jewels.

With tears in her eyes and a tight knot in her throat, she spoke quietly, "I wore these to the Ball. Ash...Aunt Anna gave them to me."

Blaine stopped talking. She picked up the emerald engagement ring; vaguely she heard Ashton's voice. She ran her hand softly over the ring.

Clutching the ring to her chest, with tears streaming down her soft cheeks. She spoke with a broken voice. "Thank you for my things, this means so much to me may I please go now?"

Not realizing Blaine's strained emotions, King Aviv continued, "Madam Blaine, I desire to speak to you about some important matters."

Blaine covered her face. She said softly. "Please, your Highness, I beg you I..., I cannot."

Blaine stood and hurried back to her chamber. When she entered her bedchamber, something was very wrong.

The window was open and her light had been put out. Blaine called. "Lome are you awake dear?"

There was no answer. Blaine lifted the lantern and lit it. "Lome where are you?" Lome was not in the bed where Blaine had left her. She was not worried thinking Lome became scared and went to the girls to wait for her.

Blaine went down the hall to the girl's room "Is Lome here with you?"

Tiki and Zuni were still awake. They both answered. "No we have not seen her since we left you earlier."

Blaine became frantic it was not like Lome to wonder. Blaine started running, yelling for Sobbo. "Sobbo. "Sobbo! Sobbo! Come quick!"

Sobbo and King Aviv came running along with many others.

. Sobbo took Blaine by the shoulders. "My friend what happened?" "Lome…. she is gone! I left her sleeping in my bed. I Came back and the window was open and the lantern was out."

One of the house servants spoke, "Maybe she ran away."

Sobbo replied. "No! Madam Blaine be mother to Lome now. Lome not leave on her own."

They went to Blaine's room. Sobbo look out the window, there was a rope tied to the window.

Sobbo pulled the rope in, there was a torn piece of Lome's sari on the window ledge. Blaine turned and fell into King Aviv's arms sobbing mournful tears, as a mother who just lost a child. There was no comforting her.

Sobbo looked at King Aviv. "I know who took her child! It is Bogota; he did not come for the babe. He was after Madam Blaine."

Anger flared in King Aviv. "How dare that treasonous viper come here?" Gently he handed Blaine to Sobbo as if somehow she would break.

"I will deal with this snake myself."

Sobbo protested. "No my King I must go with you."

"No, Sobbo you stay with Madam Blaine. Make sure she is kept safe."

Sobbo carried Blaine to her bedchamber gently placing her on her bed. Blaine cried herself to sleep. Sobbo sat by his friend.

King Aviv and six of his men went to where Bogotá lived. Bogota owned a large estate several miles from the palace.

Bogota always had his estate surrounded by armed men, as if he were an important person or someone afraid for his life.

King Aviv knew it was that Bogota had so many enemies' he needed all those men to keep his treasonous hide alive.

Once Bogota's men realized it was the King approaching, they moved out of the way without a word.

Many of the men worked for Bogotá but their loyalty was to their King.

Bogota came out to meet King Aviv. "Israel what a pleasant surprise. What brings you to my humble home tonight?"

King Aviv cautiously demounted, keeping his eye on Bogota.

"Capitan Bogota please do not address me so informally, I am your King you address me as such. I am here because someone from your house entered the palace tonight and kidnapped a young madden in my care. I order you to return her unharmed this instant."

"Pardon me King Aviv, (Bogota bowed arrogantly) what if I do not return this young maiden you claim I have in my possession.

"Then Capitan my six best swordsmen and myself will strike down any man who tries to protect you and I will gladly take your life for the treasonous acts you have performed as Capitan of my ship, for now, all I demand is the child."

One of Bogota's guards loyal to the King let Lome go free.

Bogota tried to grab her but he missed.

The King looked at Bogota. "It is good you used your head tonight Bogota. As for the matter of treason, we will speak again soon."

King Aviv mounted his horse lifting Lome to ride in front of him; the six guards surrounded their King to protect him. Lome buried her face in the Kings chest holding tight as they made haste to the palace.

Sobbo had been sitting by Blaine's side all night.

King Aviv carried Lome into Blaine's bedchamber laying her next to Blaine. Feeling movement beside her, Blaine opened her eyes to see Lome lying next to her. Blaine was so overcome with joy could not speak.

She pet Lome's hair, and touched her face, she had to make sure she was not dreaming.

Lome curled up next to Blaine's body; it was as if Lome could sense that she was back in her mother's arms again.

King Aviv made sure all the windows were locked the men left the two together sleeping safely neither waking until morning.

Blaine awoke early in the morning, dressing quietly she tucked the blankets around Lome, never rousing her from her slumber.

Blaine went to the kitchen of the palace to find something to eat.

Food was very different in her new home Blaine had to get used to eating things she never heard of before. Some things she was not sure she would ever get accustom too. Blaine finally found some fruit and walked outside for the first time. Entering an enchanted garden. A potent intoxicating sent of tropical flowers surrounded her teasing her senses. The wind was warm and caressed as gentle breath against her flesh, sounds from the ocean in the distance had a hypnotic rhythm. The sun had begun to gently heat the sky.

Blaine felt she could sit there and be taken away by her new found treasure. Blaine reclined on soft grass with her eyes closed. Soaking in the warmth and beauty around her.

Breaking her trance a voice came from behind. "Am I disturbing you?" Blaine slowly opened her eyes to see a handsome vision standing in the sun. Blaine smiled. "No, I was just enjoying something new."

The King was taken with her, "do you mind if I sit with you Madam Blaine?" Blaine touched the ground next to her. "No, I don't mind at all, please sit."

King Aviv sat down beside her, interested in what she found new. "Please, if you do not mind, I would like to hear about these new thing you are enjoying "Alright, you know, your highness this could be fun."

Blaine closed her eyes taking a deep breath, "I smell the aroma of these incredible flowers their fragrance is so intoxicating I think if I breathed them in for very long that I could become drunk off their sweetness. The wind is warm and light, it cresses me like breath on my bare flesh. It is so beautiful, soft and warm. And the distant rhythm of the ocean is hypnotic; I do believe a person could be put into a Trance just by listening to the rhythm of the ocean."

Blaine opened her eyes to meet King Aviv's very dark sensual eyes studying her face. Before Blaine could say anything, the King said in a soft tone, "I wish for you to call me Israel, please."

"Is that your given name?"

"Yes, it is. And you would honor me if you would use my given name not my title." "Then Israel, I ask you to call me Blaine."

"Blaine, I think your new discoveries are most priceless."

Blaine closed her eyes again breathing in deeply. "Mmm, I have to agree." Blaine's scarf had fallen from her shoulder. Israel did not want Blaine to become uncomfortable so he reached down and placed her scarf back upon her shoulder. Making Blaine aware of her exposure, she pulling her scarf back around her, Blaine blushed. "Please, excuse me your Highness I had no idea I was revealing so much." Not wanting the pleasant moment to end, Israel replied "It is quite alright no harm was done Blaine. Please call me Israel"

Their quiet peaceful moment came to an end when Sobbo brought Lome out into the garden.

Lome came running up to Blaine and hugged her so tight she knocked her over onto the ground.

When Lome caught sight of the King sitting next to her Blaine, she jumped on him giving him a hug.

All three of them were laying on the ground laughing. Blaine pet Lome's hair and adjusted her little sari. "Lome my love, are you alright?"

"Yes, my Blaine, I was afraid, but the bad men did not hurt me, my King saved me!" giving King Aviv a big smile.

Israel asked. "Lome, did you see any other young women there?"

Lome expression changed she was no longer smiling. Lome bowed her head as she answered in a sad voice.

"Yes, my King, I think there were three. They not took care of." Lome began to cry. "He... he is a bad man."

Israel put his arms around her. "Please, do not cry Lome, I did not mean to upset you.

We will never speak of this again. Now, you go find your sister and play." Blaine looked at Israel. "Sister?"

"Yes, Blaine, Lome views you as her mother, the other little girl Sobbo brought here, as her sister."

"Actually there is one more little girl."

Israel looked puzzled. "From where did I acquire another young house guest?" Blaine smiled. "You sent for her, her name is Tiki, she is the young girl from the dress makers shop. Israel, I could not send her back to that dreadful place. She told me the children are sleeping on the floor. I told her I would keep her I hope this is alright." Israel sat quiet for a moment, with a smile he answered. "Now Lome has two sisters." Blaine stated to laugh. "And what do you think she sees you as Israel?"

"I am not certain, perhaps her father!" Israel had a big smile on his face.

Sobbo waked away with a robust laugh, adding in. "King not even find Queen yet and already have three beautiful daughters. two the same age!"

Sobbo left them alone in the garden.

The cook came out to tell King Aviv the evening meal would be in one hour. Israel offered his arm to Blaine as they entered the palace, the cook informed them of the menu. The main course for the night was fish; Blaine was not accustomed to fish. As they all sat at the large table, the cook brought out the whole fish, head to tail and everything in between.

Blaine did not want to make a problem so she decided to forgo the fish and try something else. She had no idea how offended the cook would become if a person did not eat his cooking... he insisted she eat the fish.

Finally, Blaine leaned over to Israel and whispered. "I have never eaten fish like this, could you please help me?"

Israel did not say a word he reached over cut a boneless piece of fish removing the skin and gills for Blaine.

Blaine nodded in gratitude then reluctantly tried the fish.

It was wonderful! Better than any creek or stream caught fish she had ever eaten.

Much to his surprise, Blaine even asked Israel to get her seconds.

Zuni, Tiki and Lome displayed very good table manners, on which the King felt he had to comment. "Young ladies where did you learn such fine table manners?"

Zuni spoke up first. "Miss Blaine taught us my King. She is even teaching us how to read!"

Tiki added. "And Madam Blaine wants to keep me forever! She is not going to send me back to the dressmaker!"

Israel turned to Blaine. "I can see you have made a few happy pupils."

Blaine smiled at Israel, her eyes aglow with appreciation for Israel allowing her to care for Tiki.

"Speaking of pupils, Israel, I have something I would like to talk to you about privately, after we have had our dinner."

"Certainly, but it will have to be at another time. I must deal with a traitor tonight." Blaine had no idea what Israel's statement meant, so the impact of what was about to take place went over her head.

Blaine knew if Israel gave his word to speak to her later, he would do just as he said.

King Aviv was proving to be a man of his word.

After everyone finished their diner, Blaine took the girls back to her room for a story.

Lome touched Blaine's arm. "My Blaine, tell us about where you are from."

Blaine thought for a moment. "Alright, I will tell you about a special night called the night of the Ball. It is grand! This night, is a party people plan for months. Women wear fancy gowns. Here let me show you."

Blaine took a lead and paper and drew a picture of a gown. The girls giggled.

Tiki said. "Looks big and hot to me. Was this gown very heavy?"

Blaine replied. "Yes, Tiki, the gowns were very heavy and sometimes hot. But most balls were held when it was getting cold outside. We couldn't wear gowns like this here because it is so hot all year round. But at a Ball men and women dance together. People who are falling in love walk in the garden together and dance just with each other. There is lots of food and happy people; it is a very special time."

Zuni smiled. "So, if we had a Ball, Madam Blaine, you and King Aviv could dance just together." The other girls agreed.

Blaine shook her head. "What are you three up to?"

Tiki said. "Lome said you and King Aviv are falling in love. She saw you with him in the garden."

"Well, you three need not be snoops that will get you into a lot of trouble. King Aviv and I are friends. Now, you two scoot to your room and go to sleep. And you miss matchmakers get in bed here."

Lome crawled into Blaine's bed away from the window. Blaine checked the window to make sure it was locked. Blaine turned down the lantern and cuddled next to Lome. After all was quiet, Blaine kept thinking about what Israel said.

'He was going to deal with a trader tonight.' What he said had begun to worry her…. King Aviv had fifty of his men riding with him. King Aviv would give Bogotá the option to fight or leave the island for good.

He was not afraid of Bogota; nevertheless, he wanted peace on his island.

The King hoped Bogota would leave the island peacefully.

However, he had known this man long before he became King, Bogota had always been a violent cutthroat, from what the King had been told, Bogota was worse now.

Israel rode up to Bogota's estate, he had half his men stay hidden behind.

Bogota's gate front was guarded by fifteen men with muskets'.

King Aviv addressed the men, "Men, I know you are aware of who I am and why I am here. Are there any of you loyal to your King? If you are and you remain as you stand, you will die. If you show your loyalty now, you will be, at this moment, made part of the King's guard."

Seven of the fifteen men turned their muskets' on the man next to him and told him to lower his weapon and surrender. The eight remaining surrendered without incident.

The seven knelt in front of the King he swore them as part of the King's guards.

King Aviv asked of the seven, "Are you aware of anymore that are loyal?" "We know of two others and they are inside with Bogota."

The King said. "You seven men go to the windows call the others over to talk, when they come, those not loyal, pull them out bind and gag them."

Before the King and half his men entered, over half of Bogota's men had been pulled thru the windows, bound and gagged.

One of the seven entered inside finding one man he knew to be loyal to the King. Pulling the loyal man aside. "The King says go find the women Bogota brought from the ship and bring them to the back window."

The man was gone for some time. He finally came with three young women.

The guard outside asked, "What took you so long?" "I had to convince them I wasn't going to hurt them."

The outside guard said to the girls. "I am here with King Aviv. I am to take you to Madam Blaine."

The young women became very excited and one yelled aloud. "Miss Blaine!"

Both men said. "shhh! be quiet! Now climb thru the window."

Before going in, King Aviv gave the signal for the rest of his men to surround Bogota's place.

The King entered with twenty-five men. Bogota was armed; he met them in the courtyard. "King Aviv, why have you come back!"

"I told you, Capitan Bogota, there have been changes of treason brought against you.

Even by many of your men here." "This is a lie! I have committed no treason"

"No, I believe this is true, I have many witnesses against you. You only have yourself." "Baugh! And who are these trusted witnesses?"

"One, is my most trusted man with me here tonight, Sobbo. The second is the fine young woman you kidnapped thinking her a house servant but she is not, Madam Blaine Ewen. The third is the young child Lome whose sister you had savagely murdered aboard my ship. Moreover, there are the three young women you no longer have in your possession here. For all the treachery, you have been accused and found guilty of, I could sentence you to death Bogota. Or… you can leave my island and never return again."

At that instant, a shot rang out, one of Bogota's men shot one of the King's guards. King Aviv turned, just for an instant, to see his man who had been hit. In that moment, Bogota drew his sword striking King Aviv in the side.

Sobbo drew his dagger, throwing it, he pinned Bogota thru the chest to the wall.

Bogota expelled his final words, "She was mine Aviv! The red head was mine"! Then Bogota breathed his last. Sobbo went and withdrew his dagger Bogota's limp body. The treasonous snake slumped to the floor. Sobbo wiped his dagger off on Bogota's body.

Sobbo turned, lifting his King from the floor. Sobbo gentle carried his friend to his horse.

Sobbo said, "Come my King, I take you home. Now justice is done."

CHAPTER 16

The guards brought the three young women to Blaine. Blaine could see they had been badly abused. She decided not to ask any questions about what happened to them. However, she did want to know what happened to the other girl that had been left on the ship.

As the girls bathed and washed their hair, Blaine asked Ebina. "What happened to Kenya?"

"That nasty man Bogota went a sold err."

Nettie added. "He say she weren't pretty enough for him and his men." Malina was very quiet. Blaine asked, "Malina are you alright?"

"Yes, Miss Blaine, it's just I can't believe my eyes. This is the most beautiful place I've ever seen."

Blaine smiled noticing Malian's speech. "Yes, it is Malina. I am happy you did not give up on all I taught you."

Ebina started laughing. "Give up on it! Little Miss Malina finds out she cans use err proper ways to gets extra fine treatment… If'n you gets what I mean."

Blaine was puzzled. "No, Ebina I do not. Moreover, from the way it sounds, I would rather not. Now, if you ladies do not mind. Follow me I will show you to your chambers." As Blaine and the three young women came out from Blaine's chamber, they witnessed Sobbo carrying the King up the stairs.

One of the girls said. "If that be da King he's aint lookin to good." Another said. "Yea, it looks like mean ole Bogota gots a hold of em." Blaine hurried the young women down the hall opening two doors.

"You three decide who shares a room; I have to hurry Israel... I mean King Aviv, he needs me!"

Blaine turned and ran back down the hall and up the stairs to Israel's bedchamber. Blaine came thru the door unannounced just as they were taking, Israel's tunic off he had lost a lot of blood. Blaine did not wait for an invitation.

She lit a lantern and sent one of the house staff to get boiled water and strips of clean cloth she had the men move back. "Please move away, I need to tend to the King." At first, the men did not move, until they looked at Sobbo.

He motioned for them to move and give Blaine room to tend to their King. Blaine examined at the gash. It was deep but it did not look to have struck any major organs.

"Sobbo do we have a doctor on the island?"

"Yes, but he has gone to the other side of island to care for a sick child."

Blaine looked at Sobbo and asked. "Sobbo, my friend, I need the strongest proof whisky or rum which ever you can find and hurry!"

Sobbo left, in a short time, he was back with both rum and whisky. Blaine asked, "Which has more alcohol in it?"

Sobbo did not know for sure so he chose the rum. Blaine sterilized the strips of cloth in the boiling water.

Blaine spoke with worry in her voice, "Thank heavens he is unconscious." She poured the rum over the wound.

Blaine made sure she had cleaned the wound well. Then she took out a basket with needle and thread.

Sobbo asked. "My friend, what is that for?"

"Sobbo, if we don't sew up this wound, Israel could get an infection. I have sanitized the wound I have to close it now."

"Alright my friend."

Blaine held the needle in the fire to sterilize it.

She had Sobbo hold the wound together while she sewed as quickly and neatly as she could. After she finished she placed herbs Sobbo had brought on the wound and wrapped it with the sterilized cloth. Blaine kept the whisky incase Israel needed a painkiller. She asked Sobbo to check on Lome.

Blaine fell asleep with her head on Israel's bed. Israel was out for several days. Israel awoke moaning in pain. Blaine sat up to feel his head. Letting out a sigh of relief, "Oh thank heavens you don't have a fever."

Israel tried to smile, then he tried to move. Quickly realizing his mistake, he winced in pain.

Blaine jumped to his side. "Israel, darling, don't move. You have a very bad gash in you side. Now, Sobbo and I have tended to it. However, you must not move for several days. I have whisky here for you as a painkiller. My Da' swears it will cure anything." Weakly Israel asked, "Who is your Da'?"

Blaine smiled. "He is my father. I have called him Da' my whole life." "You miss you family very much, don't you Blaine?"

"Yes, Israel I do."

Blaine reached to tend the dressing on Israel's wound. Touching her hand, "Blaine, Sobbo can do this."

"Well, Israel he could. But at the moment he has woman problems." "What?"

"It seems the three young ladies you brought back are on a man hunt, of a Kingly nature. I believe Sobbo is trying to keep them as far away from you as possible." Squeezing her hand. "And to keep you close to me."

"Yes, because you need me to tend to you."

Blaine slowly removed the cloth strips. Israel could tell by the look on Blaine's face something was wrong. Israel laid his hand on Blaine's arm.

"The wound is infected isn't it?" Blaine covered her mouth she looked at Israel and shook her head yes. Israel patted her arm, "Blaine I can tell you what to do. But you must be strong and do exactly as I say."

"Alright, I will do whatever you say."

"First, stoke the fire, get it very hot." Blaine stoked the fire making it very hot. "Now, Blaine, go get my dagger and place it in the hottest part of the fire." As she complied with his directions, Blaine asked. "Israel, what is next?"

"Next, my dear, will be difficult. Take the dagger and cut the string holding the wound together. Now, I must warn you, once it is loosened the infection will push out quickly so have a cloth there so you won't be hit by it."

Blaine took a deep breath. She picked up the dagger from the fire.

Trying to be careful not to touch his skin, she barely touched the thread with the dagger, the thread-disintegrated, puss pushed forth liked an explosion, and the smell was overwhelming.

Blaine was able to catch the infection with the cloth. She turned quickly throwing the cloth into the fire.

Then Blaine placed the dagger back into the fire. Blaine closed her eyes took a deep breath then turned back to Israel. "Now, what do we need to do?"

"Blaine, please, listen to the next few instructions carefully. After the next step I may not be conscious."

"Oh, Israel, I don't want to hurt you."

"Blaine, my dear, what you are doing is saving my life, first, pour the whisky over the wound. Second, take the dagger while it is burning hot and place it on both sides of the wound. The burning flesh will stink, it will make noise. Leave the dagger there until this stops. Then remove the dagger. Place it back in the fire. Wrap my wound in gauze lying on that table over there. Squeezing her hand, I have faith in you Blaine."

Blaine knew Israel's life was in her hands. She would do exactly what he instructed her to do.

Motioning for Blaine to come close, "one more thing Blaine." Blaine came close, "Yes Israel."

"I want to thank you, come closer."

Blaine leaned closer. Israel gently kissed Blaine and whispered. "Thank you, my Blaine."

Blaine stood and went to her task, she apologized to Israel, as she poured the whiskey over the wound. Israel moaned loudly in pain.

Silently, Blaine, said a prayer, picked up the dagger, kissed Israel on the shoulder and lanced the wound.

Lancing a wound did everything Israel said it would. Israel refused to yell out in pain. All around him went dark. Israel was unconscious. Once the dagger cooled, she removed it, placing it back in the fire.

Quickly, Blaine covered the wound with gauze. She stayed by his side for many hours. Blaine left Israel only long enough to get herself cleaned up. Hastily, Blaine changed into a clean sari. Making her way back by Israel's side.

The sun had risen high another day had come and Israel had been unconscious for several days. Blaine never left his side.

Blaine sat quietly, playing with her emerald ring with sadness written on her face.

Israel had been awake for some time silently watching her.

Finally, he spoke. "What is it about that ring that makes you so sad, my Blaine?" Blaine turned to Israel with a huge smile. "Oh, how wonderful! You are awake! You have been asleep for so long, how do you feel?"

"You answer my question first. Why does this ring bring you sadness?" "Israel it's a long story."

"Well, my Blaine, I am not going anywhere soon, so tell me your long story." "Alright, several months before I was brought here I was engaged. We would have been married close to eight months ago, if things had not gone horribly wrong. You see, my beautiful cousin Roslyn came to visit. It seems she was quite fond of my fiancé, so fond in fact that she took to throwing herself at him when I wasn't around."

Israel interjected. "Well, most surely this fiancé of yours rejected these love gestures from your cousin."

Sighing, Blaine continued. "Israel, if only he had been more like you. Sadly, no he did not reject her love gestures and for that, he is no longer my fiancé. From what I witnessed between them, he was not only flattered by them he even welcomed her advances. As our relationship became closer, he wanted... more from me."

"What do you mean my Blaine, more from you?"

"He wanted things romantically from me that I wouldn't give until we were married." "Oh I see"

"The insane thing is, the night I found them together is the night my Da' said we could get married any time we wanted. I found Ashton with Roslyn rolling around in the hay. Giggling and playing like lovers. My cousin's bodice was off. Ashton's shirt was off. He had fingernail scratches all over his back. I am sure they would have continued had I not interrupted."

"What did you do?"

"I was so hurt, I started running. I ran... I ran until I could not run anymore. So I walked to Ashton's old hunting cabin. I was fixing it up for our honeymoon. That is where I met Capitan Bogota and Sobbo. And now I am here."

"Would you mind if we analyzed this situation with your fiancé and your cousin together?"

"No, I don't mind, it really doesn't upset me anymore. What I cannot figure it out is why this all happened, maybe, you can help."

"First, this man, you say his name is Ashton?" "Yes"

"How long did you know him before he proppose?" "Oh, not long, only a few weeks."

"Alright, in that few weeks, what was his behavior?" Blaine had a puzzled look on her face.

"What I mean, is did he want to know about you, who you are, what kind of person is Blaine Ewen. Or was he more enthralled with your beauty "Well, I cannot recall him ever asking about me as a person. He always seemed to be interested in...well, umm physical things."

"I see, he was interested in your beautiful red hair, your stunning emerald green eyes and your skin that is like the purest white silk in the sun."

Blaine blushed profusely. "Why do you blush Blaine?"

"I have never heard myself described in such a way." What Ashton seemed to be after did not sound so beautiful."

"You were engaged to this man yet he did not make love to you?"

Blaine turned three shades of red then she replied, "Israel Aviv, I do not understand why every man thinks that once he gets a girl engaged he can do as he pleases. There is a saying in Ireland...

"Why buy the cow if you get the milk for free." "Blaine I am confused what does this mean?"

"It simply means this, what is the point of a man marrying a woman if he gets what he wants from her without having to marry her. That is how I knew Ashton was no good for me. All he had been trying to do is to get me to make love to him. He did not care about me, as a person, he did not care that it was important to me to wait until we said 'I do'. It was all about what he wanted. So he found some fancy piece of fluff willing to satisfy his lust. And it was not me!"

Blaine could feel her temper rising." I am really upset Israel! You need your rest and I need to go check on the girls. I will come back later." Blaine left without giving Israel a chance to say anything else.

She was in a fine fit! Leaving Israel, Blaine walked right into an older man she had never seen before.

"Please excuse me Sir, I did not see you." Before he could say a word, Blaine was gone.

The older man knocked on Israel's door. "Come in."

Israel hoped it was Blaine returning to apologize for being so abrupt.

Much to his surprise it was not Blaine who entered his room but his father, Omar Aviv. "I heard of your injury on my arrival today. My son, how are you?"

"I am better father; I am surprised to see you, what has brought you on such a long journey?"

"To see my eldest son, to make sure you are faring well. By the way, who was the red haired beauty I saw leaving your chamber just now, is she a servant?"

"Her name is Blaine Ewen, no father she is not a servant. Now, I know you did not travel alone, did Shri come also?"

"Yes Israel, Shri is here along with Samira. Do you remember Samira, Israel?" "Of course I remember Samira she was so little when I left."

"She is all grown up now, Israel." "It will be good to see her again."

"I will leave you to rest now my son." With that, Omar left him.

Blaine had first gone to her room. With her temper raging, she decided it was best to stay secluded. In time, she calmed down. Realizing Sobbo has been with the young women for a long while, Blaine set out find her friend, to give poor Sobbo a rest. Running out of ideas, Sobbo had taken them out into the garden to pick flowers. Blaine came up to Sobbo. "You go now my friend, get some rest. I can take care of them.

Sobbo let out a sigh. "Thank you my friend. It would be easier to fight twenty men, I am thinking."

Sobbo walked away rubbing his head. Giggling to herself, Blaine could only imagine the headache the girls must have given him.

Sobbo entered the King's chamber. Israel was up donning his robe. "My King! You need to be in bed!"

"No Sobbo I have been in this bed to long." "My King, your wound!"

"My wound is fine and if I feel tired I promise to come lay down. My father and my brother are here. I am not sure of the purpose of their visit."

Sobbo eyed his King and said. "I know the purpose my King. Your father has brought a woman for you to have as Queen."

"Are you sure about this Sobbo?"

"Yes, my King, I hear your brother argue with your father about you not having a Queen, and that he should be made King of your island. Your father tells him you have Queen, that he brings you your Queen."

Israel thought for a moment. "Sobbo, did my brother say anything else?" Sobbo had a solemn look on his face. "Yes, he said he would be King one way or another. Then he left the palace."

Israel finished dressing; Sobbo helped his King down stairs.

. "Sobbo I am hungry, I would like to eat out in the garden." Sobbo's face looked worried.

"Sobbo what is wrong with you?"

"My King, the young women are in the garden."

"I see, and do you feel somehow these women will do me harm?" Sobbo was still troubled, "No my King, they all want to be your Queen."

Israel raised his eyebrows, "I wonder who informed them that I may be in search of a Queen?"

Sobbo shook his head. "I do not know my King."

"Well, my friend let me go meet my new guests."

King Aviv and Sobbo walked out into the garden. Samira was the first to notice Israel.

She smiled, making her way to him confident she would be Queen soon.

"Israel, I am so happy to see you. I am concerned for you, are you sure it is not too soon for you to be out?"

Israel smiled; his father had told the truth. Samira was all grown, and quite beautiful. "It has been a long time Samira, the last time I saw you, you were just a little girl."

"Yes, I was only eight when you left. I am not a little girl anymore, Israel, I am eighteen now."

"I can see that you are not a little girl Samira. You have grown into a fine woman." Blaine noticed Israel; she came to see how he was feeling. Not realizing she was interrupting a conversation, she placing her hand on Israel's arm. "Israel, are you sure you should be out of bed?"

Israel looked into Blaine's eyes and smiled. He thought to himself, 'This is where I could be hypnotized, by the beauty of her emerald eyes.' Finally, he replied. "I am fine, my Blaine."

Shocked Samira took notice of the intimacy of this woman, calling the King by his given name and putting her hand on him. Seeing the Kings affectionate reply to this strange, red haired, woman, jealousy shot up inside her.

Ebina and Nettie looked up to see the King and came running to greet him.

One of the girls, Malina, kept her distance, while the other two girls were fussing over King Aviv.

Nettie spoke first, "your lordship, I be happy you all better now. I mean I knows you wasn't gonna die, you too strong for that."

Ebina nudged Nettie out of the way. "King Aviv's I was a prayin' fer you, I jest knowz the good lord not lets a good man as you go. I wanna thank you fer savin' our lives a riskin' yers the way you did. I be truly thankin you."

"I thank you for your concern, and it is nice to see you again Samira but now I would ask you all for some privacy."

The three young women left the garden. Blaine was about to leave too. Israel took her by the hand. "Blaine, please, stay with me. I wish to talk with you."

"Alright Israel, I'll stay."

Samira waited for Blaine to enter the palace. She intended to make her intentions known.

She would let this strange woman know **she** had been hand chosen by Israel's father to be Queen.

When Blaine did not return from the garden, Samira went to see where she had gone.

Israel took Blaine to a beautiful garden table he pulled out her chair. He lifted her hand and kissed it. Blaine's cheeks blushed bright pink.

She just did not understand the slightest touch from him sent heat racing thru her like a whirlwind.

Israel was in pain and took his time, sitting down very slowly. Blaine noticed, reaching out to him. "Israel are you sure you want to do this. I could bring you some food to your room. I think you should go lay down."

"I am fine. I choose to be with you, right here."

The cook brought out fruit, cheese, and bread, to drink he brought them coffee and fresh juice.

They ate together quietly enjoying each other's company.

As Samira watched, she was outraged. She had seen enough.

She felt she should be the one sitting with Israel not this strange woman.

Samira set off to find Omar and tell him of this affront to her.

Blaine broke the silence. "Everything is so different here, living on an island." Israel looked at her and asked. "Different, in what way Blaine?"

"Well, where I came from, we never had fruit like this. And the weather is beautiful here almost all the time I mean it never snows. It never even gets cold. Never in my life have I seen such beautiful flowers as the ones in the garden. The ocean, I love the sound and the smell of the ocean. People are different here, life is different."

Israel studied Blaine's face; he took her hand in his. "So you like living here Blaine?" Blaine thought for a few moments before giving her answer. "Israel, I miss my parents. Here, I have the little ones to care for. And yes, I do like it here."

Israel decided to change the subject. "Blaine you had something you wanted to ask something about pupils?"

Blaine became very excited. "Oh yes! "Israel I would like to take all the children out of the dressmaker's storehouse and give them a real home and a school."

Blaine thought Israel might object she had mental list of positive reasons to undertake such a project.

She was completely taken by surprise when Israel did not object.

"That would be a fine thing my Blaine. Now, we need to think of where to build such a place for the children."

"I was thinking, since Capitan Bogota did so much badness. Maybe we could clean up his empty estate and possibly use the estate as a home and a school for the children. Sobbo told me this is a very large place, this way something good would be done with it."

Israel looked at Blaine in amazement for a woman so young she was wise. "It will be done my Blaine."

Blaine felt as if her heart was about to burst she was so happy.

Now she would be able to care for all the children like Tiki!

Blaine's curiosity was getting the best of her she had one more request. "Israel, may I ask, why do you call me my Blaine?"

"Because my Blaine, you saved my life and you are my dear friend."

Blaine felt touched to her heart. At that moment, she knew she had a special connection with Israel.

She took Israel's hand in hers. "And you are my dear friend too, Israel." Blaine could see Israel was getting tired so she helped him back to his chamber. She helped Israel into bed and covered him up.

Israel took her by the hand. "Blaine, will you just lie here with me while I sleep. Please, I do not wish to be alone."

Blaine smiled she went around to the other side of the bed climbed up and lay next to Israel.

Blaine found herself running her hand thru Israel's hair the way she did Lome's hair to help her sleep.

As Blaine watched Israel sleep, Blaine thought to herself, 'This man is different from any man I have I ever met he is so kind, he is a beautiful person, what a truly handsome man he is.'

Finally, she curled up next to him and fell asleep.

Sobbo came in to check on his King. A wide grin came across his face when he found his two friends sleeping together peacefully.

He took a blanket and covered Blaine. Then quietly Sobbo left the room.

That evening, Blaine awoke to Israel watching her. She smiled. "How long have you been awake?"

"Long enough."

"Long enough for what, Israel?" "To know I wish to kiss you."

Color deepened in Blaine's cheeks. "Oh." "I will not, if this would offend you."

Blaine's heart was beating fast she desired for him to kiss her! Softly Blaine replied. "I don't believe I would be offended, Israel."

Israel gently swept his lips over Blaine's. The warmth of his nearness sent chills racing thru her body. Blaine parted her lips, inviting Israel to explore further, sending a crashing wave of desire pulsating thru him. Teasing him with her tongue, Blaine provocatively traced his lips, sliding her arms around Israel's neck, gently drawing him closer. Desire set aflame, passionately he claimed her mouth. Blaine moaned under his ardent kiss. She ran her hands thru Israel's long black hair, desiring to be closer. Craving to continue down passions path, Israel desired to lead Blaine in the ways of love. Drawing back away from her, he looked into Blaine's emerald eyes smoldering with desire.

Blaine was breathless, oh how she did not want Israel to stop. Regaining a small measure of his senses, Israel knew he must stop.

Israel spoke softly. "Blaine, my love, is it true you have never been with a man before?" "Yes, Israel, I told you, I have never made love."

Israel pushed back to put more distance between them.

Blaine was completely confused by her feelings. She knew to be with him was wrong but the thought that he might not want her tore at her heart. Tears welled up in her eyes. She turned away from him. Quickly, Blaine climbed out of the bed. Blaine felt embarrassed and hurt as she said. "I am sorry, Israel, I guess you want someone I am not. Blaine ran out from Israel's bedchamber.

Omar witnessed Blaine leave his son's bedchamber, again. Again, this beautiful woman was not happy.

He decided to have a talk with his son, to discover what could be between this beauty and his son.

Omar knocked on his son's door. Israel was in no mood for intrusion. Gruffly he answered." Who is it?"

"It is your father, my son, may I come in?"

Israel was not in the mood for his father's match making games however, he knew he could not turn him away either.

Israel took a deep breath, "Please, come in father."

"Son, I just past the beautiful red head again. It would seem every time I see her coming from your chamber she is not a happy woman, why is that?"

Israel was stunned by his father's bluntness. After thinking for a moment, Israel replied. "Father, it would seem Madam Blaine finds my manners somewhat rough."

"I think, perhaps, your heart is tied with this woman my son."

"Father, please do not try to play matchmaker. I know why you brought Samira here. I am not happy about this game you are playing." "Son, do you not find Samira attractive?"

"Yes, Father, Samira is a beautiful woman, but beauty is not all there is to choosing a Queen, you know this."

"My son, the law is clear. You must be married by the time you turn twenty-eight. You are running out of time. I do not consider what I have done as playing games. I consider this a father helping his son, shall we say, with a slight problem."

"Father, I am very aware of the law. However, I do not see the choice of my Queen as a problem. I will not be choosing Samira, Father."

Not wanting to continue the conversation Israel decided to change the subject. "Father, I must go and take care of some important matters. Please excuse me."

As Blaine reached her bedchamber, Samira called her name. "Madam Blaine, may I have a word with you please."

Blaine tried to pull herself together. Samira had not spoken to her since her arrival two days earlier and Blaine did not want to offend Israel's guest.

Nevertheless, it did not take long to see Samira was not worried about offending Blaine. In a matter of minutes, it became clear to Blaine this woman was intent on offending her. "Madam Blaine, I have an important matter to discuss with you."

"I can't imagine what that could be Miss, since you and I have never met until this moment."

"Can't you, Madam Blaine? I suppose it is possible, Israel did not tell you about me. But I will remedy that now."

"Miss, I truly do not want to be rude. However, I am not in the mood for games. So please get to your point."

"As you wish, Madam Blaine, my name is Samira; I have been selected to be King Aviv's Queen. Moreover, I insist you end your tryst with King Aviv at once. Your affair was fine when I was not here but now I want it to end. Do I make myself clear Madam Blaine?"

Blaine's temper flared! At this moment, she was speechless! How could she be so stupid! King Aviv had played her for a fool.

All she could think to say was. "Samira you have made yourself more than clear." Blaine turned, entered her chamber, quickly closing the door before another word could be spoken. She leaned against the door, releasing the flood of tears she had held inside.

Lome was in their room playing, Blaine had not noticed her. Wanting to comfort Blaine, Lome came to her putting her arms around her. "My Blaine did someone hurt you?"

"No, Lome, I just don't feel good please go play with the other girls." Lome left Blaine but she did not go play she went to find the King. Lome had searched for some time finally, she found the King.

King Aviv was giving instructions to his men regarding Bogota's estate.

Lome came up and pulled at the King's robe. King Aviv excused himself. "Just one moment men."

"Lome, you need to wait until I am thru speaking with my men." Lome stood to the side and waited patiently.

The King finished giving instructions to his men. Noticing Lome still waiting, he turned his attention to his little friend.

"Alright, Lome, what can I do for you?"

"Not for me, my King, for my Blaine, she is very sick." "sick?"

"Yes! my King, she came to our bedchamber crying and holding her stomach. She said she is sick. You must to go to her, make her better. Please!"

"Alright Lome, I will go."

Israel entered Blaine's chamber it was dark all the windows were closed. Blaine was lying in her bed facing the wall. As Israel approached the bed, he heard Blaine crying.

Blaine said in a broken tearful voice. "Lome, honey I told you I don't feel good please go play."

Israel said softly. "Lome sent me to help you."

"Israel, you need to go find someone else to play with too!" Blaine broke into tears. Israel sat on the side of her bed. "Blaine, my love, what is wrong? I have offended you. Please talk to me."

"First, you pretend that you want me, then you don't. Then I find out you are to be married! I…I" Blaine broke out into a sob.

Israel took Blaine into his arms and held her until she stopped crying.

Once she was calm he spoke. "What do you mean you found out I am to be married?" Blaine pushed Israel away from her. "Do not play games with me Israel! You know what I mean. You and Samira! Your father brought her here to be your Queen. What were you doing with me Israel? Seeing if I would fill in for her till she arrived? Guess I was a bit of a disappointment wasn't I?"

"Blaine, my father may have brought Samira here for me. However, I never agreed to marry her. Nor did I send for her. I do not intend to make Samira my Queen.

I never said I did not want you. The way you make me feel when we are together I … Blaine, you said you had no experience in regards to the art of love. That is why I asked you again if you had ever made love to a man, because of the way you touched me, the way you kissed me. You set my soul on fire. had I not stopped then I would have taken you at that moment. Blaine, my love, you have already told me how you value your virtue. I would be a thief to steal something so valuable from you."

Blaine fell into Israel arms. "Oh Israel."

"Blaine, please, listen to what I say, what you possess is something of great value. I would be honored to have you give this as a gift to me"

"Let us not talk of this anymore. I want to show you something. Please, come with me." Blaine dried her tears, put on her slippers and her scarf.

She followed Israel thru the garden down a hidden sandy path, which opened up to a breath taking white sand beach.

Blaine quickly took her slippers off to feel the soft warm sand between her toes. Israel loved watching this fiery flower. He was amazed how she could transform from being passionate to playful and childlike so quickly.

She was intoxicating she was puzzlement to him.

Blaine just had to get her feet wet so she walked up to the water rushing in.

The hypnotic waves breaking in rhythm. The water was a turquoise blue as far as her eye could see, until ocean met sky.

The water was much warmer than Blaine had expected, it felt incredible, water rushing over her feet and the sand washing out from under where she stood.

Excitedly Blaine turned to Israel. "Israel, you just have to try this, it feels wonderful!" Israel hesitated at first, then took off his slippers and joined her.

He was surprised how incredible the sand felt on his feet he thought to himself. 'Why have I never notice this before?'

Israel and Blaine walked along the beach for hours. Picking up seashells, watching the waves.

Finally, Israel asked. "Blaine how old are you?"

Blaine had to think. "Well, I had just turned sixteen when I was taken on the ship by Capitan Bogota. I was on the ship six months, and I have been here with you, three and a half months. So, that makes me almost seventeen. Actually sixteen and nine and a half months."

Israel shook his head smiling, "you make me smile my Blaine."

"And what about you King Israel Aviv, how old are you? And why are these women chasing you"

"I am twenty-six years old. And I am assuming these women have caught wind of the fact that I must find a Queen, and produce an heir before I turn thirty. Or my younger brother may be able to take over ruler ship of my island."

"Israel, you cannot let that happen! This is yours! You built it! These people are loyal to you…, you are their King!"

Israel took Blaine by the hands. "Then you must become my Queen, Blaine. And live here with me, forever."

Nervously Blaine looked at the ground and replied. "And produce an heir?" "Yes, Blaine, this is how my Kingdom will be saved."

Israel could see the shock on Blaine's face. Seriously, Israel asked. "My Blaine, will you think about it?"

Blaine was stunned, Israel had just asked her to become his Queen and have his baby.

Moreover, he was not being funny. he actually wanted her to be his Queen! Blaine was overwhelmed so she thought she would change the subject. "Israel would it be alright if we walk along the beach for a while longer?" Israel shook his head in agreement.

Together they walked in the warm sand watching and listening to the sound of the ocean.

After some time of walking silently, Israel took Blaine by the hand.

"Please sit with me Blaine."

"Alright Israel." Blaine's heart was racing. Israel held her hand. "Blaine, I desire to kiss you."

Israel laid Blaine back in the sand kissing her gently, softly.

Israel lifted his head peering into Blaine's eyes, losing himself in the pools of emerald.. "My love, I will teach you about love and ecstasy there is so much to explore, to experience together. I will make you a happy Queen."

She touched Israel's face, "Please tell me you do not believe in taking other wives or anything like that do you?"

"I will admit to you, my love, some from my country do this, but I do not believe this is good. I believe one-man one woman."

"Then I promise to do my best to make you a happy King." Holding Blaine close, "this means you accept?"

Blaine kissed Israel softly. She whispered against her kiss. "Yes, I love you my King." They lay in the sand holding each other listening to the ocean talking of their future.

After some time past Israel stood taking Blaine's hand in his, he walked with her back to the palace.

He kissed Blaine goodnight and told her to get some sleep.

Blaine went to her bedchamber floating on air never did she think she would find happiness again. Now she had found both love and happiness.

Even at the late hour, the King sent a runner to the dressmaker and the baker. Israel was in the middle of giving Sobbo directions when Omar and Shri approached. "Brother, what is this I hear, you do not want Samira. Did your wound leave you impotent?"

Omar stopped his younger son, "Shri! You do not speak so bold to your brother!"

Normally Shri's insult would have angered Israel but not tonight.

"Shri, I assure you my body is working quite well. As a matter of fact, I do have good news to share I will be getting married, tomorrow!"

With that being said, Israel bid them all good evening and retired to his bedchamber.

Sobbo left quickly not wanting any questions to be asked of him.

Omar and Shri were left standing in shock of Israel's announcement both wondering who this could be since he had rejected Samira.

The next morning things were abuzz in the palace. The King decided to take care of a few things before Blaine arose. The dressmaker personally delivered the kings request. With questions of her own, she hoped the King would give her audience to her dismay her questions remained unanswered.

The two young women who had been trying to catch the Kings eye, without success, emerged from their bedchamber curious as to what was happening.

Israel stood at his balcony and called the entire palace to attention, including his father, brother and Samira for his important announcement.

The King spoke with a commanding voice, "Finally! My Kingdom will be complete. I have chosen Blaine Ewen to be my Queen and take my side. As my kingdom is completed there will be a celebration in honor of this most joyous event."

Samira turned to Omar pleading, "what does this mean for me?" "Samira you will wed Shri when we return home."

Samira was not pleased, but she knew this was the way of things. Israel had not chosen her and Shri had made his desire for her known.

Ebina and Nettie walked away disheartened by the unexpected announcement.

Nettie whispered. "Well maybe the King is keepin others you know."

Malina shook her head. "You mean concubines I doubt it. His Queen is Miss Blaine he won't want anyone else.

"Blaine awoke with her three little girls smiling at her. Blaine stretched smiling at her three little observers. "What are you three little sneaks up to?"

Tiki said. "We are here to pamper you. Now, you get into the tub."

Blaine started laughing. The tub was full of bubbles as the girls tried to wash Blaine one by one, Blaine pulled them into the water.

They splashed and played until they were all wrinkle.

Israel knocked on the door.

Tiki yelled. "Come in!"

Blaine tried to stop her but Zuni and Lome grabbed her legs and pulled her under. Israel stood smiling watching his Queen at play.

When Blaine came up for air, she had soap in her eyes and could not see.

She started fussing at the girls but they would not answer her. Israel motioned for them to go out of the room quietly the three ran out.

Blaine was still fussing trying to find a towel she said in a playfully demanding tone, "Girls, this is not funny my eyes are burning now please give me the towel!" Silently Israel handed Blaine the towel.

Blaine wiped her face fussing how she was going to tan their bottoms once she could see again.

She threw the towel and opened her eyes to her surprise Israel was kneeling there in front of her watching her!

Blaine's breath caught in her throat she wrapped her arms up around her breasts. drawing Israel's eyes to what she tried to hide.

He reached out to wipe the bubbles from her face. "Are you cold my love?" "No Israel I am not cold."

Israel bent closer. "I wish to kiss you." "But Israel I am…"

Israel placed his fingers over Blaine's lips to quiet her moving his fingers to replace them with his lips slowly caressing her lips with his.

Blaine sighed, "Oh Israel I love you."

She gave him a seductive look. "but you should not be in here."

"I wanted to show my bride how eager I am to be with her tonight." Confused Blaine replied, "Tonight?"

"Yes my love we are to be wed tonight."

"But Israel isn't there supposed to be an engagement time?"

"No, my dear Blaine, once a King has chosen a Queen, and in our case, the Queen has agreed, the wedding takes place very quickly. Come, get dried off, I have something special for you my love." Israel turned to give Blaine privacy.

Blaine dried off then put on her pink robe.

Israel said "go to your bed, I have something for you for our special day." Blaine found the most beautifully elaborate sari she had ever seen.

It was white smooth silk with diamonds sewn all over. The wrap had small glistening jewels sewn in the pattern of stars. It was simply breath taking.

Blaine turned to Israel wrapping her arms around him she kissed him softly. "I have another surprise for you my love."

Blaine smiled at Israel joyfully, "and what might that be my King?"

"Sobbo left last night to bring your father, I mean your Da', here to see you. I know he will miss our wedding but you will see him soon my love."

"I do love you Israel. Just think my Da' will be here soon!"

Blaine planted kisses all over Israel's face. "Thank you, thank you so much." Israel was overjoyed to see how happy Blaine was to know she would get to see her father.

But this also worried him. Would her love for him be strong enough for her to remain his Queen? Or would she leave for her life she was taken from? Israel's heart grew heavy.

Israel left Blaine alone to prepare herself for their special day. The other young women thought they would offer their help.

Nettie started trouble while brushing Blaine's hair, "Miss Blaine, we don't want to scare ya none, but ya ain't never been wit a man"

Ebina laughed. Mens ruff and mean and dey does what dey wants."

Nettie added. "I had my first man do what he wanted, it hurt too. No matter what men says, it is fer dim."

Blaine was becoming more afraid by the minute never had she thought of making love as being cruel and painful.

Seeing how upset Blaine was becoming Malina spoke up. "Miss Blaine what does your heart tell you about the King? You need to know not all men are as they say." Quickly, Blaine excused herself and left her chamber.

Ebina and Nettie turned on Malina. "What was that all about, what's your heart say. We was trying to tell her the truth."

Malina stood and walked to the door, "The problem is its your truth not hers. We have been slaves and treated as slaves, she has not. I know not all men are bad but you two believe they are."

Malina left and went to the garden. Blaine went to Israel's bedchamber.

At first she hesitated, Blaine was not sure she wanted to talk to Israel about this. hoping he was not there, she decided to knock.

"Come in."

Blaine entered the room slightly hysterical, "Israel, I have to say something, I just don't think I can do this! There are just something's I did not know about and I just do not think I can be a wife!"

Israel could see something had Blaine very emotional, he had her sit down. "Now my love what has distressed you so?"

"Well the girls were helping me get ready and they started telling me what to expect tonight when we…. Israel this making love thing does not sound like love to me at all! It sounds horrible! Why do men want to do such bad things to women?"

"Alright, my love, I insist you listen to me now. Blaine, I promise to be gentle with you because I love you. I will never do anything to hurt you. Now, I will go and find the ones who have filled your head with such disquieting thoughts."

Israel found Nettie and Ebina in their bedchamber preparing for the wedding they bowed when King Aviv entered.

He said. "I find it odd that the two women my Queen risked her life for, sent myself and my men after, show their gratitude by telling her horror stories about her wedding night. Do you women see me as a monster? Was it not even a week ago you were trying to catch my eye, Israel stood quiet for a moment then said, "Neither of you are welcome to the wedding. In addition, you are no longer welcome in this palace. If decent employment is what you seek, the dressmaker will hire you. If you choose to keep to your wayward ways there is a brothel two miles down the road near the water front." Nettie said. "But my lord what about Malina?"

The King turned replying in a firm voice. "You two do as I say and worry not about anyone else."

The two women left with the King watching them go. Then he went to find Malina. The King found Malina kneeling in the garden facing the ocean. The King came to Malina, "Am I disturbing you?"

"No my King."

"Are you one who tried to frighten the Queen earlier?"

"No my King. I told her to listen to her heart about you and not the others." "I made the others leave the palace for their badness."

"You are wise as is Queen Blaine, do you wish for me to go also my King?" "Are you loyal to my Queen, Malina?"

"I am, my King."

"May I ask what you are doing Malina?"

"Praying my King, for you and your Queen. And that the ocean will be at peace for Sobbo to return safely."

"Malina, do you have feelings for Sobbo?"

"Yes, my King, but I am not fit for him I just want him to return safely."

King Aviv stood with Malina silently watching the ocean peacefully. Then he turned to leave, "Malina, if you are going to attend the wedding you must get ready."

"Yes my King."

As Tiki helped the Queen ready herself for the weeding, all the people had gathered outside to watch the ceremony. Blaine was very nervous.

Lome asked. "My Blaine, do you love the King?" "Yes Lome I do"

"More than your other man before?"

Blaine thought for a moment then said. "What I felt before was different. It was not real love. Real love is based on friendship and understanding and physical attraction. All I had before was physical attraction and one can't have a happy marriage with only physical attraction."

Lome smiled "I think you and the King will be most happy and have many pretty babies too."

Blaine blushed. "Lome, you surprise me with what comes out of your mouth!" There came a knock at the door Blaine opened it. Israel stood in his fine kingly attire he bowed, "You are more beautiful than the heavens my Queen."

He took her hand and they walked through a procession of people. To a balcony built above very one. In the balcony sat three people, Israel's father Omar, his brother Shri and Samira. Blaine thought it odd that neither Israel's father nor brother had spoken to her since their arrival. She dismissed the thought for Israel began to speak.

"Tonight my people, I introduce your beautiful Queen." Taking Blaine's hand having her rise.

"She is wise and beautiful. She has ordered the completion of the first home and school for homeless children. There will no longer be child labor on this island. My Queens first decree."

"There will no longer be women sold or traded on this island or to be carried on by any ship making its birth at these docks. This is the King and Queens first decree together." "This is a peaceful island and our goal is to maintain that state as long as possible. However, the world around us is changing. Therefore, I am instituting an armed army to be trained. In addition, we are to build more ships. This is only for a precaution. not to cause threat or cause any alarm." now on to happier matters."

"My Queen is Christian. I have ordered our wedding to be blessed by a Christian minister." One of the men seated behind came forward.

"Are you truly of a Christian upbringing my Queen?"

"Yes I am Sir."

"And it be of yer own free will and choice to marry King Israel Aviv?" "Yes it truly is." Blaine smiled at Israel.

The minister looked at Israel, "Do you promise King Israel Aviv to care for Blaine Ewen in sickness and health? And forsaking all other women and sharing your love only with this woman?"

Proudly Israel answered, "Yes I do."

"And do you Blaine Ewen promise to care for this man in sickness and in health, to be in subjection only to him forsaking all others?

Blaine smiled, Yes, I do.

"Then by the Holy Scriptures and all these witnesses, I pronounce you King and Queen, husband and wife. For as long as you both live together on earth."

The minister cleared his throat and said. "King you can kiss your Queen. I think the people are waiting for it."

Israel turned to Blaine and gently kissed her.

All the excited on lookers cheered.

Afterward, there was an elaborate celebration held at the Palace.

Israel finally introduced the people Blaine did not know. Israel stood and said. "my Queen, I would like you to meet my brother, Shri and this is…"

Shri interrupted, "this is Samira my future bride."

Blaine was shocked seeing Samira had been so determined to marry Israel. She could not imagine why she would have changed her mind so quickly.

Israel took Blaine to meet his father. "Father, this is Blaine. Blaine, this is my father, Omar Aviv."

Israel's father was very pleasant, he welcomed Blaine to the family. "I do believe I am your father too now my dear."

However, his brother was not so friendly. When Blaine went to get Israel, something to drink, Shri followed her, he cornered her.

"Woman! If you think forcing my brother to have a Christian marriage ceremony will change who he is you are wrong, if I were ruler here."

Israel walked up at that very moment. "Shri, it is a good thing you are not ruler here.

Now, step away from my Queen before you spend the night in stocks."

Israel took Blaine by the hand, bidding every one goodnight, "Please, everyone, enjoy yourselves. My Queen and I will retire now. Thank you for sharing in our joy. Good night to you all."

The guests were wishing them well, waving and bidding good night to their King and new Queen.

Israel took Blaine upstairs to a different bedchamber. Until this night, this chamber had remained locked at the end of a long hall.

The fire in the large ornate fireplace lit the chamber.

The decor was deep red and gold. Israel directed Blaine to the veranda. "Go, open the window my love."

When Blaine opened the window the ocean breeze rushed in., they were right over the water.

Israel lit a lantern, Blaine viewed chamber, the bed was breath taking, decorated in dark red velvet and gold. The tub area was twice the size of hers.

Blaine walked out onto the veranda, staring at the ocean. Israel came to her with a drink.

Blaine smiled at him and took the drink. "What is this?" "Just fruit juice and something to help you relax a little."

"Oh I see." Blaine took a drink she looked at Israel and said. "I much prefer this to wine.

Wine is nasty stuff, this is good." Blaine drank more.

Israel took the glass from Blaine's hand and started laughing. Blaine, my love, you drink too much you will make yourself loopy."

With seductive look in her eyes, she slid her arms around Israel's neck, "But I thought that's what you wanted."

Israel held her in his arms.

"Blaine my love I have something on the bed for you to change into. Please, change and come to me by the fire.

Lifting up on her toes, she pressed her body close to his playfully rubbing against him. Israel claimed his Queens mouth. Hunger for her consumed him. Now he did not have to stop himself. Now he could explore this beauty for she was his.

He was starving for her flesh, he kissed her mouth the curve of her chin down to her neck. Slowly Blaine let out a soft moan.

"I love your kisses my King." "And I yours, my temptress, now go."

Blaine turned and went into the room lying on the bed, she found a rose-colored sheer silk sift.

She removed her sari and slid the silk over her flesh.

Blaine thought never had any fabric ever felt so stimulating caressing her whole body all at once.

She came to Israel who sat in a sea of pillows in front of the fire.

Her fair body glistening beneath the silken shift. Blaine's body reacted as its own at the sight of Israel sitting in the sea of pillows wearing only white silk pants, with his muscular bronze chest and arms shinning in the fire light.

She felt the heat of excitement rising inside of her.

Israel's voice was deep with desire when he spoke. "Come my love." he held out his hand and brought Blaine to his playground.

"I am with you Blaine, I am guiding you, you have nothing to fear." Blaine looked into Israel's eyes. "I know my …." Gently Israel took her in his arms, softly he traced his lips across the palms of her hands sending a delicious wave of fire thru her body. Working his way up her arm, leaving a trail of heat in the wake of his lips he found her lips. Passionately their lips met, teasing the desire growing between them. Blaine's hands wondered across Israel's bare flesh hungry to explore. His kiss deepend sending Blaine's mind whirling. His hands desperate to pull her closer. He needed her now! Their bodies molded as one as they reached their zenith together their worlds collided, exploding into crystal passion then drifting back to earth intertwined as one.

Israel lifted his wife into his arms carrying her to the bed, they laid there together sleeping in each other's arms.

When Blaine awoke, Israel was not beside her. She donned her silk robe and slippers then went to find him. She did not have to go far, Israel stood on the balcony looking out at the ocean. Blaine quietly came up behind him slipping her arms around his bare waist.

"Good morning my King. You are up early, is something wrong?"

Israel turned holding Blaine in his arms. "No, my love all is well. I woke feeling...the need to wake you but you looked so beautiful sleeping I decided I should let you sleep." Playfully, Blaine rose up wrapping her arms around Israel's neck. "And for what did you have a need?"

Israel's voice was deep with desire, running his hands down her back squeezing her bottom. "For you my love, for all of you."

Blaine kissed her husband slow and seductively. "You can have me my lord...if...you can catch me."

Blaine turned and ran from him, he chased after her. She was laughing, she ran across the bed and the around the tub.

She started taking one piece of clothing off at a time and tossing it at Israel. Israel had not expected love play like this, he was very happy.

First one slipper then the other, next her robe then she dove into the tub. Israel quickly undressed and dove in after her. He grabbed hold of her. Wrapping her arms and legs around him.

"It would seem you have caught me my lord. Now what would you do to me?" Israel laughed, "Blaine Aviv you my breath."

Laying her head on his chest, "Blaine Aviv. I love the way my name sounds. Israel and Blaine Aviv. This is not a dream; we are really married aren't we?"

"Yes, my Queen we are."

"You are intoxicating, you consume me, my love." Blaine felt his passion, surrendering to ecstasy, reaching the crescendo of passion together.

Israel carried Blaine from the tub and laid her on the sea of pillows in front of the fireplace. He closed the window so she would not be chilled. Israel came over her. Blaine reached up pulling him to her. Slowly they made love, drowning in passions sea. Later Blaine awoke to find Israel lying peacefully next to her.

She studied the beautiful man of hers. He was so handsome, dark and muscular. Oh, how she loved his hair. Black like a raven and so soft. Blaine rose up over him kissing her husband. His eyes opened.

"How are you feeling my love?"

Blaine smiled and said. I am very well, my lord." Israel sat up. "I wonder if any food is left, I am hungry." Blaine stretched "me too"

They both put on their robes quietly descending stairs.

Blaine asked. "Is it normal for the King and Queen to have to sneak down stairs of their own palace?"

Israel looked at Blaine with a mischievous smile "well, usually the King and Queen do not leave the bed chamber for several days after their marriage."

"Oh! And I guess we are to live on love?"

Israel smiled and shook his head. "No my love food would be brought, but not until later this morning."

They made it to the kitchen; Blaine made them two big plates of food.

Israel retrieved two glasses and juice without the liquor.

As they, started back to their room Israel's brother came around the corner.

Shri stopped them, with a haughty tone he asked. "Where are you two going?"

Israel did not like the way his brother was looking at his wife.

"Brother, this is my palace and where I maybe going is none of your concern." Shri looked around his older brother leering at Blaine.

"Brother, if you are having a problem with the marital due. I will be more than happy to assist you."

Before Israel could react, a strong voice echoed from behind.

"Shri! How dare you insult your brother, the King, in his own home! Do you have no shame at all! Your stupidity prevents you from becoming King. You must be wise, just and fair. Qualities, you Shri, you refuse to develop.

Now you have brought shame to your father. Go... out of my sight!

Please, Israel, I am sorry, my son, and to you my daughter for Shri's ignorance. For some reason this boy think brute action is wisdom. Please, Israel, do not hold his stupidity tonight against him."

"Father, only for you, I will let his behavior tonight go, but this cannot continue." "I will talk to him my son."

Blaine and Israel went to their chamber. Blaine had a worried look on her face.

Israel turned to her. "What concerns you so my love?"

"Israel, I have seen the look your brother has in the men who sailed with Bogota. They were blood thirsty and crazy. Be careful my love. You see him as your brother, he sees you as an enemy. Israel, I believe he will come after you with all the hate he has inside of him."

"I will be careful, I will watch him."

They ate and cuddled up together. Blaine was very shaken up by Shri and his wild behavior.

Later in the morning Israel rolled toward Blaine, he ran his hands over her stomach. Going to the end of the bed he slowly crawled under the covers starting at her feet, gently Israel began kissing each toe on each foot. Israel kissed the center of Blaine's foot sending incredible chills thru Blaine's body making her giggle. "What are you doing?"

"I am exploring **my** new treasure." trailing kisses from her toes to her lips. Blaine was breathless with the boldness of his touch. Heat pulsing through her body, she could take no more of this passionate torture. Pulling him to her, kissing him deep, boldly touching him, expressing her mounting desire. As one, they reached the precipice of passion, colliding with fire and light. Then descending softly back to earth. Sleeping soundly, together as lovers as husband and wife.

The next day a light knock came at the door awakening Israel, "Who is it?" Omar replied, "It is your father, son."

Israel made sure Blaine was covered. "Come in."

"My sons, forgive my intrusion. But you brother is trying to start an uprising. He has found several men not loyal to you and I believe he will now try to take kingdom from you.

"Thank you, father, I will handle this."

Omar left. Blaine held Israel's arm. "I beg you to please be cautious." Israel kissed Blaine. "I will be careful."

Israel called his men together. He sent out two spies to see how many men his brother had with him.

Blaine decided not to take any chances either she had all the upstairs windows shut and bolted.

After the men left to meet Shri and his men, she had all children and women brought into the palace.

And all outside doors and windows double bolted. Any man left in the palace the Queen had armed all the children were kept in the center away from any window.

Israel rode to the other side of the island to confront his brother.

His two spies had already told Israel about the traps set. The King and his men were able to avoid them.

The King approached his brother Shri. "Brother! What is this that you are doing?" Shri answered. "I will claim what is mine."

"How is what I built with my two hands yours Shri?"

Shri laughed. "You are too soft! You do not know how to be a King. You must be firm.

Subjects must fear their King. Not honor and respect him!"

"Shri, this is not yours to rule! Not now not ever. I ask you to stop this insanity and return with father."

Shri was becoming angrier. "Father is nothing to me, as you are nothing to me. I will not live in your shadow anymore Israel!" if you want me gone you will have to fight. If you have the courage."

Shri turned to his men. "My brother, *the King*, could not even bed his new Queen last night! She will not have that problem once I am King. I doubt she will be able to walk." That was it, Israel had heard enough. He gave the signal for his men to dismount. "Alright, little brother, what will we fight with today, will it be sword or dagger, you choose."

Shri was over confident he chose the dagger.

The two men circled each other, studying each other.

Finally, Shri lunged at Israel.

Israel spun away, not wanting to kill his brother.

Shri had the look of a wild man. He started poking and lunging. Shri was starting to get close to Israel.

Shri jabbed at Israel, he was determined to kill him. Israel grabbed Shri's wrist and flipped him to the ground.

Shri jumped up, he charged Israel, Israel moved quickly. Shri stumbled over a pile of rocks, in his heated rush, he fell taking his own life upon the dagger. King Aviv's men quickly subdued the would be rivals.

Israel fell to his knees next to his brother and cried. King Aviv's men arrested the men not loyal to the King and took them to the stocks.

Israel picked up the lifeless body of his brother, put him on his horse and rode back to the palace.

When Israel and his men reached the palace, they saw it closed up tight.

Israel called out. "My Queen, is all well inside!"

The front gate opened. And all the children ran out. Israel shook his head and thought my wife is truly a Queen. Israel found his father and Samaria, he carried Shri's limp body to them.

Israel knelt before his father holding his brother.

"My father I did all I could to prevent this from happening. And in the end, it was Shri's own dagger that took his life. When in anger he charged at me and fell upon his own dagger. I am sorry father I am sorry to you too Samara."

Samara said nothing she turned and walked back to her bedchamber.

Omar placed his hands on Israel's head.

"My dear son, your brother has been headed for this path for a long time. I wish with all my heart that it could have been someone else to finish it for him.

But now my son, take comfort in your beautiful wife who was willing to save the entire town today by bringing them all here for safety if something had gone wrong. You my son, have found your Queen."

Blaine could see two men and one dead body from where she stood on the staircase. She ran down the stairs as quickly as she could then she realized the man kneeling was her husband. Flooding stream of tears ran down her face she ran to him, kneeling next to him.

"My lord, are you alright?"

Israel looked into Blaine's eyes he could see the love and concern she felt.

Israel noticed she called him lord in front of all the people. He touched her face and answered.

"I am now, my Queen."

Blaine looked down, "Oh, your brother, I am sorry for both of you." she stood and hugged Omar "Please if there is anything I can do for you just ask."

Omar smiled and said. "Please my lady, do not think I did not care about my son. I truly loved him before he turned into the person you met here. His end, as unfortunate as it is, was inevitable. But as what you can do for me, my dear, I want a grandson."

Blaine blushed deeply "I believe, Sir that will be up to the King."

Blaine turned and walked away before the conversation turned even more personal. Israel decided to be cleaned up and then he had a surprise for his bride. But his bride had a surprise for her King first. Israel floated in the tub relaxing all the tension away. Blaine entered the room without a sound slipped out of her sari. She waited for Israel to go under then she entered the water on the far side. She swam up behind him and said in a seductive voice.

"How would my King like to be bathed today?" Israel answered. "What does my lover have in mind?" Blaine came up behind I will wash you my lord."

Then she rubbed soap all over his back. Then she had him lay back against her body while she shampooed his hair and massaged his scalp.

Israel thought he was in heaven. Then she oiled her hands and rubbed his back and chest.

. Israel took the oil pouring down his stomach. Blaine could see in Israel's eyes his desire for her. She grew with desire for him. Once again, they made love in the water slow and beautiful. Blaine let out a cry of ecstasy. The room seemed as if it was spinning. They spun off into ecstasy together.

Clinging to each other holding tight not wanting their passion to end. Once the lovers came back to earth, Blaine asked. "Would you like me to get you a towel my love?"

"I will get out with you I have something important to show you I was going to wait but I think today will be good. So we need to get dresses."

Blaine and Israel got dressed and went down stairs. There were two horses waiting for them. Israel took Blaine for a long ride.

Blaine heard children singing. Blaine looked at Israel "the home and school! You did it!" Blaine dismounted and ran to the school. When the children saw her coming, the all yelled "the Queen! Here is our Queen!" the children ran out to meet her. Along with the teacher. Israel came in behind. Blaine wanted a tour. The schoolhouse was well equipped. However, Blaine was not at all happy with the children's wardrobes or bedding. She promised to be back later that day. Blaine turned to Israel. "Is it alright for me to do this?" Israel smiled and replied. "My love, this is your home for these children you do as you please. I am only here to assist."

Blaine and Israel rode to the mill and market. They bought every blanket, doll, boat and ball the store had.

Then they stopped at the dressmaker and order twenty saris for girls and ten tunics with pants for boys. The dressmaker complained. "You will have those little urchins dressing better than the rest of us."

The King addressed the dressmaker. "My Queen has opened a school for the less fortunate Madam and she will see to it that when they finish they will be a pleasant addition to our community not a blemish."

The King turned and followed his Queen, they returned to the school. The children were overjoyed most had never had a toy of their own.

Blaine turned to Israel with an excited look on her face. "Israel I just had the most wonderful idea."

"Well, my excited beauty what is your idea."

"As an incentive for the children to do well in school and behave why don't we let one new child a week come stay the weekend at the palace with us."

Israel thought for a moment then he replied. "How about once a month one new child can stay with us, because I still have plans on working on mine."

Blaine blushed and agreed to once a month. Blaine stood before the class and described the new incentive program. Moreover, that it would be the one who carried thru for the whole month that would get to come and stay with the King and herself for the weekend. The children loved the idea.

Israel and Blaine rode back to the palace. They decided to eat lunch in the garden.

There they found Malina sitting staring at the sea again.

Blaine went to her and sat down. "Malina, did you tell Sobbo how you felt before he left?"

"No my Queen I did not."

"Do you plan to tell him when he returns?" "I can't my Queen."

"Malina, with all we have been through together you can call me Blaine." Blaine sat tiring to figure out why Malina would not tell Sobbo how deeply she cared for him. "Malina I do not understand if you love Sobbo you should tell him."

"You can't understand because you have never been a slave. You have never been forced to do things that make you feel worthless. You are pure and clean. I am not. You had a beautiful gift to offer the King. I have nothing to offer Sobbo. He would think of me as dirty and used. I know he would want someone more like you."

"Malina, a very dear friend once told me privilege in life is not given to everyone some are smart enough to find it or they work real hard for it. On the other hand, they just happen to be born into it. On the other hand, they marry into it. Malina, you have the same chance my friend gave me. I have taught you how to carry yourself how to speak and how to behave. The other two had the same training but what do you think was the difference?"

"I suppose they just did not want it."

"Exactly, Malina, you have completely changed. Moreover, Sobbo will see that. And do not think that man put his life on the line just for me on that ship he did it for all of us." Malina started to cry. "My Queen, please don't think I wanted any of the ones to be left behind. But, if Sobbo cared for me at all why did he leave me?"

Tears came to Blaine's eyes. "I don't know Malina that will be something to ask Sobbo when he returns." Blaine hugged Malina leaving her to find Israel.

"I am not feeling well, Israel, I want to go lay down." Israel stood up. "My love, why are you crying?"

"Please, Israel, would you take me to our bed chamber."

Israel asked the cook to bring the food upstairs. Israel laid Blaine in bed and asked. "Now, my love, tell me what is wrong."

"Would you have still wanted me if those horrible men had...?" Blaine started to cry again.

"Blaine, my love for you is not founded on the fact you were a virgin. Although it makes me happy knowing I am the only man you have ever made love to. What has brought this up?"

"Malina is in love with Sobbo but she feels she is worthless because she has been a slave and been used. When Sobbo had the chance to save her from those horrible men, he left her there, taking the two little ones and me. She did not want him to leave us. She just thought he would have tried to take her if he cared." Oh, Israel the abuse she must have endured while she was there. I cannot even bring myself to ask her for fear I couldn't bear it."

"What would you like me to do my love?"

"If you could please, speak to Sobbo, even if his feelings are not romantic, he might at least talk to Malina."

"Do not worry my love; I will try to speak to him when he returns. Now come here to me so I can take the worry off your beautiful mind.

Israel made gentle love to Blaine, soft, slow and sweet. His touch like silk his kisses like velvet he moved with a slow passionate rhythm that sent them swirling into another world. Then cradled in each other's arms back in their bed to sleep.

CHAPTER 17

Sobbo's ship was preparing to dock in the New York harbor. He was not sure how difficult convincing Mister Ewen would be.

He hitched up the coach and followed the map. He came to the cabin. There were now people living there. Sobbo had the carriage stop.

He went to the cabin door and knocked.

Aggie opened the door and yelled, "Great merciful heavens! Seth there is a half naked giant at the door!"

Seth came running from the back with an ax in his hand. Sobbo held out his hand to shake.

"Aggie, he might be savage lookin, but, see he's friendly." Seth shook Sobbo's hand. "And he's strong too. What can we do for you Sir?"

"My name Sobbo, I seek Mister Ewen. Can you help Sobbo?" Seth smiled that pearly white smile and said. "You come to the right place, Mister Sobbo; I can take you right to him."

"My name not Sir or Mister just Sobbo."

"Alright, wouldn't want to offend such a large man as yourself so Sobbo it is."

Seth brought his horse around and they were off to the Rossi estate. As they rode Seth, realize he knew Sobbo from the trade ship. He did not mention he recognized this man not sure of the stranger's intent.

They reached the stable.

Seth asked. "Sobbo do you want me to tie your carriage out here?"

Sobbo looked around and said. "Yes maybe horses get to know each other again. You take very good care of them I happy we trade with you."

That let all the wind out of Seth sails he thought for sure they could ambush the big man and find out what happened to Blaine.

Seth took Sobbo in thru the front door, everyone was sitting down for dinner. Seth walked into the dinning room and said. "This is Sobbo he is here in search of Mister Ewen."

Ashton jumped up." I bet you are! You piece of trash what have you done to Blaine?

Sobbo did not move nor say a word.

Seth said. "Ashton, don't make him mad or I don't think we will find out anything." Anna spoke up "Seth is right dear we have waited a long time for something like this by heaven stay calm."

Shamus stood up and had Carlin stand with him.

Shamus said. "I am Mister Ewen and this is my wife Carlin. We are Blaine's parents." A big smile came over Sobbo's face. "Honorable parents of Blaine. I come long way to find Da'. Which one is Da'?"

Shamus scratched his head and said. "Well, that would be me." Sobbo continued. "King say I must bring Da' for my friend Madam Blaine… So please Da' you must come, we have long trip."

Shamus started waving his hands. "Wait a minute a King has Blaine?" "Oh, yes, they are to be married they may be by now."

Carlin and Shamus looked at each other and said, "Married!"

Sobbo said. "Do not worry, my King good King, he take good care of Madam Blaine, she will be Queen."

Anna stepped in and said. "Sobbo, Blaine was engaged to my son Ashton." Sobbo walked up to Ashton and said. "You big horse trader yes?"

Ashton answered. "Yes, I made many trades with your Capitan Bogota." "Capitan Bogota was killed for treason. For buying young redhead from golden hair, your wife."

"No, Sobbo, she pretended to be my wife." "Did golden hair come with you that night?"

"Yes, but I had no idea what her plan was she is a very ill person." "Were this ill person now?"

Carlin spoke up. "She is in prison for the crime she committed against my daughter." Sobbo shook his head and said. "I suppose good justice was done."

Ashton said. "No, it is not! What about Blaine?"

"My friend Blaine is good. I have come to bring her Da' to her. Will you come honorable one?"

Shamus looked at Carlin then he looked at Sobbo. "I must bring my wife." Sobbo said. "The trip is not easy."

Shamus stuck out his chest and said. "We are Irish my big fellow and yer taken us both to our daughter."

Sobbo handed Anna a silk purse, inside was her jewelry she gave Blaine to wear to the Ball and the antique ring. Along with this note. [My dearest friend Anna, oh how I love you. and your lessons I have shared with others. I have found a new life here a happy one. You will never be forgotten. Love always, Blaine.] Anna went to her room to put the jewelry away before anyone asked any questions.

Anna came into the study to find Ashton arguing with his father.

"Son, I just don't think it is a wise thing for you to impose. Let her parents go first then, if the situation needs, you can go." "No, father! I am not going to set by and have Blaine forced into marrying some barbarous King. Who knows what kind of uncivilized person he is. I, for one, plan to be on that ship!" Sobbo came into the study with Shamus and Carlin. Ashton looked at Sobbo.

"Sobbo, you are going to have one more passenger. I plan to go too." "King is not going to be happy, he sent me for Da' Ewen."

That night Sobbo slept outside he did not trust this man Ashton. The next morning the carriage was filled. Anna and Joseph said their good byes then Sobbo, Shamus, Carlin and Ashton were off to the ship. As they approached the ship, Carlin asked. "Does this ship belong to your King Sobbo?"

"Yes Madam Ewen." Sobbo replied.

Sobbo gave Blaine's parents the Captain's quarters. Shamus and Carlin were surprised at the luxury a trade ship held. Their birth had ornate carvings in wood and brass. Both thought it beautiful. Ashton and Sobbo stayed below with the crew.

Things were very different now that Sobbo was Capitan. The men kept themselves clean and the ship clean. The King made sure they were well rewarded for it.

Ashton looked around the ship, he noticed how well kept it was and how all the men spoke highly of Sobbo and this King Aviv.

Ashton had never heard men so loyal to one person.

Ashton wondered how much they had all been paid to sing his praises or maybe he was a good King.

He had read about great commanders and kings but never thought he would hear people talk about one this just made Ashton dislike the man even more. It was going to be a long trip so he had plenty of time to think about it.

Sobbo went to check in on the Ewen's. He knocked. Shamus answered, "Come in." Sobbo asked. "Is all good for you?"

Carlin answered. "Everything is very good." Sobbo smiled. "You sound like Madam Blaine."

Carlin smiled. "You really care for my girl don't you?" "I only have two real friends one is my King the other, Madam Blaine. She is brave and strong. She will fight for others who cannot protect themselves. She has big heart. And much love in her. She special. You should be proud." I leave now so you can rest. Close window so you do not get cold."

"Good night Sobbo."

"Oh Shamus it doesn't sound like our daughter is a little girl anymore."

"Yea and she did not have to get married to grow up. But I am wondering what our girl did have to go thru."

"Well, Shamus dear, she may or may not tell us, it will be up to her." Finally, Shamus and Carlin were rocked to sleep by the rhythm of the ocean.

The next morning Sobbo came to their door. "Please stay inside today. Weather will be bad."

With that, Sobbo hurried away. Ashton did not receive the same comfort. "Mister Ashton we face a storm will you help on deck?"

Sobbo knew he could make no demands on this unwelcome guest. Ashton did not want to be out in a storm but he would not look weak in front of King Aviv's man.

"Of course I will help, just show me what to do."

Ashton tied off riggings, lowered sails, battled waves. He had to fight he storm with the rest of the men.

He could not believe what went into keeping a ship going. And by the end of the storm, he was completely worn out. But what amazed him was the other men; they were jolly, singing and ready to eat. The crew acted as if nothing had happened.

Ashton asked Sobbo, "How do they do it? How do they fight a storm that could take their lives and then turn and celebrate?"

Sobbo patted Ashton on the back. "They celebrate that the sea let them live this day. Now, come let us eat." The men ate their fill Sobbo made sure Blaine's parents had food brought to them. Then everyone slept for the sea was calm again. They had now been on the ocean nearly three months.

Shamus went to Sobbo. "Sobbo please how much longer?"

"The sea and wind have been good to us. We will port early. Maybe Two full moons if weather holds."

"Thank you, so much Sobbo we can't tell you how much this means to us."

Shamus went back to the room to tell Carlin.

Ashton was getting anxious himself he wanted off this ship. He felt like he was being treated like a slave. He needed to vent, he went to complain to Shamus and Carlin. He knocked on the door. Carlin answered. "Come in."

Ashton came in looking like a whipped puppy. "My heavens, Ashton, what has happened to you?"

"Carlin, I came on this trip to help find Blaine and bring her home. Not to swab decks and tie in lines in the middle of a hurricane! I could have been blown overboard last night. Now I am so sore I can barely walk."

"Son, did Sobbo make you go above with the others?"

"Well, not exactly. But he puts me down there with the men who have been doing this all their life. I did not want to look foolish or cowardly by not helping. I am sure Sobbo knew that."

"Seems to me lad you have been doing a lot of assuming. Without askin Sobbo himself. Now, if you would rather stay here with me and Carlin until the soreness goes away you are welcome. And those men wont have any idea where ya gone to."

Before Shamus said another word. Carlin was covering Ashton with a blanket and he was fast asleep.

Five months had past, Israel had become slightly distracted with the new fleet and army he was putting together. Blaine was right by his most of the time and even offering some ideas. One day Blaine decided, spend her time at the school. She visited the dressmaker to make sure the clothing she ordered were being readied. When the dressmaker had several, finished Blaine took them to her children at their new home. The children were in awe. None of them had ever had such nice things. Malina had joined the staff and now taught English in the school, Malina loved being with the children. Blaine also bought more toys for the kids. Once Blaine delivered the clothing and toys, she left the school. She decided to go by the beach. Blaine sat in the warm sand enjoying the ocean for some time.

Israel raced up the beach like a wild man jumping off his horse and grabbed Blaine, he was angry. "Do not ever do that to me again!"

Blaine was confused and upset Israel had never acted like this before. "Israel what have I done?"

"You know better than to disappear and not tell anyone where you are going. Anything could happen to you. Get on this horse we are going home!"

Blaine got on the horse with Israel but her temper was building. How dare this man come and scold her as if she were a five year old. As if, she had no brain in her head. When they returned to the palace, Israel went to help Blaine down.

She jumped down by herself. Marched into the palace, up the stairs and slammed the door of their bedchamber everyone in the palace turned to look at the King.

Therefore, he marched into the palace up the stairs and closed the door behind him.

Blaine was in a royal Irish fit. She was pacing the floor trying to figure out what to say to the three-headed mule she married.

"Blaine, I know you are upset."

Blaine swung her head around and her eyes were greener than Israel had ever seen them. "I am not upset Israel Aviv, I am livid! You come riding up yelling at me as if I am some idle minded child. Do not ever scold me like that again! I am your wife Israel, not a slave, not someone to be talked down too. You made me feel like dirt. Why? Did it make you feel good?"

Israel was trying hard to stay calm. "Blaine, one minute you were with me. You said you had something to do for the school. I expected you to come back to me. When you did not, I became afraid. I started looking for you, I looked for two hours then I found you at the beach."

Israel came up and grabbed Blaine in a very possessive hold. "You are mine woman and I protect what is mine. You made me angry today by not telling me where you would be." He held her even tighter. "I did not mean to insult you or make you feel belittled because you are the most important person in the world to me."

Israel looked into Blaine's deep flashing green eyes and could tell she was not over her anger... yet. Therefore, he thought 'let us use this in a good way.'

Israel twisted his hands in Blaine's hair and claimed her mouth with his.

At first, she tried with all her might not to respond. he kissed her deeper, harder forcing her lips apart for his pleasure. Blaine could not resist his ardor; she willingly parted her lips drawing him deeper. Israel was surprised at her willingness. He swooped her up into his arms tossing Blaine on the bed. Pulling him to her tearing at his clothing not wanting anything between them... once their passion had been spent Israel kissed Blaine lightly moving to dress Blaine reached for him. "Please don't go."

"I have to my love; I have many things to attend to. You rest. I will be back soon." Blaine curled up on Israel's side of the bed falling into a deep sleep.

Israel dressed and went to meet his general of the guards. Israel was gone for several hours. When he returned, He asked Lome. "Where is Blaine?" "My lord I don't think my Blaine is well. She has been asleep since you left. I checked on her several times but she was always sleeping."

"Thank you Lome. I will go and see to her now."

Israel went up to their chamber Blaine was just waking up. Blaine smiled. "You were not gone very long." Israel had a very concerned look on his face.

"My love, I have been gone for hours. You have been asleep the entire time. I am concerned. I want the doctor to see you right away."

"Israel, do not be silly I just slept a long time that's all. I do not need a doctor." Israel was still very concerned. "Blaine, if anything out of the ordinary happens you will see the doctor. Do you agree?"

"Yes, my King, I agree." Blaine wrapped her arms around him and kissed him passionately.

Then a knock at the door and a small voice. "My lord, its Lome, is my Blaine alright?" Israel answered. "Come in little one and see for yourself." Lome opened the door. Seeing Blaine sitting up in bed she ran and jumped in bed with her and hugged her tight.

"Oh, my Blaine I thought you were sick. You slept so long. I was worried." "Lome, honey, I am fine. I was obviously very tired. Our King has kept me very busy." Israel looked at Blaine with a surprised look. After Lome left, Israel smacked Blaine's bottom as she climbed out of bed.

"Ouch! What was that for?"

"For referring to our love play in front of Lome. I should spank you again!" "Only if you can catch me your lordship."

"Blaine you are a little imp."

Blaine ran from Israel giggling the whole time. He chased her around the bed, then over it. Around the tub and back around the tub.

Then Israel diapered. Blaine crept around trying not to giggle. "Israel where are you?" He did not make a sound. Blaine looked under the bed he was not there. She looked in the tub he was not in the water.

"Israel, please, I don't like this, where are you?" she walked past her vanity and opened the closet suddenly Israel grabbed her!

Blaine screamed. Not a scream of play but on of sheer fright, she fainted in Israel's arms.

Israel was ashamed of himself for frightening her so badly.

He carried her to the bed. He ran to the door. His father was downstairs. "Father, please send a runner to get the doctor, Blaine has fainted.

Omar did so right away. The doctor was there in less than half an hour. By this time, Blaine had come to and insisted she was fine. Nevertheless, under Israel's insistence, Blaine agreed to see the doctor.

Israel did not like the fact the doctor told him to leave the room. However, he listened and went downstairs with his father.

Omar put his arm around his son. "I have never seen a man love a woman the way you love her. And if it is true that love concurs all, you have nothing to worry about."

"Father that scream, I cannot imagine the terror she went thru." "Son, if she has not told you about it she probably cannot. Just don't go popping out of closets anymore." "I can promise I won't try to scare her ever again. What is taking so long?"

"Son, be calm, it really has not been that long."

A few minutes later, the door open and the doctor came down stairs. The doctor bowed to the King.

"King Aviv, the Queen is fine she just needs rest. In addition, please, your lordship no more hide and seek. And I do believe you should go speak with the Queen she said she had something she wanted to tell you."

The doctor left Israel looked at his father. "Go on son."

Israel went upstairs thinking Blaine was going to scream at him for doing such a foolish thing to her.

He opened the door. Blaine was still in bed. "Are you alright my love?"

"Yes, Israel I am fine. Come here and sit with me." Israel sat beside Blaine.

"Please forgive me, Blaine, I didn't mean to frighten you so badly."

Israel took her in his arms holding her tight Blaine ran her hands thru his black hair and rub her face against his.

"I am not upset with you Israel. But I do have to tell you something." Israel looked into Blaine's beaming emerald eyes.

"What is it my love?"

Blaine took Israel's hands placed them on her stomach.

"You're going to be a father, Israel." Israel's heart caught in his throat. He could not speak.

He started to cry. He lifted Blaine's gown and look at her stomach.

He touched it and rubbed it he bent and kissed the safe haven of his unborn child.

Then he kissed the mother of his child.

He knew he loved Blaine. At that moment, something came over him. That depend his love for her. He realized he not only loved her he cherished her. She was not only his wife, friend, and lover she was now the mother of his child. She was his Queen in every way.

"Are you hungry my love?" "Yes, Israel, I am."

"Do you want me to bring your food to you here?" "No, actually I think I would like to eat in the garden." They went to the garden. dining at their special table. "Israel, I wonder when the ship will be arriving?"

Israel had mixed emotions about her father coming he had tried to keep them hid from Blaine.

"The weather has been good. And Sobbo had a light load. I would think the ship should be here in the next month."

"Oh, Israel, this is so exciting my Da' is coming to meet the man I love and to find out he's going to be a papa."

"My love, do not be disappointed if your father is less than happy to meet me. And don't be surprised if he at first tries to talk you in to going back with him."

"Why would he do that, once he sees how happy we are together?"

"I am sure your father may think I took you from him even if Sobbo explained what really happened. If you were my daughter I would believe, only someone stole you from me. I would be angry."

"Israel, why did you want him to come?"

"To see with his own eye's I am no thief. That I love you. That you are honored as my Queen."

Blaine came to Israel's side she could see the worry in his eyes.

"Israel, my Da' is a good man, sometimes short tempered, but a good man. I know if we give him enough time he will see the truth."

Sobbo spent much of the time with Shamus and Carlin.

"I like you Mister Ewen you funny man. Shamus would sing Sobbo Irish songs and do his dances. Most of the ones Blaine loved.

Sobbo told the Irish fairy tale, Blaine told to the little ones at night. Sobbo would listen at the door.

Carlin asked. "Sobbo, where did you learn that story?"

"Madam Blaine, she told it to the little ones every night. I guard Madam Blaine's door so I learn story."

Shamus asked. "Why, may I ask, were you guarding Blaine's door?"

"I protect Madam Blaine, she my friend, no one will hurt her so I guard door." Carlin was relieved.

"Oh, I see so Blaine could go out, but you made sure no one went in right?" "Only one go in is King."

Carlin and Shamus held each other's hand imagining this rouge of a King taking advantage of their daughter. Ashton was having the same thoughts.

Sobbo continued talking about Blaine. "Madam Blaine she strong.'

"When first in palace King had all doors locked. Madam Blaine climbs out window and climb right in Kings window. Want to know why her door locked. King not know what to say. Madam Blaine was a mess she still wore gown from six moons ago had no real bath in all that time.

She tell King she not going to be no used woman for the King. The King promised she be safe. No one harm her, King protect her. I guard door make sure."

Ashton spoke up. "So you mean the King has not used Blaine as you said." "King Aviv honorable man. He never do harm to a woman."

Ashton replied. "What about Bogota? Doesn't he work for the King? He is not honorable he buys and sells women."

"Bogotá bad man! Go against King. King says no buy and sells women against the law. Bogota does anyway. King gives Bogota chance to leave Kings Island forever. Bogota tried to kill King. Sobbo kill Bogota. Justice was done.

King was hurt bad. Madam Blaine took care of him did not want anyone else to touch him. Madam Blaine strong she saved Kings life."

Carlin asked. "Sobbo, did Blaine want the King to live?" "Yes, she never left his side. I believe them one now." "One, in what way?"

"When you save a person's life the two are connected forever. The King and Madam Blaine have a special connection you see." After that, Sobbo left for the night.

Ashton turned to Shamus. "It's too bad old Bogota missed his mark."

"Ashton, I am tended to believe Sobbo there more here than we know. So let's not jump to conclusions."

"Shamus, please, tell me you're not going to fall for his special connection story." "Ashton, I don't *fall* for much of anything but there are on occasion things I believe. Now, I am tired and I am going to sleep."

Carlin spoke up. "Shamus is right, Ashton, we will just have to wait until we get there.

Now please get some sleep."

The next morning Carlin decided to have a talk alone with Sobbo. "Sobbo I would like to speak with you alone please."

"Yes Madam Carlin."

"Sobbo, you say you are Blaine's friend?"

Sobbo smiled. "Yes, Madam Carlin, we both are friend to each other."

"Good, then I need you to tell me please, the relationship between Blaine and King Aviv is theirs like yours and Blaine's or is it different?"

"Sobbo, never have what they have, Madam Carlin, they like the wind and the sea. One cannot be without the other. Do you believe in sole mates Madam Carlin?"

"Do you mean two people that just fit together so well it was as if they were made for each other?"

"No, when to people are so connected, it reaches all the way to the soul of the two people and they are one."

"Oh, Sobbo, that is beautiful. Is that how you see Blaine and the King?" "Yes, Madam, I only hope to find love like that someday."

"Sobbo, I am sure you will you are a very good man too. You deserve a woman who loves you."

"You honor me Madam Carlin." Carlin went off to find Shamus.

Sobbo stayed looking over the side wondering if any woman would ever love a man like him.

Time had passed quickly. Finally, they could see the island. Excitement was growing in anticipation of their arrival.

A runner came to the palace to alert the King and Queen of the ships arrival.

Blaine was now seven along but with the sari, she wore, no one would notice. She picked one of gold silk. Israel wore his Kingly silk red robe with a gold silk shirt and black silk pants.

At first, they thought to go to the dock but there being so much trouble down at the docks Israel decided to send a carriage for them. Blaine had Malina wait with them Blaine had Malina wear a purple sari, knowing purple to be Sobbo's favorite color. Sobbo escorted the Ewen's and Ashton into the palace carriage and whisked them away from the docks.

Within twenty minutes, they were at the palace gate. They were escorted out of the carriage and in thru the grand palace gates. As they walked into the palace, Blaine could not believe her eye's there stood her Mama and her Da'! She hugged Israel and ran down the stairs.

"Mama, Da'! I cannot believe it you are really here!"

Blaine grabbed both of them hugging and kissing. Israel stood back and watched his wife glow.

Then he noticed another man standing next to Sobbo. This man was watching him with a glare in his eye. Israel was determined to find out who he was. In addition, what seemed to be his problem?

Israel motioned to Sobbo to bring their new houseguest over.

Sobbo escorted Ashton over to King Aviv. Sobbo reluctantly introduced the two men. "Mister Ashton Rossi this is King Aviv."

Ashton kept his manners and bowed to the King, "King Aviv you have a beautiful place here."

"Thank you Mister Rossi. Your name rings a bell. Ah! Horses. Do you still deal in horses Mister Rossi?"

"Yes, your Highness that is our family business."

"Please, excuse me, your highness I would like to see Blaine."

Ashton walked toward Blaine. Israel turned to Sobbo. "What has happened my friend?

Of course, I do not mind her mother, but him? How did this happen?"

"My King, I tried to stop him. He thought you were hiding something I do not know. The man makes me crazy. He makes no since. He insisted to come."

Blaine turned to call Israel over and came face to face with Ashton Rossi. Blaine's demeanor changed quietly she asked. "Ashton, what are you doing here?" "Blaine, I came to see you."

"Well, now you've seen me you can leave."

She turned back to her parents, "I am really tired if you don't mind I need to go lay down.

Malina will show you where your rooms are. Israel, could you please help me." Israel took Blaine to their bedchamber. As soon as the door closed, she fell apart. She cried so hard she had no more tears left.

Finally, Israel asked his most feared question. "Blaine, do you still love this man? Blaine did not have time to answer there was a knock at the door Israel opened and there was Malina crying. Blaine asked if she could talk to Malina alone.

Israel left closing the door. Blaine put her arms around her. "Malina, what has happened?"

"I was going to talk to Sobbo like you told me. After I showed the guests their rooms. When I showed Mister Rossi his room. He asked me to come in; he said he wanted to ask a few questions. Then he asked if there were any other women like me, here in the palace. I told him I did not know what he meant. That I lived here and worked at the school. He acted like the others Blaine."

"Malina, did he touch you or try to touch you?"

"No, my Queen, he just wanted to know if I was kept for the King." Malina started crying again.

"Oh, my dear Malina, that man is not a smart man. You stay away from him. If he even comes close to you, you run to Sobbo. And if Sobbo is not, there you run to the King or myself do you understand. Malina, do not even speak to him and do not be alone with him. Now, let us go find Sobbo so you can talk. I will help you."

Sobbo was down stairs with Ashton.

"Excuse me, please, but we need Sobbo for a moment." Blaine never paid any attention to Ashton.

Blaine took both Sobbo and Malina to the garden she had Malina sit at the table.

She took Sobbo to the spot Malina watched for him every day.

"Sobbo, my friend, there is something you should know. Malina sat in this very spot every day, even in the rain and prayed for your safe return. Malina did not want you to know because she is ashamed of her past. She feels you could never love a woman who has been a slave. Is that true, Sobbo, could you not love someone because of their past?"

"No, my Queen, I have a past too. But, Malina is a beautiful woman. Look at me. Why would she want me?"

"You are not like other men Sobbo. You are caring, protective, sweet, Malina has felt insecure her whole life, used and unloved. You have a big heart full of love Sobbo. Go talk to her, It will not hurt to talk to her."

"Yes, my Queen." Sobbo went and sat with Malina. Blaine went back inside. She came in smiling.

Israel was coming toward her. "Who were you with out there with?" Blaine smiled even bigger. And she whispered "Sobbo and Malina."

"I thought you wanted me to speak to Sobbo. You were to be upstairs resting."

"I was but wouldn't it be wonderful if they were married too." "Israel smiled, "yes, my love, it would be."

Blaine's stomach protested loudly letting her know she needed to eat soon "Israel, do you think it is too late to ask the cook to fix that wonderful fish of his. I really want some."

"My Queen, I thought you hated the head and tail business." "Well, you can pick the fish off for me, right?"

Israel laughed, "Yes I can. I will go speak to the cook."

Blaine went looking for her parents hoping to find them in their chamber, she knocked, Carlin opened the door "well hello dear we were just talking about you." Blaine hugged her Mama, "Why, are you two sitting here, there is so much to see. Carlin and Shamus got up and went with Blaine. Blaine met up with Israel.

"Oh Israel please come with us I want to show my parent the garden and the beach." "I would be honored to come with you." Carlin asked "Blaine, dear don't you think we should ask Ashton to go?"

."No, Mama, I do not. He can find his own way around."

Shamus put his arm around Blaine's shoulders "But, darlin, he did take this trip to see you that's all your Mama meant."

"I appreciate that you are trying to be nice. But I am not ready to be nice." "Blaine, you listen to your Da'. You are just not given the man a chance to say his peace."

"Da' I do respect you but I do not give a toads behind about his peace." Israel came up to Blaine taking her arm gently. "Blaine, my love I agree with your parents we should include Ashton in our walk."

"But Israel I am."

Israel placed his fingers to her lips. "My love, have I ever let harm come to you?" "No."

"Then trust me now." "Alright my love. I trust you."

Blaine's parent listened to the conversation and they were amazed at King Aviv's ability to reason with Blaine without argument.

King Aviv offered. "I will go and invite Mister Rossi to come with us." Israel went to Ashton's room. He knocked. Ashton answered. "Who is it?"

"It is King Aviv, I am sorry to disturb you but there is a small group of us taking a tour of the palace gardens and the beach. The Queen and I thought you might enjoy coming along."

Ashton swung open the door. "The Queen and you?" are you referring to Blaine as your Queen!"

"Yes Mister Rossi I am, because she is my Queen. Now, I know your journey was hard but if you would care to come with us you are welcome."

"Yes, King Aviv, I do believe a walk would do me good." "Fine, Sir follows me."

They met the others out in the garden. Israel came and took Blaine's arm they were giggling and talking together. Blaine finally stepped back with her parents.

"These are the most beautiful flowers I have ever seen or smelt." Blaine stopped to pick an arm full for her Mama's room when they came to a bell; Blaine rang it and out ran a happy young man.

"Please, take these to Madam Ewen's room and make sure they have a proper amount of water."

The young man bowed, "Yes my Queen."

Carlin caught what the young man said. "Blaine have you and the King married?" Blaine was Quiet for a moment because she did not want to hurt her parents. "Yes Mama, Israel is my husband and I love him every much."

"But darlin, you were engaged to Ashton."

This was finally it. She let the others go ahead. Blaine asked her Mama to sit in the grass with her.

"Mama, I don't know what Ashton told you. But I know what I heard and witnessed that night in the stable. Ashton was rolling around half-naked with Roslyn. Ashton had scratches all over his back. Roslyn was telling him how she wanted to be his love slave and how I would never have to know. I know they would have done exactly what they were out there for if I had not walked in to give him the good news about us being able to get married anytime we wanted. The problem with Ashton, Mama, is he did not want to be married he wanted sex. And he found an easier way to get it, Roslyn. And I have been through the closest thing to hell to get here and there is nothing that man can say that can make up for what he has done or what I have had to go thru because of him. I am tired, please; tell Israel I went to our room."

Blaine turned and went into the palace up to her chamber to lie down. Later a knock came at the door Israel entered.

He woke her with a kiss Blaine wrapped her arms around Israel only to realize this was not Israel!

She tried to push the intruder away but he would not let her go. She was finally able to kick him and he stumbled back.

Blaine screamed for Sobbo he came running with a lantern. Standing beside the bed was Ashton. Sobbo was angry.

Blaine calmed him and asked. "Where is my King?" "King Aviv is out with the general, my Queen."

"Sobbo, my friend, this did not happen. If Israel hears of this he will have Ashton killed." "Ashton, do not ever! I mean ever! Come anywhere near my bedchamber again! Because if there is a next time I will not stop Sobbo! "Now, Ashton, please go back to your room.

Sobbo stayed. "Thank you my friend for coming so quickly."

"My Queen, why do you want to hide this from your King? This is bad what he has done."

"Sobbo I don't think he meant to harm me."

"My Queen, I should tell you something. When I arrived to get honorable Da' Ewen I was angry when I saw Mister Rossi. The golden hair who sold you to Bogota said she his wife. I was thinking he in trade of you to. But Sobbo was wrong girl tricked him too. When they find out who responsible for you being lost your honorable

Mama and Mister Rossi go find golden hair girl. They trick her to tell truth now she in prison. Mister Rossi thinks you go back with him and leave King and all your people."

Blaine was stunned at all the news but especially that Ashton would think she would go back to him.

"Sobbo, see if you can find my Da' and bring him to me." Sobbo was back in a few moments with Blaine's Da'. Shamus came in and sat next to his girl.

"Da' do I look happy to you?" "Actually, my girl, you look very happy."

"And now that we are alone wouldn't I tell you if something is wrong here with Israel?" "I know ya would darlin. What are you getting at girl?" "Da' I am Israel's Queen. We married over seven months ago."

"Please, child, was there and Christian minister?" "Yes, Da' Israel made sure we had one."

"Do you love him?"

"More than the heavens love the stars, Da'." "Pardon me for bringing this up but what about Ashton."

"My love for Ashton died the night I was taken. Please, ask mama to tell you what happened. My love for Israel goes far beyond anything I felt for Ashton. I just have to calm Ashton down enough to talk to him."

"We'll not worry about that tonight you go on to bed. We can talk more in the morning." Shamus went back to his room. He sat down and asked Carlin to repeat the story Blaine had told to her.

"It seems Ashton sure knows how to cover his behind now doesn't he. He might as well have been in the thick of the plot the entire time. Then for him to say he was passed out drunk and she come in takin advantage of him and all long he was playin out of the two sides of his face. Carlin, my dear, I've been drunk many a time, but never, would I even look at any woman let alone lay my hands on her unless her name was Carlin Ewen and she was as beautiful as you."

"Shamus, no wonder Blaine can't stand the sight of him. She wants him gone. And I am sure her husband cannot wait for him to leave either."

They turned out their lantern and went to sleep.

Israel came in quietly undressed and cuddled up with Blaine. She wiggled and moved herself into the safety of his arms. They slept peacefully; Israel's hand cradled around Blaine's stomach.

The next morning Israel asked. "Have you told your parents our good news?" "I plan to tell them this morning."

"You better because I have a surprise planed for everyone in the garden tonight." "What kind of surprise?"

"If I told you it wouldn't be a surprise." Israel kissed Blaine. "Just tell them and I will be back soon." Blaine was getting dressed and noticed her stomach was showing thru she added another layer of silk to cover it a little better.

She went down stairs.

The cook came out and asked. "My Queen, when would you like the fish served?"

"I think tonight at the surprise the King is giving. Has he spoken to you about a menu?" "I am sorry my Queen he did not." "Well we can keep it simple." Blaine went on to give the cook some ideas and left the rest to him, which she knew he loved. She left the kitchen to find her parents.

They were sitting in the sunroom with Omar. As Blaine entered Omar brought his attention to her, "You are a vision of light today my dear."

Blaine took a seat next to her Mama picked up her Mama's hand and placed it on her stomach.

Carlin's eyes widened. "Blaine is that a baby I feel moving!" Blaine's face lit up. "Yes Mama, Israel and I are going to have a baby." Shamus was stunned again. "I am going to be a papa!"

Carlin grabbed Shamus's hand. "Come here papa before the wee one stops moving." Shamus was able to feel his grandchild move for the first time. He was overjoyed. "Omar have you felt this! Come over here this is your grandchild too."

Omar felt the small movement of his first grandchild too. He leaned over and kissed Blaine. "You truly are the Queen.

Blaine had tears in her eyes. She did not expect such an over whelming acceptance of her and Israel and their baby to come.

That night was a beautiful gala in their garden Blaine even talked her mother into wearing a sari. Carlin was beautiful.

Blaine noticed Malina and Sobbo came together.

All their friends were there.

The cook out did himself. He truly made a banquet fit for a King and everything was so nice. King Aviv had the Champaign poured and said.

"This night my Queen and I make an official announcement we are having a baby. Due to come, according to the doctor, in about three months. This celebration is for our baby, our love and for the safe arrival of my Queen's parents." Everyone applauded. Then the most amazing thing.

Israel had every one line up at the waterfront.

Then the sky lit up with the most amazing colors. Loud booms and more colors. "Israel, it looks like the stars have fallen from heaven. What is it?" "It is call fireworks." "Oh my love this is beautiful."

"As you are my Queen."

Blaine wrapped herself in Israel's arms.

Her parents were happy because they were sure of this man's devotion to their daughter.

Moreover, both felt Sobbo's words on the ship were right. Somehow, Ashton would have to move on and leave Blaine in her happy life. The fireworks lasted twenty minutes. Then the cook came out and proudly announcing, "Dinner is served."

Israel looked at Blaine. "Did you do this part?" "Well me and the cook."

Everyone entered the room. It was set up in crystal and gold. Everything was buffet style and the cook had small tables and chairs for the people to sit.

Blaine walked up to the cook. "You, Sir, are amazing, I consider you a chef not a cook." "Oh, thank you, my Queen."

After that, the chef was beaming all night. The food was excellent and Israel made sure Blaine got her fish. Everyone had a fabulous time. Shamus leaned over to

Carlin. "You see the way he cares for her." "Yes, darlin, I have, and did you notice who deliberately refused to come to the party?" "Yes, Carlin love, I noticed. Seein he was not invited to start with; you would think he would act as if he has some manners."

"Carlin, I think I'd like to get to know my son in-law a little better." Shamus walked up to Blaine and Israel.

"Blaine, honey, your Mama would like a word with you. And if you don't mind I would like to get to know you better son."

"I would enjoy this very much." "Where are you from originally?"

"I was born in a small country in the middle east. I left and took to the sea at sixteen. I love the sea but the men were wicked. So at twenty I went home. My father purchased this island and told me if I could clean it up brings order upon it I would be King here. Then last year my father tells me I must find a Queen and produce a hire before I am thirty."

"How old are you?"

"I am twenty-seven. Until now, I had not met a woman I wished to be my Queen then I meet Blaine. She is strong and full of life. She is not afraid to stand up when she thinks others are being treated badly. She has an amazing mind. Did you know she took a traitors home and turned it into a school and home for the homeless children on the island? She made her first decree that child labor was illegal. Our first decree together was no person would be bought or sold on this island. And no ship with that purpose will be allowed to birth here."

"I have known Blaine was a special person all her life, she is all that you say and more son. What about your religious beliefs, how will the child be brought up.

Israel smiled. "I believe in the Bible and so does my man Sobbo. We are not immoral men nor are we cruel men. I believe the peace the Bible teaches. Unfortunately, others do not. Therefore, we have to protect our home and the ones we love. Sobbo bought Blaine a Bible while she was on the ship. She taught the other girls how to read from it." "How many girls were there?"

"Nine is the number Blaine gave me." "What happened to them?"

"The journey was a difficult one, three died. I want to tell you I had not given the command to my captain for the taking of women. He has been punished for his crimes. One young woman was sold before captain Bogota was brought to justice. Bogota would have destroyed them. Sobbo saved three lives by carrying them off the ship here to the safety of the palace. The other women had been slaves for some time. Though Sobbo did not want to leave them, he had no choice. We went back later and saved them. Sobbo gave Bogota justice."

"Yes, I know Sobbo told us about the justice." "May, I call you Israel?" Israel smiled. "Yes please."

"You have a beautiful place here. Carlin and I love it."

"Then, please, do not leave. Stay here as our family. Be with Blaine, me, my father and our new baby."

"Israel, that is very generous, I will talk it over with my wife and we will let you know. Please, do not say anything to Blaine. If we decide to stay we will want to surprise her." "That will be fine."

All retired to their places of rest, the gates were locked and everyone was safe asleep in their Bedchambers. The next morning the guards opened the gate. There laid Ashton pasted out against the palace doors. One of the guards recognized him and brought him in.

King Aviv was just coming down the stairs when the guard dragging Ashton in. "Guard who is that you are dragging in?"

"My lord, it is Mister Rossi. We found him past out against the palace doors." Blaine heard the commotion and came to see what happened.

"Oh, my heavens, Israel, what happened to him?"

Israel looked at Blaine, he was worried about her concern for this man and the fact she never answered his question about her feelings for Mister Rossi. The guard asked. "My King, what should we do with him?"

"For now take him to his chamber."

"Israel he may be hurt or sick shouldn't someone check on him?" "Are you volunteering my love?"

"Israel I don't really want to."

"But you will to make sure your old friend is alright."

"Thank you for understanding." Blaine kissed Israel and went down to Ashton's room. To make sure there would be no reason for talk she placed a chair to prop open the door. Ashton lay moaning in his bed. He was dirty and reeked of rum. This made Blaine's stomach turn.

She called two guards to come, take him to the general bath, and redress him in clean clothes. When they brought him back, the one guard told Blaine Ashton's ribs had been badly bruised possibly broken. Blaine wrapped his ribs tightly.

When he finally came to, he smiled. There was Blaine sitting in a chair taking care of him.

"You are my angel of light Blaine Ewen."

"Good you're awake now. You best not move. Looks like whatever trouble you got into last night you took a beating on your ribs. They are badly bruised Ashton and may even be broken. Therefore, I suggest you stay in bed. I'll have someone bring you some food."

"Blaine, I need to talk to you. I came all this way to talk to you."

"Ashton, I know you did. I know that day is coming but it will not be today not until you are feeling better." Blaine stood up moved the chair letting the door close behind her as she left.

She wanted so badly to take a bath where no one could find her. Blaine went to her old bedchamber and opened the window filled the tub with bubbles and splashed and played by herself. When she was done, she laid out a towel in front of the window were the sun was glowing intensely warm and she laid there naked, her and her belly basking in the sun. Blaine's red hair spread out like fire her white skin glowing like flawless silk in the sun. She looked like a work of art.

Israel had been looking for her. Knowing she would not have spent that much time with Mister Rossi. However, he was unable to find her any place else so he knocked on Ashton's door.

"Who is it?"

"It is King Aviv, may I come in?"

"Yes please come in." Israel came in and looked around the room. Ashton knew right away that the King was not so comfortable with him.

"If you are looking for Blaine she just left." "Was my Queen here with you the entire time?"

"Blaine is a very good nurse. She got me all cleaned up wrapped my broken ribs and sat here with me for some time. She even got me these nice clean clothes to wear. She is something."

"Yes *my wife* is a good person. Now if you will please excuse me I must find her." Israel was not mad he was hurt. For Blaine had done the same things for him when he was injured. Moreover, it was out of her love for him that she did this. Israel could see the light coming out from under Blaine's old bedchamber. He thought, maybe she had gone into her old chamber to think the door was locked. King Aviv unlocked the door, when he opened the door and walked toward the window he saw the vision beautiful red hair in a spray of fire glowing in the sun. A perfect silken white body with her arm cradling her growing belly protectively as she slept soundly in the warmth of the suns glowing heat.

Israel pulled the covers back on the bed. He went and gently lifted his wifely work of art carefully placing her in the bed. Israel took off his shirt holding her in his arms they slept. Israel awoke to his wife kissing his chest. Caressing his arms then she kisses his face brushing her lips over his. Israel pretended to be a sleep. Seductively her tongue played over his lips. Blaine was amazed at how handsome and how wonderfully made her husband was. She kept caressing him and kissing him. Israel could take no more of love's torture. He took his wife passionately. They felt the world would explode, at their climax Blaine yelled Israel's name then fell into his arms.

Israel asked. "My love, did I hurt you?"

All Blaine had the energy to say was. "No, I love you Israel." and she was asleep. Cling to the man she loved.

Two months had past.

That night at dinner, Sobbo made an announcement.

"I would like to tell my friends. Malina wants to marry Sobbo!" Everyone was so excited.

Blaine asked. "When Sobbo, when are you getting married?" Sobbo looked at Malina. Malina spoke. "We wanted to ask you and the King if we could have our wedding here in the garden."

Israel said to Blaine. "We should have the wedding this weekend." "My love that is only five days away."

"That is plenty of time; we did ours in one day."

"I know Israel but shouldn't we ask them if that is alright?"

"Yes my love I'll ask" Sobbo and Malina do you have any objection to being married in the palace garden this weekend if everything is cared for?"

The two lovers looked at each other and said. "Thank you my King!"

King Aviv stood. "Please everyone I have an announcement. We will be having a wedding in the palace garden this weekend! My man Sobbo will wed the beautiful Malina! Everyone is welcome."

Several days had past and the wedding was getting close. Carlin and Blaine were having a time helping Malina prepare.

The dressmaker was preparing a white sari trimmed in dark purple.

Blaine no longer referred to the cook as the cook he was now the palace chef. He put much work into proving he was a chef.

All was going well and the wedding was now two days away.

Blaine could not sleep one night so she went down stairs to get some warm milk.

Ashton happened to be in the kitchen too. "Are your ribs feeling better Ashton?" "Well enough to travel soon I hope." "You plan on leaving soon then?" "Blaine, I need to talk to you now."

"Alright Ashton, it's obvious neither one of us can sleep so let's talk."

"Blaine, when you disappeared I went out of my mind. I searched everywhere for you. Seth and me spent months riding in the mountains tiring to find you." "Then when we found out Roslyn was behind your disappearance your Ma'am and me went straight out there to set her up and catch her and we did. She admitted she sold you to a ship Capitan."

"Come back with me! Blaine, I know we can have a good life! This man is no good." "I had these women down at the docks tell me he was cruel to them. That he used them and threw them out on the street!"

"Ashton these two women, their names didn't happen to be Nettie and Ebina?" "Yes how did you know?"

"Because Ashton, those two were after the King to become Queen! When he did not pay any attention to them, they started trouble. The King did not throw them out on the street. He offered them decent jobs with the dressmaker. They chose to go back and be prostitutes. I should have known you would take the word of a prostitute as a valuable source of information. Ashton you will never change."

"Blaine, listen to me, you have no idea what I've gone thru for you, you have to come back with me! You are all I think about!"

"Ashton, you have no idea what I have gone thru because of you! How long do think I stood at the stable door that night before I walked in?" "I assumed you just walked in."

"Well you assumed wrong! I stood there long enough for you to ask Roslyn what else she wanted from you. For her to say she would be your love slave and I would never have to know. I was not drinking that night Ashton, I noticed your shirt was off and the scratches down your back. Roslyn's bodice was off. So I am sure if there had not been any interruptions you would have gotten exactly what you wanted minus the wedding." "Blaine she tricked me."

"Ashton, the only thing she tricked you in was making you think she really cared for you.

Because Roslyn can only love Roslyn! Really all she wanted to do was to hurt me. Which you both managed to do! You! Rolled around with her like her lover! She did not make you do that. You! Broke any vow between us, when you lay down with her. Now! You let me tell you what I went thru I was on a filthy stinky ship with men that would have used and killed every young girl in that hold if it wasn't for Sobbo. I had to live in conditions

you wouldn't even put your horses in. I had no clothes for
six months except for the gown I had at the Ball. We had
to bathe out of a wooden bucket once a week. We lived
on bread and fruit Sobbo brought to us. The food the
Capitan sent was rotten. Sobbo had to sneak us blankets,
Ashton, one blanket to each girl with no way to wash
them for six months. I had to listen to the men drag one
of the girls away to use her until she was dead! Leaving
her tiny sister all alone. Then I had to care for two girls
with fever who had become my dear friends and watch
them drift into death. I could do nothing. Then at the end
of this voyage from hell Bogota pulls a gun and tells my
friend Sobbo to carry those he could, anyone left behind
belongs to that evil man. Sobbo chose me and the two
smallest ones but he has to leave behind the woman who
loves him, and the two you met the other night. Israel
did not bring me here but because of him, I was kept
safe. He has taken care of me. Israel let me know how he
felt but unlike you, he never pushed himself on me. He
has always treated me like a lady. With you, I was your
possession. Because of you Ashton, my life was almost
ended. Because of Israel and Sobbo, my life is complete.
I am married!"

"No you are not!"

"Ashton do not be belligerent! A Christian minister
married Israel and me and I am pregnant with our first
child.

Ashton went wild violently he grabbed Blaine.

"You listen to me Blaine, I came all this way to bring
you back and I intend to bring you back!".

"Ashton let me go!"

341

"No we are going down to the dock and find the first ship back to New York." "I can't Ashton I am pregnant!"

"Israel! Israel! Help! Blaine yelled at the top of her lungs. Israel came running along with Sobbo, Shamus and Omar. They could not believe their eyes. The sight of Ashton dragging Blaine toward the door. He had completely lost s his mind. Sobbo grabbed Ashton from behind the neck causing him to lose consciousness. Israel wrapped his arms around Blaine.

"Oh Israel, I tried to tell him I wouldn't leave you and I kept telling him we are married. That we are going to have a baby. I told him I did not want him here but he went crazy.

Please Israel make him leave." Blaine was crying.

Shamus came to Israel's side and said. "Israel, Ashton has a problem, once he thinks something belongs to him he won't let go. I am sure you have your ways of justice about matters like this. But if you would let me handle this for you, I think all will be able to sleep tonight. I will need the assistance of your man Sobbo."

"Alright, I will attend to Blaine."

Shamus and Sobbo carried Ashton down to the docks. They took him to the bar. Shamus ordered the three of them Irish whiskey. Shamus splashed water on Ashton's face to wake him up.

"Oh my head, Shamus where are we?" "In the bar at the docks."

"What are we doing here?"

"You just drink your whiskey it will help yer headache." Sobbo came in, leaned over Shamus shoulder, and whispered.

"There is a ship to New York it leaves in twenty minutes, Capitan said he will take the kings guest." Then Sobbo sat down next to Ashton.

Ashton said.

"Well, that answers the question about the third whiskey."

"Now, Shamus, are you going to tell me how I got here and why we are here?"

"As to the how you got here, it seems Ashton, you got a bit out of hand with the Queen so, Sobbo had to show you how to relax. by knocking you out, and we carried you here to celebrate."

"celebrated what?"

"Your immediate departure to New York."

"What are you talking about Shamus? I am not leaving here without Blaine."

"Oh, yes, you are son, because she has no intensions of going anywhere with you. And it seems Ashton that attacking a Queen, whether you know her or not. Is a serious offense. Caring the death sentence. The King was good enough to allow Sobbo and myself to find you the first passage back to New York, with your solemn promise to never return. For if, you do, Ashton, I do believe you will be put to death. So drink up! Your ship leaves in about fifteen minutes.

And please tell your parents we have decided to stay ourselves. The men finished their whiskey Sobbo and Shamus watched Ashton reluctantly get on board the ship and cast off.

Shamus slapped Sobbo on the back. "That boy is probably so scared he'll be willing to swim back to New York."

They made it back to the palace and Sobbo and Shamus were laughing when they came in. Everyone else was very solemn.

Shamus asked. What has happened?"

Carlin said. "Its Blaine, the doctor and Israel are up with her right now. Shamus ran up the stairs and knocked on the door. Israel let him in.

Shamus went to her bedside and said. "Blaine my girl he's gone. Sobbo and me we made him go away and he won't come back."

Blaine lifted her hand and touched her Da's face. He kissed her hand.

"Blaine girl your Mama and me we want to live here with you and Israel and the baby.

We don't want to go back. Do you want us to stay here with you darlin?" Blaine answered in a weak voice.

"Yes Da' I want you to stay. Where is Israel?" "I am right here my love."

"Here love feel this." Blaine placed Israel's hands on her stomach the baby was very active. Israel had never felt the baby move so much before. Israel tuned to the doctor. "Is this normal for the baby to move so much?"

"My King, the Queen has suffered a shock but she will be alright and your baby will too. the wee one is just responding to all the excitement that is all."

The doctor decided to stay the night just in case something else happened. Blaine slept peacefully in Israel's arms knowing Ashton was gone and her parents would be living with them from now on. The next day Blaine felt much better.

Sobbo and Malian's wedding would be that afternoon everything was ready.

That morning as she stood at the window looking out at the sea. Israel came up behind her.

"What is on your mind my Queen?" "Names."

"Names for the baby?"

"Yes, I have a few I wanted to ask you about."

"Alright, what names have you decided you prefer, my love?"

"For a girl I like Jasmine like the beautiful flower. And for a boy I like Abishai. He was a mighty man who protected King David in the bible."

"I do believe I like your choices my Queen. Jasmine or Abishai very nice I approve of both."

"Now about the wedding today you must stay very calm as the doctor said." "Yes my King." Blaine answered in a slight sarcastic tone.

"Blaine, do not be coy you must promise not to tire yourself today."

Blaine changed her tone realizing Israel only wanted what was best for her and the baby.

"Yes, my love, I will tell you if I begin to tire, I promise."

The afternoon had come quickly everyone was ready for the wedding to begin.

King Aviv escorted his Queen to their places.

The music began and Sobbo escorted Malina out to the minister. They took their vows promising to love one another for the rest of their lives. Blaine just knew Sobbo would love Malina forever.

Malian's sari was most beautiful. White silk trimmed in dark purple silk. Sobbo had on his gold silk pants and a dark purple shirt. They looked perfect together. The chef had out done himself; again, everything was perfect, the way it should be.

Blaine was getting tired after they ate she turned to Israel. "Israel, would you mind taking me back to our room."

"Is everything all right Blaine?" Israel was concern.

"I am very tired." Israel gently helped his very pregnant wife up and went to say their well wishes to the new couple. Israel explained Blaine was tired and needed her rest. Israel and Blaine made it to their room, "Israel, I would like to look out the window for moment." Blaine peered out at the ocean while she leaned against Israel. He decided to ask his love the question he feared.

"Blaine did the thought ever cross your mind when Mister Rossi asked you to go back that you might wish to go?"

Blaine turned looking into Israel's eyes. "No, not for one instant."

With an imploring tone in his voice he asked, "Was it because of the baby?" Blaine could sense Israel's insecurity she rose up softly kissed him tenderly, with love and gentleness then she said, "I stayed for the love of my King."

Israel gently took Blaine in his arms and kissed her deeply caressing her beautiful red hair.

She wrapped her arms around his neck twisting her hands in his long black hair.

Israel lifted his head to look into Blaine's emerald eyes. Blaine had a sweet but strange look on her face she asked, "Israel, is the doctor still here?"

"Yes he is, he chose to stay in case there were any more problems." "Israel my love, you may want to go get him I am in labor." "Labor! Are you sure?"

"Yes my King, I believe I am. Could you find my Mama too?" Israel lifted Blaine and put her to bed. He kissed her once more.

"I love you Blaine Aviv. He raced out the door to find the doctor and Blaine' Mama. Blaine was alone her contractions were getting stronger. She rubbed her stomach and spoke softly to her little one.

"We can do this little one for the love of our King."

The doctor came in first as he prepared to check Blaine he noticed how strong her contractions were and how fast they were coming.

"Dear let me know when this one ends."

Her Mama came in and sat by her side holding her hand. "Now, doctor it is gone."

The doctor checked her. "Dear I can already feel the baby's head. On the next contraction push hard."

Blaine pushed and pushed she cried out in her labor pains she pushed for an hour.

Finally, she heard the baby cry.

The doctor wrapped the baby up and said, "You have a healthy boy my Queen." Blaine cradled her son in her arms. "Mama please gets Israel."

Carlin hurried to find him.

Israel came running into the room tears streaming down his face. Blaine laid his son in his arms. "Israel meets your son, Abishai."

Israel kissed Blaine on the forehead. "We have a son."

Israel marveled at the beautiful tiny creation he held in his arms then his son let out a loud cry of protest.

Carlin said, "A son who probably needs to nurses."

Israel handed Abishai back to Blaine, Carlin helped set her up so she could nurse her eager son. Israel sat and watched in amazement as Blaine fed their baby. How she held him so protectively. He watched the smile on her face how she glowed with love for this new little person.

She looked at Israel. "Thank you Israel." Israel was not sure why she was thanking him. "No my Queen I thank you."

Blaine and the baby fell asleep. Israel gently picked up his son kissing him softly on the forehead he walked to the window to look out over the sea. Looking at their beautiful son Israel understood Blaine's words, for her voice came to him over the sea, 'I stayed, for the love of my King.' At that moment, Israel knew the depth of Blaine's love. His love for *his Queen* grew even deeper.

Printed in the United States
By Bookmasters